AN UNFORGETTABLE KISS

Captivating Kisses
Book 7

Alexa Aston

© Copyright 2026 by Alexa Aston
Text by Alexa Aston
Cover by Dar Albert

Dragonblade Publishing, Inc. is an imprint of Kathryn Le Veque Novels, Inc.
P.O. Box 23
Moreno Valley, CA 92556
ceo@dragonbladepublishing.com

Produced in the United States of America

First Edition March 2026
Trade Paperback Edition

Reproduction of any kind except where it pertains to short quotes in relation to advertising or promotion is strictly prohibited.

All Rights Reserved.

The characters and events portrayed in this book are fictitious. Any similarity to real persons, living or dead, is purely coincidental and not intended by the author.

AI Statement: No AI or ghostwriting was used in the creation of this story, or any story, published by Dragonblade Publishing. All text, structure, content, ideas, and concept are 100% human generated solely by the author whose name appears on the cover. It is prohibited to use this material, or any copyrighted material, for AI engine training.

ARE YOU SIGNED UP FOR DRAGONBLADE'S BLOG?

You'll get the latest news and information on exclusive giveaways, exclusive excerpts, coming releases, sales, free books, cover reveals and more.

Check out our complete list of authors, too!

No spam, no junk. That's a promise!

Sign Up Here

www.dragonbladepublishing.com

Dearest Reader;

Thank you for your support of a small press. At Dragonblade Publishing, we strive to bring you the highest quality Historical Romance from some of the best authors in the business. Without your support, there is no 'us', so we sincerely hope you adore these stories and find some new favorite authors along the way.

Happy Reading!

CEO, Dragonblade Publishing

Additional Dragonblade books by Author Alexa Aston

Captivating Kisses Series
An Unexpected Kiss (Book 1)
An Impulsive Kiss (Book 2)
An Innocent Kiss (Book 3)
An Unforeseen Kiss (Book 4)
An Enchanting Kiss (Book 5)
An Urgent Kiss (Book 6)
An Unforgettable Kiss (Book 7)

The Strongs of Shadowcrest Series
The Duke's Unexpected Love (Book 1)
The Perks of Loving a Viscount (Book 2)
Falling for the Marquess (Book 3)
The Captain and the Duchess (Book 4)
Courtship at Shadowcrest (Book 5)
The Marquess' Quest for Love (Book 6)
The Duke's Guide to Winning a Lady (Book 7)

Suddenly a Duke Series
Portrait of the Duke (Book 1)
Music for the Duke (Book 2)
Polishing the Duke (Book 3)
Designs on the Duke (Book 4)
Fashioning the Duke (Book 5)
Love Blooms with the Duke (Book 6)
Training the Duke (Book 7)
Investigating the Duke (Book 8)

Second Sons of London Series
Educated By The Earl (Book 1)
Debating With The Duke (Book 2)

Empowered By The Earl (Book 3)
Made for the Marquess (Book 4)
Dubious about the Duke (Book 5)
Valued by the Viscount (Book 6)
Meant for the Marquess (Book 7)

Dukes Done Wrong Series
Discouraging the Duke (Book 1)
Deflecting the Duke (Book 2)
Disrupting the Duke (Book 3)
Delighting the Duke (Book 4)
Destiny with a Duke (Book 5)

Dukes of Distinction Series
Duke of Renown (Book 1)
Duke of Charm (Book 2)
Duke of Disrepute (Book 3)
Duke of Arrogance (Book 4)
Duke of Honor (Book 5)
The Duke That I Want (Book 6)

The St. Clairs Series
Devoted to the Duke (Book 1)
Midnight with the Marquess (Book 2)
Embracing the Earl (Book 3)
Defending the Duke (Book 4)
Suddenly a St. Clair (Book 5)
Starlight Night (Novella)
The Twelve Days of Love (Novella)

Soldiers & Soulmates Series
To Heal an Earl (Book 1)
To Tame a Rogue (Book 2)
To Trust a Duke (Book 3)
To Save a Love (Book 4)
To Win a Widow (Book 5)
Yuletide at Gillingham (Novella)

King's Cousins Series
The Pawn (Book 1)
The Heir (Book 2)
The Bastard (Book 3)

Medieval Runaway Wives
Song of the Heart (Book 1)
A Promise of Tomorrow (Book 2)
Destined for Love (Book 3)

Knights of Honor Series
Word of Honor (Book 1)
Marked by Honor (Book 2)
Code of Honor (Book 3)
Journey to Honor (Book 4)
Heart of Honor (Book 5)
Bold in Honor (Book 6)
Love and Honor (Book 7)
Gift of Honor (Book 8)
Path to Honor (Book 9)
Return to Honor (Book 10)

The Lyon's Den Series
The Lyon's Lady Love

Pirates of Britannia Series
God of the Seas

De Wolfe Pack: The Series
Rise of de Wolfe

The de Wolfes of Esterley Castle
Diana
Derek
Thea

Also from Alexa Aston
The Bridge to Love (Novella)
One Magic Night

CHAPTER ONE

London—July 1808

"Do we truly have to attend a wedding?" asked Viscount Samuel.

Rowena Stanhope looked at her father as a governess would a petulant child and responded, "Yes, Papa. And it is just not *a* wedding. It is *the* wedding of the Season. At least, according to the newspapers. Besides, many of your friends will be there."

"Who is the couple? I cannot keep up with all the gossip." He smiled benignly at her. "That is why I have you, my dear."

"It is actually a double wedding ceremony," she informed him. "Two brides and two grooms will be speaking their vows at St. George's Church today."

He frowned in disapproval. "I have never heard of such a thing."

"The first bride is the Duke of Millbrooke's sister, Lady Tia Worthington. She will marry the Earl of Merriman."

Her father thought a moment. "Oh, the one who stammers. He made that awful scene at the card party we attended at Lady Swarthmore's. Dreadful. Simply dreadful."

Disappointment filled her. Though she loved her father, he was quick to judge others, as were so many members of Polite Society.

"You know as well as I do that Lord Balch and Lord Calley goaded Lord Merriman that evening. Their behavior was reprehensible. Yes, Lord Merriman stammered as a boy and did so that night, but he works very hard at keeping the stammer at bay. At least, that is what I am told. I have attended other events with him present, and I have yet to hear the earl misspeak."

She and her aunt been present at the garden party a month ago, where Lord Merriman had made a very public proposal to Lady Tia. That afternoon's events had seemingly changed the opinions of the *ton* regarding the earl and Lady Tia. Now, Lord Calley and Lord Balch were the black sheep, thrust from the bosom of Polite Society, while Lord Merriman and his betrothed were the new darlings.

"Who else will wed?" her father asked gruffly.

"Lord Merriman's sister, Lady Delilah Drake, is the other bride. She will wed the Earl of Forsythe. I think it sweet the two siblings wish to marry at the same time."

Her father said nothing, merely turning back to his newspaper. Rowena did likewise, motioning for a footman to pour more tea for her.

Usually, she was not much for attending weddings, but she had actually met and spoken with Lady Tia during the brief time the beauty was an outcast in Polite Society. Lady Tia, whose dance programme filled before anyone else's in the ballroom, had been shunned. Not given the cut direct—since her brother was a duke—but she had been judged and found lacking by those who influenced the *ton*'s opinions. Rowena thought her courageous for standing up for Lord Merriman. She could have stayed home or even gone to the country and not returned until next Season. Instead, Lady Tia had remained in town and braved the wrath of Polite Society. She had taken her place amongst the wallflowers at a ball, where she had sat next to Rowena. The two had engaged in a very interesting conversation, and she found herself liking the formerly popular girl quite a bit.

She had almost invited her new acquaintance to attend the Literary Ladies Book Society, but she held off. Now that Lady Tia's imagined sins had been forgiven by the *ton* and she wed Lord Merriman today, she doubted that the new countess would have much interest in joining Rowena's little book club. It was composed of wallflowers such as herself, women who had an intellect and were not afraid to show it. Of course, by doing so, they were deemed unsuitable to wed, marked as bluestockings.

It did not matter to her. She had never held a desire to wed, much less have children. She had her hands full taking care of her father and his household. Besides, Papa usually left her to her own resources, and a husband would not have done the same. Rowena did everything to make herself unappealing to the bachelors of the *ton*, from wearing ill-fitting gowns to donning spectacles which she did not need. At five and twenty, she would be given access to her dowry, arranged in the marriage settlements between her parents long before her birth. At that point, she wished to retire from Polite Society and move back to Dorset. It was where her father's country estate lay. They had not visited it in many years, but she loved the green beauty of Dorset, as well as being near the sea.

Papa never wished to go to Stanfield, it being the scene of where he had lost his young wife. Rowena's mother had died two days after giving birth to her, and Papa had found he could not bear going through rooms without seeing his beloved wife's presence. Because of that, they lived in town year-round, only occasionally leaving to visit friends at their country estates. Rowena had only been back to Stanfield three times in her life. The rest of the time, Papa's tenants were cared for by her cousin Ollie, the only son of her late uncle, who served as their estate's manager. Ollie was Papa's heir apparent since Rowena was his only child.

Rowena finished her tea and closed her newspaper. Giving her father ample warning, she said, "We will be leaving in a quarter-hour, Papa. Be ready."

He sighed. "I shall meet you in the foyer."

She returned to her bedchamber to claim her reticule and don a bonnet. She knew she was not fashionably dressed. It would not matter. Hundreds would be in attendance at St. George's today.

And not one eye would come to rest upon her.

An hour later, they were seated inside the Mayfair church they attended each Sunday. Rowena had been to weddings at St. George's before, but she believed this one to be special. Simply from observing Lord Merriman and Lady Tia, she could tell they were a love match. The same could be said of Lady Delilah and Lord Forsythe. Love matches were rare within the *ton*. She herself had not truly believed in them until she had witnessed Lord Merriman's emotional, heartfelt proposal to Lady Tia. Still, she found the idea of romantic love odd and was happy in her decision never to seek a husband, much less love.

The organist began to play, and the doors to St. George's were opened. The guests all turned, watching Lady Delilah escorted down the aisle by the Duke of Reddington. Rowena knew that His Grace and Merriman were very close friends. Since Lady Delilah's father was deceased—and the brother who would have escorted her to her groom was already waiting at the altar for his own bride—she thought it lovely that Reddington had stepped into the role to see Lady Delilah to her groom.

Then the Duke of Millbrooke started down the aisle with his sister on his arm. They made a striking pair, the duke tall and handsome with his chestnut hair, Lady Tia tall and willowy, her strawberry blond hair piled high atop her head. Red hair must run in the family because the other two Worthington siblings also possessed hair with shades of red. Lady Tia's twin, Viscountess Cressley, had auburn hair, while her older sister, the Marchioness of Aldridge, possessed a magnificent head of copper tresses.

Her eyes followed Lady Tia and His Grace down the aisle. She saw the bride did not look at a single guest because her focus was on the groom who awaited her.

Rowena's throat grew thick with unshed tears, and she thought it very unlike herself. She was most stoic in all situations and could not ever recall crying. Perhaps it was because she had been raised only by a father, one who was level-headed and rarely showed emotion himself. Papa had not known what to do with any child, much less a female one. Because of that, she had been brought up more as a son than daughter. He had taught her to ride and play cards. She had received a first-class education, with a male tutor living in instead of a governess. Rowena was fluent in French and Italian, and she could also write in Latin and Greek. She excelled at maths and was not only in charge of the household accounts and paying their servants, but she also read every report from Ollie regarding their tenants and the crops produced. It was she who replied to her cousin's requests, not her father, and she was the de facto viscount in many aspects.

She did have a love for literature and history, also fostered by Papa. If she could do anything with her life, she wished she could be a don at Cambridge or Oxford and guide those university students as they read history. Being a woman, however, she would never be allowed to be a part of the academic community. She satisfied her urge to teach others by guiding her fellow bluestockings through the book society she had founded.

The wedding ceremony took a bit longer than usual, simply because there were two couples having to repeat their vows to one another. Knowing she would never be a bride herself had been something Rowena thought she had come to terms with, but seeing the joy on Lady Tia's and Lady Delilah's faces as they marched up the aisle on the arms of their new husbands gave her pause. She shook her head, trying to rid herself of such nonsense. She neither wanted nor needed a gentleman in her life. A husband would put her under his thumb and expect her to do his bidding. Rowena had a stubborn streak and the more she was told to do something, the more she resisted doing that very thing. She would trade marriage for her freedom to do as she pleased any day.

With the ceremony completed, she and her father left St. George's, taking almost an hour to say their goodbyes to other guests. She found it a waste of time since they would see these very same people at social affairs throughout the remainder of the Season. At least tonight was a card party, something she shined at. In fact, she had partnered with Lord Merriman a few months ago at a card party. They had lost their match on the last hand of the game to Lady Tia and Lord Balch.

Though Rowena knew she would be amongst the last to gain a partner at cards this evening, most likely she would carry her partner because of her strategies and skill at cards.

Once they arrived home, she changed from the gown she had been wearing to a simpler, drab one. She removed the spectacles and rubbed the bridge of her nose. Sitting at her dressing table, she gazed into the mirror, thinking herself a bit pretty. She did not wish to attract any suitors, however, and used her wardrobe and the spectacles to hide behind. The spectacles were made of regular glass since her eyes needed no correction. Once she gained access to her dowry in three years' time, she would throw them away and dress as she wished.

She looked forward to moving to a cottage near the sea on her father's estate. Papa would be surprised when she left him, but she would hire a competent housekeeper to look after the household. Eventually, her cousin would take his uncle's title. She had already spoken to Ollie, and he was willing to allow her to remain in the cottage as long as she wished.

It was close to time for her to leave again, and Rowena stopped by her father's study, telling him she was heading to the bookshop. He mumbled a goodbye and most likely would not recall where she was five minutes from now.

Setting out on foot, she did not bother to take a maid as her chaperone, knowing she would be invisible on the streets. If anyone from Polite Society were out and about and recognized her, she was of so little interest that they would not even bother to gossip about her being unwed and unsupervised.

She arrived at Mr. Washington's bookshop, which included a subscription library within it. The owner, like so many in his profession, adored books—and those who loved them. Because of that, he allowed Rowena and her small circle of friends to meet at his bookshop for their monthly meetings.

Going now to greet him, she said, "Good afternoon, Mr.

Washington."

"Why, good afternoon to you, Miss Stanhope. I hope you are doing well. By chance, did you have time to read *Tristam Shandy*, which I lent to you?"

She handed the Laurence Sterne book to him. "I most certainly did. You were absolutely right about it. Perhaps when you have some free time, we could discuss it together. Parson Yorick was quite an entertaining character."

His eyes lit up. "I would appreciate hearing your comments, Miss Stanhope. Not many can make their way through it because of the number of times the author digresses, but satisfaction is guaranteed by the time a reader comes to its end."

Mr. Washington glanced over her shoulder and then back to her. "I see two of your friends have already arrived."

"Then I should join them. Thank you again for loaning Sterne's book to me."

She moved to the other side of the bookshop, which had a few chairs available, and joined Miss Tweedham and Lady Sarah.

"Were you at the wedding?" Miss Tweedham asked.

"Indeed, I was. Lady Tia and Lady Delilah made for two beautiful brides."

Lady Sarah looked wistful. "I have heard that they are both in love with their new husbands. I thought it obvious by looking at them that the rumors are true. Oh, what I wouldn't give to be in love."

Rowena doubted love would come to Lady Sarah. She was already on the shelf at six and twenty. Very plain of face. Still, she had an enticing dowry. At some point, a gentleman in need of that dowry would no doubt speak to Lady Sarah's father and receive permission to wed her. Sadly for Lady Sarah, love would not be a part of that union.

Miss Tweedham sniffed. "I, for one, am not interested in marriage and have made that perfectly clear. I will grant that it was a lovely wedding, though."

Miss Tweedham was her closest friend amongst the book

society's members. She, like Rowena, was a bluestocking, through and through. Miss Tweedham was average looking but possessed a keen intellect. She was also the fifth of five daughters, all of whom had very small dowries. Her four older sisters had all previously wed, and Miss Tweedham's mother had high hopes this final daughter would, as well. This was her friend's second Season, however, and it did not seem as if she had any prospects, the same as Rowena. The only difference between the pair was that Miss Tweedham hoped to one day wed, despite her voicing otherwise.

"Do we know if any of the others are coming today?" she asked.

Lady Sarah said, "I think it will just be the three of us today, Miss Stanhope." She named three other members whom she had seen at today's wedding, and they had all cried off coming to their meeting.

Miss Smythe rushed up. "Am I late? Oh, I hope I am not late. Have you begun the discussion?"

Of all the book society's members, Miss Smythe rubbed Rowena the wrong way. Miss Smythe leaned more toward gossip than she did discussing the books they read. She was unpleasant to be around and seemed to have no other friends. Rowena had taken pity upon her and allowed Miss Smythe to join their group, but she doubted the woman ever read any of the books they chose to discuss. Her contributions to the group revolved around repeating comments others had made in a new way or asking irrelevant questions.

Still, Rowena placed a smile on her face. "No, you are right on time. It shall be the four of us today. Shall we begin?"

They took their seats, and she began her discussion of Jonathan Swift's *Gulliver's Travels*, consulting the notes she had brought along to help guide their time together. As usual, Miss Smythe contributed nothing. Lady Sarah did make a few good points, while Miss Tweedham showed the most insight into the book.

"I still am a bit vague on all the symbolism," Lady Sarah admitted.

She bit back a smile and noticed Miss Tweedham did the same. Though Lady Sarah was an avid reader, she avoided newspapers and knew next to nothing about politics, which put her at a disadvantage. Swift's satire was rife with political symbolism, and Rowena did not think flogging a dead horse would bring any more understanding to Lady Sarah.

"I think we have discussed Gulliver's adventures enough. I wanted to share with you the novel we will take up next."

"I hope it is not as boring as this one was," Miss Smythe commented. "I plodded through it."

"Of course, you did," Rowena said, knowing the woman had most likely not cracked open the book—and the sarcasm in her tone would go over Miss Smythe's head. "I think you will find next month's choice to be unusual."

"Please tell us it is not as thick as today's selection," Miss Smythe said.

"It is barely a hundred pages," she told them. "The author is French. His name is Voltaire, and we will be reading *Candide*."

"Oh, I already like the sound of it," Miss Tweedham said. "Would you share something about it with us, Miss Stanhope?"

"Gladly," she said, smiling at her friend. "It is a picaresque novel. Candide is known for being overly optimistic."

"Does Mr. Washington have copies of it?" Lady Sarah asked. "If so, I will purchase one while I am here."

"He does. I informed him of our next choice, and he has graciously held back copies for our group."

The four went to the counter, where Mr. Washington sold them three copies, Rowena already having bought hers previously.

"A very important work of literature," the bookshop owner said. "Miss Stanhope always makes wonderful choices for you ladies to read."

Rowena bid them all goodbye after confirming with Miss

Tweedham that she would be at tonight's card party.

"I am hopeless at cards, but the hosts are friends of my parents," her friend said. "I simply must attend."

"Then I will see you tonight."

"Tomorrow night's ball will be the last event I will attend," Miss Tweedham informed her. "Mama grows tired of town. And tired of my lack of prospects."

"I am sorry to hear that," she said. "I will miss your company."

"I have run out of ballgowns, as well as prospects," her friend told her.

She knew Miss Tweedham wore hand-me-down gowns from her various sisters, and though a modiste tried to tailor them to fit better and change their appearance somewhat, her friend was usually as poorly dressed as Rowena herself.

"There is always next year," Rowena proclaimed brightly.

"I will read *Candide* and write to you regarding my thoughts," Miss Tweedham promised.

They said their goodbyes, and she walked home. At least Papa did not push all kinds of suitors upon her. Selfishly, he seemed to like the fact that she had not wed and was able to care for him and his household.

Still, the remainder of the Season would be lonely without Miss Tweedham's company.

Chapter Two

Constantine Alington, Viscount Dyer, dressed for tonight's ball. He had no valet, so he had shaved himself and donned his black evening wear on his own.

He looked about the rooms he lived in, which seemed a bit forlorn ever since his cousin and best friend had moved out last year. Val's father, the Duke of Millbrooke, had died, making Val the new duke. He had left their shared, rented rooms for his ducal townhouse and country estate. It was at Millvale that Val had meet Eden, who had since become the Duchess of Millbrooke, and provided Val with William, his heir.

While Con was pleased at the happy turn of events, he couldn't help but feel his cousin had moved on. Val now had a wife and child and was head of the Worthington family. He also had access to unlimited wealth, while Con continued to live frugally. His own father, the Earl of Marley, was in excellent health, so Con did not expect to inherit for years to come. He and Val had made a pact that they would not look for a bride on the Marriage Mart until they had claimed their titles. It made sense. What woman would want to come and live in these dark, dusty rooms, especially on the pitiful quarterly allowance given to him?

Mama was to thank for his lack of funds. She was the true power in the Alington family. His kind-hearted father may have had the title, but Lady Marley ran the family and made decisions both large and small. Her word was law. She did not want Con becoming a lazy, worthless rake. While she did pay his tailoring bills, wanting him to appear fashionably dressed at events in Polite Society, he lived frugally the remainder of the time. Walking to many places to save the hansom cab fare. Not visiting gaming dens because he would not have the funds to pay off his debts if he lost.

At least his membership at White's gave him a place to visit with his friends. He could read the newspapers there, saving on any subscriptions, and drink all the coffee he wished. Oftentimes, he dined at White's for his evening meal since that, too, came with his membership. He did not mind living carefully. In truth, he had few needs.

Except for his growing need for companionship.

Female companionship, to be specific. He had plenty of men he was friendly with. In addition to Val, Con was also close to several of his sisters' and cousins' husbands. Julian, Marquess of Aldridge. Judson, Marquess of Huntsberry. Rupert, Viscount Cressley. Hugo, Earl of Merriman. He was just getting to know Lord Forsythe and the Duke of Reddington better. Both men were friends of Merriman's and had joined his circle. Con also looked forward to making his sister Dru's husband, Perry, a part of their group when the couple came to town next Season.

No, his group of friends was more than adequate. What he now wanted was what he saw amongst all those married men. They each carried an air of happiness which surrounded them. They were not only husbands to their wives, but best friends and lovers to those wives, as well. It stirred a bit of jealousy within him. *He* wanted that shared closeness.

Of course, what his friends had in common—and which he lacked—was a title. Con could not purse a woman of quality until he possessed that. For now, he tried to keep himself occupied with brief affairs with a variety of women, usually pretty widows. He knew he could be a bit of a flirt. The fact he was handsome and very willing to couple with a willing woman also was to his advantage. He was able to move from one lady's bed to the next with no consequences.

But even he understood there was something lacking in his life. Especially with Val no longer a bachelor and living with him, Con grew lonely at times in his rooms. It had caused him to take to the streets, walking for hours, even heading toward Hyde Park and walking there. He wished he had the funds to stable a horse here in town, but that cost would be prohibitive. Instead, he carefully saved his coin and would rent a horse upon occasion.

What he wouldn't give to be able to peruse the Marriage Mart this Season and find love for himself. Of course, others in the *ton* might laugh at him for seeking a love match, but Con had seen both his sisters make one, as well as all four of his Worthington cousins. He had witnessed the power of love and knew it existed. Yet he would never wish ill of his father. Papa, along with his aunt Agnes, mother to his Fulton cousins, were the two most popular members of their large family. The day Con lost his father would be a dark day, indeed.

For now, he needed to be happy with what he had. He might not be rich in material goods, but he had loving siblings and good friends.

He finished tying his cravat and set out for Lord and Lady Purlington's townhouse. They were the host and hostess of tonight's ball. The Season would conclude in another couple of weeks. He might as well enjoy the social whirl while he could. Tonight, he needed to seek out a Miss Rowena Stanhope, the daughter of Viscount Samuel. His cousin Tia, who had wed only yesterday, had asked him to do so as a favor to her. Tia had briefly made Miss Stanhope's acquaintance and had liked the young lady so much that she hoped by Con dancing with her, that Miss Stanhope's chances of escaping her time with the wallflowers might come to an end.

It was true. For all that he lacked in wealth, both Con and Val had always had the eye—and favor—of the *ton*. If he danced with this wallflower, other gentlemen would take notice and wonder what Con saw in her. It could lead to Miss Stanhope finding herself dancing quite a bit this evening, and her drawing room might actually become the home to a few suitors in it tomorrow afternoon. He could easily do this favor for Tia, whom he thought of more as a sister than the cousin she was.

The Purlington townhouse was crowded outside. He stopped to talk to a few others, everyone asking after Tia and Merriman.

"They should be present this evening," he informed those who asked.

While Tia and Hugo had left yesterday's wedding breakfast and gone to his townhouse for their wedding night, both had assured him they would attend tonight's ball. Con had a feeling, though, that the couple would depart after the midnight buffet—if not before.

He joined the receiving line, which was considerably smaller than it had been for weeks. It seemed now that July had arrived, members of Polite Society had had their fill of social affairs, as well as the heat of London. The heat brought about the stench, making that much more noticeable. He usually ignored it since he lived in town most of the year. Though he would have liked to be at Marleyfield more, he did not wish to infringe upon his father, who enjoyed having a hand in running his estate. Con wouldn't have known what to do with himself in the country with no duties to see to, and that caused him to remain in town.

Occasionally, he did go to visit one of his cousins in the country, but he avoided house parties like the plague, knowing they were hotbeds of sudden engagements. Perhaps he could visit with Dru and Perry once the Season came to an end. His sister was about to give birth sometime in the next couple of weeks. He would enjoy meeting his new nephew or niece. It would also give him a chance to visit with Lucy and Judson and their new babe, Elizabeth. Con envied his sisters, who had wed men who had estates close to one another in Surrey. Their cousin Ariadne also lived nearby. When Con inherited, he would be far away from his sisters, Marleyfield being in Somerset.

Reaching Lord and Lady Purlington, he greeted them. Lady

Purlington eyed him with interest.

"We attended your cousin's wedding yesterday, Lord Dyer," the countess said. "I believe your two sisters are also wed. When might you consider taking the plunge into marriage?"

He laughed easily. "The parson's mousetrap is not for me, Lady Purlington. At least not for several more years."

"Bachelors are becoming scarce in town with so many weddings occurring," she told him. "You must pay special attention to all the still available ladies, my lord. I do not want to see you ducking into the card room this evening."

Always one willing to please a hostess, he said, "Very well, my lady. I shall make a point of dancing every set. Only because you asked it of me," as he employed the smile that he knew made feminine hearts flutter.

Moving away from his hosts, he entered the ballroom. Right away, he saw his parents standing with Tia and Hugo, and so he made his way toward them.

"Good evening," he greeted. "How are the newlyweds?"

"The newlyweds are here reluctantly," Hugo told him. "I would have preferred staying home, but I did want Polite Society to see how happy my countess and I are with one another. We plan to make it an early evening, though."

"Will you be around for the midnight buffet?" he asked. "If so, I thought I could ask Miss Stanhope for the supper dance, so that we could sup with you and Tia."

"We might be here. We might not," his cousin said, mischief dancing in her eyes.

"Apparently, you have taken to the marriage bed, Tia," he said, causing his mother to swat him with her fan.

"Dyer, watch what you say. You are in public. You would not wish to embarrass your cousin."

"Were you embarrassed?" he asked Tia, who burst out laughing. "Where is everyone else?"

"Val and Eden are leaving in the morning for Millbrooke," Tia told him. "They will take Mama with them. I am not certain if they plan to come to tonight's ball. With the wedding now over, Lia and Rupert decided to return home today, as did Lucy and Judson. I am not certain if Ariadne and Julian will be here this evening." She glanced around the ballroom. "I do not see Miss Stanhope yet. Be sure to look for her, Con. She is quite tall, with a slender frame and golden-brown hair."

"And spectacles, you said," he reminded her. "Not many wear them to balls, even if they need to, so I believe your Miss Stanhope will be easy for me to spy. In the meantime, our hostess has instructed me to dance every set since there seems to be a dearth of bachelors this evening."

"Thank you, Con," Tia said. "I appreciate you doing this favor for me."

"For us," Hugo added. "I quite like Miss Stanhope. I do hope she can find a husband."

Con laughed. "Well, it certainly will not be me."

He bid them and his parents farewell and set out, moving about the ballroom, signing a programme here and there. He had yet to see Miss Stanhope and wondered if she would even be in attendance tonight. Then he glanced at a group of women. The wallflowers. Some were incredibly shy. Others were plain of face. Still others had little or no dowry. All these things made this particular group of women unpopular. He knew a few bluestockings would be sprinkled amongst them and recalled that Tia had indicated that Miss Stanhope was one herself.

Then he spied a lady in a most inappropriate ballgown. The color was all wrong for her, and the fit of the gown poor. She wore spectacles and was speaking with another woman close to her age, one who was short, thin, and had mousy brown hair. Con made his way toward them.

As he arrived, the lady he believed to be Miss Stanhope was saying, "I do think that is exactly what Swift meant. Lilliput and Bleufuscu are made to resemble England and France. And the loathing evident between the low heels and high heels simply has to represent the Whigs and Tories."

"But do you believe that Flimnap represents Walpole?" Con asked, referring to Sir Robert Walpole. "After all, Walpole was a Whig, and Swift's relationship with Walpole was most turbulent."

She looked up at him. "You have read *Gulliver's Travels*, my lord?"

He frowned slightly. "I would think that apparent by my statement, my lady."

"You are right," she said apologetically. "I simply know of so few gentlemen who actually *read*. They say they do, but I find beyond what is reported in the gossip columns or horse racing results, most gentlemen do not have a particular fondness for reading."

He smiled, knowing her statement to be true. "You are correct, Miss Stanhope."

"You know me?" she asked, frowning slightly. "You leave me at a disadvantage."

"Pardon me for not introducing myself. I am Lord Dyer, a cousin to Lady Tia. That is, Lady Merriman now. My cousin thinks highly of you, Miss Stanhope."

Con took her hand and kissed it. He watched the blush tinge her cheeks. He also looked beyond the spectacles, seeing she had large, expressive brown eyes, rimmed in amber.

"I am flattered to hear of Lady Merriman's high opinion of me." She turned to her companion. "May I introduce Miss Tweedham, my lord?"

"Ah, Miss Tweedham. A pleasure to meet you, as well." He also kissed her hand, causing the young lady to giggle.

Deciding he would help both of them, he said, "Might I engage both of you in a dance this evening?"

They both looked at him as if he had sprouted a second head.

"You wish to . . . *dance* with us, my lord?" Miss Stanhope managed to ask.

Clearly, these two were wallflowers who rarely got out onto the ballroom's floor. "Yes, I do. That is, if you have any available slots on your dance cards."

Quickly, Miss Tweedham thrust her programme at him. "Choose whichever set you would like, my lord."

Biting back a smile, he signed her empty card and returned it to her.

"And yours, Miss Stanhope?"

Though she had appeared flummoxed, she had now regained her composure. Handing him her programme, she said, "Obviously, you have your pick, Lord Dyer. I am rarely engaged to dance."

"Might I sign for the supper dance, my lady? If so, we could join Lord and Lady Merriman and sup with them afterward."

Miss Stanhope smiled, a very engaging smile. "Please do so, my lord."

Once he gave her programme back to her, he said, "I look forward to dancing with you both."

He heard other nearby wallflowers begin tittering and bowed, escaping before any of them thought to pounce upon and beg him for a dance, as well.

Returning to Tia and Hugo, who now stood talking with Reddington, Ariadne, and Julian, he reported, "I have scheduled my dance with Miss Stanhope, as well as one with her friend, a Miss Tweedham."

"Oh, dear," Tia fretted. "I am sorry that occurred, Con."

"No worries, Cousin. I am happy to dance with them both. I did request the supper dance from Miss Stanhope, however. I hope you and Hugo will be available to join us after it."

"Plan on it," Hugo told him. He looked to the others. "Would you care to join us?"

"We would be happy to do so," Julian said, speaking for him and Ariadne. "Tonight is our last event to attend. We plan to leave for Aldridge Manor sometime tomorrow morning. It will be a nice way to say farewell."

Reddington sighed. "I suppose I shall have to scrounge around and find a dance partner for supper then. Look for me, also."

The duke set off, and Con went in search of his first partner of the evening, now committed to dance each number with a different lady. He knew better than to dance twice in one evening with any woman. Gossips of the *ton* were always looking for someone to talk about, and he refused to show interest in any particular lady in front of them.

As he danced the first dance, his mind kept drifting back to Miss Stanhope, however. It seemed she hid her attractiveness, deliberately choosing an unflattering ballgown. No woman with her intelligence would believe she looked good in the gown she wore. And she was very pretty if you looked beyond the gold spectacles.

Con found himself looking forward to the supper dance—and his time with the pretty wallflower.

Chapter Three

After Viscount Dyer left, several women came up to her and Miss Tweedham, asking if he had claimed a dance from them. Miss Tweedham excitedly shared the news, while Rowena smiled numbly.

Why had Lord Dyer come and spoken to them, much less asked the two of them to dance? She believed it must have something to do with his cousin, Lady Tia, or else the viscount never would have sought her out. It was kind of Lady Tia to still be thinking about her, and Miss Tweedham had reaped the benefits of standing next to her when the viscount appeared. She had to give him credit for being a gentleman and asking both of them to dance. Far too many other bachelors, on a mission of mercy such as this, would have merely asked her to dance and ignored Miss Tweedham.

She tried to surreptitiously watch him on the dance floor. He was at least six feet and possessed a lean, athletic frame. He moved with grace as he danced, and it was apparent any physical activity would be easy for him. His aquiline nose gave his profile an interesting look. Overall, he was very appealing. Still, she knew his reputation. He was a gentleman who tended to flirt a bit, but he never seemed to call upon any eligible young ladies. That let her know right away that he had no intentions toward her. It was merely a single dance.

Just before it was time for him to dance with her friend,

Rowena saw her aunt motioning to her.

"I must leave you, Miss Tweedham. My aunt wishes to speak with me."

"But he is about to be here, Miss Stanhope!"

She patted Miss Tweedham's hand and smiled. "And you will be waiting here for him, as he expects."

Rowena wished to tell her friend not to make too much of this dance, but she knew Miss Tweedham had not danced a single set this entire Season. She could not take away the thrill her friend now experienced.

"Enjoy your dance with Lord Dyer. I will watch for you on the dance floor."

She left where they were seated, a section of chairs set up for those wallflowers who did not dance—or were rarely asked to do so. Making her way around the edges of the ballroom, she spoke to a few others, and then she reached Aunt Sylvia. Her aunt was Papa's only sister, a woman who had been widowed early in her marriage and had chosen not to remarry. Aunt Sylvia had been the one Rowena had turned to when she had questions which only a female mind held the answer to, including what it meant when her courses began. Rowena had thought she was dying when the blood first appeared, but Aunt Sylvia had calmed her and explained how to handle this monthly inconvenience.

Aunt Sylvia sat with Lady Pebble, whose husband's country estate was adjacent to her own father's. Lady Pebble had been a good friend of Rowena's mother, and she and Lord Pebble treated Rowena as a daughter. The couple remained childless, and she appreciated her visits with the viscountess when they came to town each spring for the Season.

"Good evening, Aunt. Lady Pebble. How are you this evening?"

"I see the wallflower section atwitter, thanks to Lord Dyer's visit to it," her aunt observed. "I assume he asked you to dance. It looked as if he signed your dance programme."

"He did," she confirmed. "He also claimed a dance from my

close friend, Miss Tweedham."

"But why?" Aunt Sylvia pressed. "How do you even know Lord Dyer?"

She knew Lord Dyer had broken protocol by speaking to them without having been previously introduced by a common acquaintance. She did not want these two women to think less of him and told a small white lie. "We met through Lady Tia Worthington, who is now Lady Merriman."

"Oh, Lord Pebble and I attended her wedding yesterday," the viscountess said. "I did not realize the two of you knew one another."

"We do," she said confidently, not bothering to share their connection.

"She is a duke's sister," Aunt Sylvia said, looking suitably impressed. "It is a good connection for you to cultivate, Rowena."

The three watched as Lord Dyer made his way toward Miss Tweedham. Even from far across the room, she could see her friend beaming at him. He led them out onto the dance floor, and Rowena watched them dance together.

"The viscount cuts a fine figure," Lady Pebble remarked.

She would have to stop this nonsense since both women eyed her expectantly. "I believe Lord Dyer is simply being kind in asking me to dance this evening. He is quite close to his cousin. I would not like for either of you to think too much of this."

"As you wish," Aunt Sylvia replied.

She bid them farewell and returned to the area of wallflowers who watched the couple with bated breath as Lord Dyer moved one of their own about the dance floor.

When the set ended, he returned Miss Tweedham, giving Rowena a smile and saying, "I will see you soon, Miss Stanhope."

She was sitting there, listening to Miss Tweedham go on and on about the dance when another gentleman came up. Rowena had met him during her first Season, so no introduction was necessary. Still, it surprised her he was here now.

"If you are not otherwise engaged for this set, Miss Stanhope,

I would be most grateful to dance it with you."

"I am not, my lord," she said, smiling at him.

As they danced, Rowena now guessed at the reason behind Lord Dyer asking her to dance. His cousin, feeling sorry for Rowena, had asked him to do so, in hopes that other gentlemen might also dance with her. A bit of disappointment filled her, knowing it had not been the viscount's idea. Still, she would graciously accept the dance simply because she enjoyed dancing. Not that she excelled at it by any means, but it was a pleasurable activity she did not have the opportunity to often indulge in.

And then it was time. He approached her, so tall and handsome. She was mesmerized by his unique amethyst eyes, a shade she had never seen in another living soul.

"I believe this is the number we are engaged for," he said, flashing a smile that made her grow weak in the knees.

She placed her fingertips on his sleeve and walked with him, where they joined another group forming on the dance floor.

Her heart beat fast as they danced. She saw some of the looks she received, other women wondering why a man such as Lord Dyer would even bother with a wallflower such as herself. Suddenly, Rowena was painfully aware of the disguise she wore. How her gown was three Seasons old and did not fit her well. She wished she could fling off the gold spectacles and let him see her face without them.

Then she chuckled to herself, thinking she was reacting as a starry-eyed girl making her come-out. She had no need of a husband. Besides, it wasn't as if Lord Dyer held any true interest in her. She decided to throw herself into the moment, knowing dances were few and far between for her.

The musicians concluded their number, and Lord Purlington announced that supper would now be served. Lord Dyer reached for her hand and slipped it through the crook of his arm in a possessive gesture, causing all kinds of new, unknown feelings to rush through her. Rowena pushed them aside, knowing her fairy tale would soon come to an end—and it would not have a happily ever after ending.

"You are a most enthusiastic dancer, my lady."

She gazed up at him. "You must have a mother who drilled good manners into you, my lord, and told you to always compliment a young lady. I know I do not dance well. You do not have to pretend otherwise."

His brow creased. "I find that I did enjoy dancing with you, Miss Stanhope. I also look forward to supping together." He glanced about the room. "I do not see Tia or Merriman anywhere. It is possible they have already gone home. After all, they are newlyweds."

She would be humiliated if he left her now, but pride stiffened her spine. "If you need to beg off, my lord, I understand. I know why you asked me to dance this evening. It had to be at Lady Merriman's request. We had an enjoyable conversation, and I think she feels a bit of pity for me."

He placed his hand over hers, causing an odd rush of sensation along her spine. "First, I never do anything I do not wish to do, Miss Stanhope. That includes dancing with you. Second, I engaged you for the supper dance because I *wanted* to share supper with you. I would never cry off—and neither should you."

Flustered, she said, "No, my lord. I simply meant . . . if you would rather . . ." Her voice faded, and then determination filled her. "Let me try that again. Thank you for asking me to dance with you this evening, Lord Dyer. I am eager to sup with you, as well."

He smiled at her, causing her to grow warm. "That is more like it."

They moved with the crowd and finally arrived in the supper room, and she couldn't help but glance at her friends, who dined together, without the company of any gentlemen present at their tables.

"There they are," Lord Dyer said leading her to the Duke of Millbrooke's table.

As a keen observer of Polite Society, she knew everyone at

this table by name and appearance, even though she had never been introduced to any of them.

The viscount seated her and took the chair next to her, saying, "This is Miss Stanhope. She is the daughter of Viscount Samuel. This is my cousin, the Duke of Millbrooke, and his duchess."

Rowena greeted them, and Lord Dyer continued. "This is the duke's sister and brother-in-law, Lord and Lady Aldridge."

Again, she greeted the pair, then Lord and Lady Merriman arrived at the table, and the countess leaned down, warmly embracing her.

"I am so glad to see you again this evening, Miss Stanhope. I heard you did well at cards last night."

"Yes, my lady. I had a most skilled partner."

Lord Merriman snorted. "I have partnered with you before, Miss Stanhope. I know that you carried the evening and your partner. Congratulations on your win."

"Thank you," she said modestly, knowing the earl was exactly right. Her partner had been quite good at following her lead, which had led them to a victory over the other couples they had faced at the card party.

The men agreed to go to the buffet and fetch plates for the ladies, and Lord Dyer asked her if she had any food she particularly favored.

"Anything sweet, my lord. I fear I am a fiend for sweets."

He smiled easily. "Then that is something we have in common, my lady. I promise I will return with plenty of sweets for us to share, as well as a few other items."

The men departed for the buffet line, and she said, "Thank you for the invitation to your wedding, Lady Merriman. It was simply lovely. You and Lady Delilah made for the most beautiful brides I have ever seen."

"I wonder where she and Lord Forsythe are this evening," Her Grace mused, looking about.

Lady Aldridge gave her sister-in-law a knowing smile. "They

are newlyweds, Eden. I am certain they have thought of better things to do than attend another boring ball."

The duchess blushed prettily. "You are right." She looked to Lady Merriman. "Then why are you here this evening, Tia?"

"Hugo thought it important that we appear at a few events together. We will leave for Merrifield by the end of the week. I believe he wanted to prove to Polite Society—and himself—that our union is no dream."

"He spoke his vows beautifully yesterday," Rowena said, having listened carefully and not having heard Lord Merriman stutter once.

Her new friend beamed. "He did, didn't he? I know he practiced a great deal and that it meant so much to him to speak them without a single stammer."

"At least the *ton* has done what they should have all along and turned away from Lord Balch and Lord Calley," Lady Aldridge said. "I am glad they have embraced you and your new husband, Tia."

The men returned with plates piled high with food, and the next half hour proved to be delightful. It was obvious the others knew one another well because there was much teasing and camaraderie between them. The conversation was also stimulating. She had never sat a duke's table before, and Rowena was surprised just how informed everyone was regarding affairs of the day, especially politics. She was eagerly embraced by this group, and her opinions solicited often.

"Miss Stanhope has read *Gulliver's Travels*," Lord Dyer told the others.

"I have read it several times," His Grace said. "Did you enjoy reading it as much as I did, Miss Stanhope?"

"I, too, have read it multiple times, Your Grace."

"Which of the four sections did you find the most appealing? I found myself enthralled by the first one in Lilliput, but the second, at Brobdingnab, was also entertaining."

"I agree, Your Grace. I rather liked how he goes from one

extreme to the other. Did you feel Swift was comparing Gulliver to Joseph from the Bible? Especially how he is sold to the queen of that realm."

"I had not thought of that, my lady. I shall give that section another read," the duke said.

For the next several minutes, she and the duke chatted about the book, the others interjecting their own thoughts occasionally. She did not think many members in Polite Society read, much less a book as lengthy as Swift's tale.

Rowena couldn't help herself and said, "I find this discussion so intellectually stimulating. Thank you for including me at your table this evening, Your Grace."

Millbrooke smiled at her. "You are always welcome here, Miss Stanhope. I have enjoyed talking about Gulliver and his travels with you."

Lady Aldridge said, "Do you do any charity work, Miss Stanhope?"

"Why, yes, my lady. I have in the past but am not engaged in any specific endeavor at the moment."

The marchioness brightened. "My husband and I own Oakbrooke Orphanage. We are always looking for new volunteers to come and help with the children. I know you must be quite busy, but perhaps when you return next Season, you might be able to donate a bit of time to our orphanage."

"I remain in town throughout the year, my lady. My father prefers town over the country."

"Splendid," Lord Aldridge said. "My wife and I come to town for two days a week, year-round, since our country home is in Surrey, and we are so close. We spend those two days with our orphans. We would be delighted to have your company at Oakbrooke. It is run by a good friend of ours, Miss Darnell. I feel the two of you would get along quite well."

"I shall look into doing so, my lord."

The marquess added, "We are leaving town tomorrow, but we will return next Wednesday and be here for two days. Would either day be convenient for you to stop by and let us show you the classrooms and meet our children?"

"I could do so on Wednesday, my lord," Rowena said, excited by the prospect of volunteering her time for a good cause. With the Season winding down, this would give her something to look forward to and make her feel useful. She had never been to an orphanage before and found it interesting a marquess and marchioness not only owned one but seemed to devote much of their time to it.

"I will write to you about the particulars," Lady Aldridge told her. "If you would like, we could call for you on our way to Oakbrooke next Wednesday. Would nine o'clock be too early for you?"

"Not at all. I am an early riser."

She shared where she and Papa lived, and they told her how much they looked forward to seeing her again next week.

"I think since we are leaving tomorrow morning, we should depart now," Lord Aldridge told the group.

Lord Merriman said to his wife, "Are you also ready to leave, my love?"

Rowena was touched by the earl's tender address, and it was obvious to see just how much this couple loved one another.

"Yes. I have had quite enough socializing for one night," Lady Merriman said. Looking to Rowena, she added, "It was most enjoyable visiting with you this evening, Miss Stanhope. I do hope we will see one another again before my husband and I leave for the country."

Lord Dyer helped her to her feet, and as the other couples departed, he asked, "Would you care to get a bit of fresh air before the musicians began playing again, my lady?"

Suddenly, a stroll on a moonlit terrace with a handsome viscount was exactly what Rowena wished to do.

Chapter Four

Con was surprised at how much he had enjoyed Miss Stanhope's company at supper. She had fit in well with his family, which was no easy thing for an outsider to do. They were so comfortable with one another, and she was a stranger to them, yet Miss Stanhope had not shied away from questions. She had also freely entered the conversation, where most young ladies in her position would have been intimidated, sitting at a duke's table. One of the most interesting discussions of supper had been listening to her and Val discuss a book Con had read once before. Now, he wanted to read the novel again.

And get to know Miss Stanhope better.

They moved to the ballroom again, which was empty, and headed for the French doors leading out to the terrace. He enjoyed the moment the cool breeze floated over him. July in a crowded London ballroom could become most unpleasant. Con decided when he became the Earl of Marley, he might consider holding a ball outdoors. Surely, it had to be better than ones held in stifling ballrooms, with ladies fanning themselves and gentlemen wishing they could shuck their coats and waistcoats.

Unfortunately, the terrace was full of others. He glanced down and saw other couples sitting on the stone steps leading down to the garden, as well as spying two couples entering the gardens.

Easing Miss Stanhope through the crowd, Con guided her

down the steps.

"Would you care to stroll the gardens?" he inquired, noting she looked immediately to them as another couple entered.

"I suppose we could," she demurred. "It seems others have the same idea."

They moved toward the entrance to the gardens, which had a group of lanterns in front of it. Picking up one, he held it in his right hand, as Miss Stanhope had hold of his left arm.

As they moved along the path, she inhaled deeply. "Oh, the scent of flowers is so pungent in the night air. It is as if flowers sleep all day and come alive at night."

"I had not thought of it that way, but you are right," he agreed. "It seems much easier to catch their scent now." He breathed in. "I smell sweet peas. And roses. How about you?"

He halted their steps, and she bent, sniffing a bloom. "Hmm. Delphiniums. And jasmine."

She righted herself, and they continued along the way. Con could see a few lanterns ahead of them when they reached a fork in the path. The lights were to the right.

Instead, he chose the path which went left, not quite certain why he did so, seeming to want a quiet moment with the lady he escorted.

"Have you enjoyed the Season this year, my lady?"

She laughed, a deep, throaty laugh that caught his attention. "This Season has been much like last Season. And the year before that one."

"So, you have been out three years?"

"Yes, my lord. Unwed—and with no prospects."

He halted again. "You say it so . . . blithely. Not many ladies would be as happy as you are in your position."

"You must know I would never be a choice of any gentleman perusing the Marriage Mart."

Con gazed at her intently. "And why is that, Miss Stanhope? You are most attractive, even if you are hiding your figure behind a poorly tailored gown. Are you trying to keep suitors at bay?"

He sensed her hesitation. "Pardon me if I have become too personal. It is not my business to comment on the cut of your gown."

She tugged on his arm, and they continued along the path.

"You are correct. I do hide myself. On purpose."

"Why so?" he asked, very curious about her reasons. "You have a great wit. You saw how those at my cousin's table flocked to you. They enjoyed conversing with you and hearing what you had to say. It surprises me that you do not have a line of bachelors at your elbow, fighting to gain your attention."

"Perhaps because I do not want a line of bachelors, my lord. I do not wish to have any suitors at all."

They had come to a bench, and he guided them toward it, indicating for them to sit. Con set the lantern on the ground and looked at Miss Stanhope. Part of her face was in shadow, but he could see enough to know she regarded him with a pensive look.

"Since we will only be together this one time on this one night, I shall tell you of myself," she began. "I am an only child. My mother died soon after giving birth to me. My father depended upon her for everything, and he transferred that dependence to me."

"Was that a heavy burden as a child?" he asked.

She shrugged. "I did not know anything else. I only know he has seemed helpless my entire life. Papa cared for Mama a great deal. He might have even loved her. The reason we remain in town all year is because he does not want to be in a place where they lived together. He has told me how painful it is to enter a room and think of her no longer being there. Playing the pianoforte in the drawing room. Sitting at the breakfast table. Because of that, we stay here."

"He must trust his estate manager a great deal to neglect it as he does."

"Oh, my cousin Ollie serves as Stanfield's steward and is its future lord. He sends monthly reports to me. I can tell you about crop yields and our tenants and their families. Why, only yesterday, I received a letter telling me of the birth of a new babe. I will embroider a blanket and send it to Mrs. Roberts."

"Does Lord Samuel also read these reports from your cousin?"

She chuckled. "No. Never. Papa does not trouble himself with anything about his estate or his household. Ollie runs one, with advice from me, while I run the other on my own."

She told him a bit about the country estate in Dorset, near Weymouth, and how much she loved the country.

"We have only been back to Stanfield a handful of times during my life, but I know it is a place I want to live when I come into control of my dowry in three years' time. And I will have lovely neighbors. Lord and Lady Pebble are nearby. Lady Pebble was my mother's dearest friend, and she and the viscount have treated me as a daughter all these years."

"Is that why you fight to keep gentlemen away? Because you enjoy your independence?" He sensed her hesitation. "You do not have to answer that question, Miss Stanhope."

"You are correct," she said softly. "I have always valued being independent. As long as my father's household runs like clockwork and all his needs are taken care of, I am left to do what I wish. I make sure rooms are cleaned properly, rugs beaten and bedclothes washed. I have hired the best cook available, and the meals placed on the table are to Papa's liking. I even visit with his tailor and recommend what additions he needs to his wardrobe and select the materials to be used in making it up. Even doing all that, I have much time to spend on my own. I pursue my interests. History. Architecture. Literature."

"No one tells you what to do," he said quietly. "It is as if you live as a man."

"Exactly," she agreed enthusiastically. "Why would I wish to have strangers woo me and wed one of them? I have everything I need for now. When I turn five and twenty, I have access to my dowry if I have not wed by then. I plan to retire to Dorset and live in a cottage on Stanfield lands. Ollie has already approved of my plan, and as he will be the viscount someday, there is no foreseeable problem."

"Except loneliness," Con said. "It is all well and good that you can come and go as you please, but won't you miss companionship? Or the idea of one day having children?"

She did not answer, so he said, "I will share with you that I am lonely. Val—Millbrooke—and I have been with one another most of our lives. We went to school together. University together. We even shared rooms in town after we completed our education. Now, I do not begrudge him finding Eden. They are madly in love, but I find myself walking about the rooms, longing for someone to talk with."

"His Grace has wed. You should do the same," she recommended.

"I cannot. My title is a courtesy one. There is no land or income attached to it. I could not court a woman and wed her, only to return to live in three tiny, dark rooms. I receive a small quarterly allowance, akin to a lady's pin money. How could I wed and expect a lady to be happy in such circumstances?"

Con shook his head. "No, I will not consider marriage until I have become the Earl of Marley."

"So, that is why you have never called upon a lady," Miss Stanhope mused.

"You know that?" he asked, shocked.

She chuckled. "Oh, I know a great deal, my lord. When a wallflower is near, others speak openly, as if she is not there. I hear a great deal of gossip. I can tell you all about which gentlemen have been unfaithful in their marriages. Which ladies are increasing and have yet to share that publicly. Which children are giving fits to their mamas. Which men have run up debts in gaming hells. I listen—and learn. I am an invisible bystander."

He took her hand, threading his fingers through hers. "You could be so much more. You are clever and kind. Full of life. Enjoyable to be around. If you let down your guard and did not dress to frighten gentlemen away, you could have numerous men eating from the palm of your hand."

Con felt the tension within her. "If I did what you said, then they would come calling. Papa would not refuse if one offered for me, and then I would be trapped. I would be as a bird whose wings had been clipped, forced to wed someone I did not wish to, spending the rest of my life in a prison, freedom just outside my grasp."

"Not all men are jailers, Miss Stanhope."

"No, but one can never be certain which ones would be. As things stand now, I have my freedom as long as I see to Papa. When I reach my majority and can access my dowry, then I will choose to live the life I wish to."

"Will this not anger your father, your leaving suddenly?"

"Frankly, I do not think Papa will live until then," she revealed. "His doctor has told me that he has a weak heart, and it is only getting weaker. The last time he examined Papa, he told me that he did not think Papa would live another year. Still, he has surprised us because that was almost nine months ago. I do notice his shortness of breath. How slowly he moves. He does nothing strenuous. I handle all his business affairs, as well as matters regarding Stanfield."

"It seems you have your life planned out," Con told her.

"I do. At first, it hurt my feelings when I was called a bluestocking during my first Season, but then I learned to embrace the term and my own independence."

"Do you regret never having been kissed?" he asked.

She jerked her hand from his. "That is a most personal question, Lord Dyer."

"You sound upset—but I do not think you are. Even now, I think you are pondering my question. Wondering why I asked it."

"Why *did* you ask it?" she demanded.

"Because I very much want to kiss you, Miss Stanhope."

It was true. The more he spoke with her, the more he liked her. And the more he wanted to kiss her.

"We have been honest with one another," he continued. "Some would say we have bared our souls to each other. For all my appearance, you know I actually live close to poverty and would never ask a woman to be my wife. I understand how you cherish your freedom and pursue intellectual matters, which forces you to hide your true self in order to keep suitors at bay."

"But why does sharing those things with one another lead you to want to kiss me?" she asked, clearly confused.

"I am lonely. In your own way, so are you. And you said it yourself. Most likely, we will never have such an intimate conversation with one another again. Since you have no plans to wed, I thought you might be interested in seeing what a kiss is like."

She studied him a moment. "You surprise me, Lord Dyer. I had written you off as a flirt. A man who could playfully tease a woman but hold no interest in her. You have more depth to you than I imagined. I am surprised by how much I like you."

He smiled. "I like you, as well, Miss Stanhope."

Con's hand cradled her nape. She wet her lips, causing desire to flare within him. Then she placed her palm against his cheek.

"Yes," she whispered. "I would like to see what a kiss is like. No obligation to one another. Just something to add to my experiences."

He placed his lips against hers, the sweet smell of the garden's blooms surrounding them. He kissed her softly, breaking the kiss and repeating it, again and again. Her other hand came up so that her hands framed his face. Increasing the pressure, he kissed her harder, wanting more from her. Wanting her to give a little of herself to him. She responded, her hands sliding down his neck, gripping his shoulders, kissing him back.

Desire flickered within him, and he slowly ran his tongue along the seam of her mouth, surprising her. She opened as if to ask him what was next, and he took advantage of that, slipping his tongue inside her mouth. Their tongues mated, and he stroked hers, the fire within him beginning to burn brightly.

He tugged gently on her hair, and her head fell back, allowing him to deepen the kiss. She murmured something indistinguishable but kept kissing him. Con longed to cup her breast or run his hand up her leg, but they had not agreed to anything beyond a kiss. Because of that, he would keep his hands off her body, even though he was still curious about what lay under the sackcloth of a gown she wore.

They kissed for some time, surprising him, because he had usually been one to kiss no longer than a minute or two before diving into the deep end. He found kissing Miss Stanhope most enjoyable.

Finally, he knew he had to stop. The ball had already begun by now. Partners whom he had arranged dances with had been left standing alone. Reluctantly, he broke the kiss, already regretting his doing so.

"We must return to the ballroom," he told her as he reached for the lantern. He brought it up and saw the glazed look in her eyes. The yearning he had left there. Despite everything Con had said about not being interested in finding a bride at this point in his life, he suddenly very much wished to call upon Miss Stanhope to get to know more about her.

"Might I see you tomorrow?" he asked huskily. "Call upon you?"

Slowly, she nodded. Then she smiled at him. He had not seen her do so all evening, and the smile affected him in ways he did not understand.

"Good."

He rose, offering her his hand. She took it, and they moved along the path, heading back to the house.

The terrace only held two couples now, and they hurried past them, entering the ballroom again. He deposited her back where he had claimed her, and he knew he had the attention of every wallflower seated there as they eagerly looked upon Miss Stanhope and him.

"I will see you tomorrow," he promised.

"Yes," she agreed, looking as if she did not trust herself to speak more than that single word.

Con hurriedly moved through the ballroom, stopping an acquaintance to ask which dance was now being performed. He found his partner awaiting him and apologized for his tardiness, taking her out onto the floor and paying close attention to her. He did the same for each of the partners who followed, forcing himself to focus on them alone, when all he wanted to do was think of Miss Stanhope and those beautiful brown eyes rimmed in amber.

The ball came to its conclusion, and he did not bother to search for a hansom cab in the crush of carriages outside the Purlington's townhouse. It would be far easier to walk home than be caught up in that crowd. Besides, it gave him time to think on the way home.

About Miss Stanhope.

He would need to call on Tia and Hugo tomorrow and let his cousin know how grateful he was for her asking him to do the simple favor of dancing with Miss Stanhope. While he knew he could not change his circumstances, much less talk her out of her desire to never wed, Con did plan to see her as much as he could for the rest of the Season—and beyond. Knowing now that she remained in town once the Season concluded, he could picture long walks in Hyde Park with her. Visits to the British Museum. Even going to Gunter's for an ice. He now yearned for her company.

Perhaps, they might form a friendship. Perhaps, it might become even more. For now, Con would settle for calling upon Miss Stanhope tomorrow afternoon.

He reached his rooms and unlocked the door. He had yet to step through the door when he heard a voice calling, "My lord! Lord Dyer! You must come at once!"

Turning, he saw one of his parents' footmen. Fear rippled through him.

"What is it?"

The footman, who had been running, now paused, panting. He placed his hands on his thighs and lowered his head, breathing hard, trying to catch his breath.

"Is it Lord Marley?" he asked, dreading the servant's response.

"Yes," replied the footman. "Lady Marley sent for the doctor. She also wants you to be there."

Con took off running, leaving his door open and the footman far behind. He raced the few blocks between his rooms and the Alington townhouse, bursting into the foyer.

"Where is he?"

A footman pointed, and he ran up the stairs and down the hallway. He reached his father's bedchamber and paused, trying to gain his breath. Tears already stung his eyes as he pushed open the door.

He saw his mother at the bedside, along with the doctor. Papa's valet stood at the foot of the bed, disbelief on his face.

Con went to the bed and clasped his father's hand. The warmth seemed to be fading.

"I am here, Papa," he said desperately. "I am here. It is Con."

His father's eyes were closed. He merely groaned. Con didn't know if Papa heard him or not. He squeezed his father's fingers, willing life from him to his father. Instead, he sensed it ebbing away.

For a moment, Papa squeezed back. Then his hand went limp.

"No!" he cried hoarsely, falling to the bed, wrapping himself around Papa.

After a moment, he heard Mama say, "He is gone, Marley."

It struck him that she now called him Marley. In a matter of a few seconds, Con's life had changed.

And not necessarily for the better.

CHAPTER FIVE

*H*E WASN'T COMING.

That was all Rowena could think of as she sat on the settee in the drawing room.

She had dressed with care this morning, not wishing to try too hard, but donning a gown that fit better than most. While the cut was slightly more flattering than most of her day gowns, the color was a drab olive, washing out her skin. Still, it was the closest thing she had to something decent.

But it had all been for naught—because Viscount Dyer had not shown up.

She glanced at the grandfather clock that stood in a corner of the drawing room. Rowena hadn't thought he would arrive at the beginning of morning calls, but she had been in the drawing room half an hour early just in case. As she had sat waiting, tension filling her, she realized she was not merely sad. She was deeply hurt. Lord Dyer had seemed different from other gentlemen of the *ton*. His honesty had been refreshing as he spoke to her of his loneliness and limited funds.

Now, she could not help but wonder if it had all been a lie.

Had he played a cruel joke on her? She still believed Lady Merriman had sent him to dance with her. Her heart wanted to believe that they had enjoyed a connection, both at supper last night and as they had talked while strolling the gardens.

And then there was that kiss.

Oh, what a glorious thing kissing was. Or was it kissing Viscount Dyer that made it thus? She would never know. She doubted she would see him again. Actually, she would see him across the room at balls or Venetian breakfasts or musicales. They simply would never allow their gazes to meet, much less acknowledge one another.

Her throat grew tight. For the first time ever, tears misted her eyes. Rowena made a conscious decision not to let any fall. She refused to cry over a wicked rake such as Lord Dyer. Well, perhaps he was not a rake. If he were, he kept his assignations with other women quiet, and none of them spoke ill of him afterward.

Why had he poured his heart out to her and asked if he could call upon her, only to leave her dangling?

The only thing she could think of was that Lord Dyer was embarrassed. Embarrassed by how much truth he had spoken to her last night. Ashamed of how openly he had been in her presence. He might be ashamed for revealing so much to a stranger and believe things would be awkward for them as they faced one another in the light of day. It was one thing to share confidences in a dimly lit garden where it was hard to read the expression on your companion's face. It was quite another thing to sit across from one another in a drawing room and know how much you had revealed to someone.

If he weren't coming, he might at least have had the decency to send around a note. A note, she could understand. He could have written and told her that some unexpected appointment came up, and he was unable to visit with her today. She could have read between the lines and figured out that he did not wish to see her again. Though she had thought much of him last night, her opinion of him had fallen. She had not taken him for a gutless milksop, yet that is exactly what she thought of him now. He could have showed up at her doorstep and told her he was uncomfortable with all that they had spoken about. That it would best to end their budding friendship before it even started.

No, Viscount Dyer had taken the coward's way out, leaving her sitting in an empty drawing room, hoping he would show up. Thank goodness she had not asked Papa to wait here with her for Lord Dyer's arrival. That would have been most humiliating. She had thought merely to send a servant for Papa when Lord Dyer arrived so that they would be suitably chaperoned.

Glancing at the clock again, she saw the time for morning calls had ended. The teacart would soon appear, along with Papa.

Five minutes later, both arrived simultaneously. She poured out for them, forcing herself to eat a few bites. Not that Papa's suspicions would be aroused. It seemed he never noticed anything about her. Not what she wore, nor how she dressed her hair. He never was interested in the books she read or the places she went. Rowena realized now that he had always been a ghost to her, present in body and yet gone in mind and spirit. He moved as if in the shadows.

Recalling what she and Lord Dyer had spoken about last night, she couldn't help but think she, too, might one day appear as a wraith, living such a quiet life as to really live no life at all. The thought depressed her. How was she to go to whatever *ton* event was scheduled for this evening and pretend all was well when it very much was not one whit.

She needed space to breathe. To think about her future and what she truly wanted.

Rowena realized she wished to go home to Dorset.

It was funny how she thought of Stanfield and Dorset as home when she had lived a majority of her life in the largest city in the world, but the country spoke to her heart.

"Papa, I would like to visit Stanfield."

He set down his saucer. "We were there not too long ago."

"No," she said, shaking her head. "We last visited when I was ten and seven. I remember because it was the year before I made my come-out." Rowena paused. "And I am now in my third Season."

"My, how time flies," he said, wincing. "Perhaps we can go in a few months."

"I do not wish to go in a few months. I wish to go now." She realized she sounded like a petulant child and softened her tone. "I need to breathe in the country air, Papa. It would not hurt to meet with Cousin Ollie and see how the estate fares, along with its tenants."

"Oh, but you do such a good job of taking care of things for me, Rowena. Ollie, too. He is a good boy."

"That boy is a man who is close to thirty years of age, Papa," she gently reminded him.

"He is?"

"Yes. Ollie is seven years my senior. I am two and twenty now."

Again, he looked at her. "You are? Where has the time gone?"

He winced again, and concern filled her. "Is everything all right, Papa? You look a bit unwell." She glanced at his plate and saw he had eaten next to nothing. "I think we should call the doctor and let him look you over."

"No need to . . ." His voice trailed off and as she watched him, he slowly crumpled, falling to the floor.

"Papa!" she screamed, falling to her knees, listening to him moan.

Rowena leapt to her feet and rang for the butler. The minute he appeared, she said, "Send for the doctor at once! His lordship has collapsed."

The butler fled the room, and she rushed back to her father. Kneeling, she sat upon her feet, placing his head in her lap. Lovingly, she stroked his cheek.

"Open your eyes, Papa. Everything is going to be fine. I promise."

She knew it was a promise which would not be kept. His heart was finally giving out.

He shuddered, as if he'd been deeply chilled. A strangled sound came from him, and his hands flew to his chest. His eyes opened, bulging.

"Rowena," he gasped.

"I am here, Papa. The doctor is coming. You are going to be fine."

"No," he said sadly. "I am . . . not."

She had asked his doctor to keep the news from him regarding his unsound heart. She had not wanted to worry him unnecessarily. He had always been so childlike, while she had been the adult in the household, despite her tender age. Now, it looked as if Papa were hanging by a thread. Suddenly, a picture of the banquet King Dionysius held for Damocles came to mind. The king had tired of Damocles' incessant flattery and placed him in a seat at the banquet which was directly beneath a sword. The sword was suspended by a single hair. All waited with bated breath to see if the sword dropped. She felt as if that sword was one of death now, and her father was about to be no more.

Rowena cursed silently, angry that she was distracted by the long-ago story a tutor had shared with her. She must focus on Papa and save him.

Looking down at him, their gazes met. He struggled but managed to say, "You are a good girl, Rowena. You . . . always cared for me."

Then he clutched his chest, crying out in pain. By now, their butler had returned, a brigade of footmen with him, ready to carry her father to his bed. As half a dozen servants looked on, he whimpered. Then his hands fell away from his chest, dropping uselessly to his sides.

"Papa!" she cried. "Papa, hold on."

But her heart told her he had slipped away. Her fingers went to his throat, searching for a beating pulse and finding none. A vast emptiness filled her. Surprisingly, her eyes remained dry. Here she had almost cried over a viscount not showing up in their drawing room, and yet the passing of her own father left her dry-eyed.

Dully, she informed the servants. "He is gone." Rowena forced herself to raise her head and saw the shock—and grief—in the eyes of those gathered.

"Please take Lord Samuel to his bedchamber," she asked quietly. "When the doctor arrives, send him up to us."

The footmen, under their butler's supervision, lifted Papa gently and carried him upstairs. Once there, she asked his valet to remain behind.

"After the doctor has seen to him, I wish for you to prepare Papa," she explained. "His body is to be bathed. Dress him in something dark blue. He always favored wearing that color."

"Yes, my lady," the valet responded, tears streaming down his cheeks.

"He is to be placed in the front parlor. I will arrange for a footman to be with him at all times. See now to the bath and the clothes he will be laid to rest in."

The valet left her, and the doctor arrived two minutes later. He examined his patient and then looked at her sadly.

"I am greatly sorry for your loss, Miss Stanhope. I hope it was the right thing to do to keep Lord Samuel's shaky health from him."

"It was," she said firmly. "With his weakened heart, any worrying on his part might have caused me to lose him sooner. As it was, he enjoyed his last year on earth." She paused. "Thank you for coming. Would you mind sending the butler to me as you leave?"

"Of course, my lady."

When the butler appeared, she said, "Send for the vicar of St. George's. I must arrange for the funeral to take place. Also, a message must be sent to my cousin at Stanhope to inform him the title is now his. I will write this, and then you must see it sent as quickly as possible."

"Yes, my lady."

"Also, gather the staff in the foyer. I will address them."

"At once, my lady."

She waited until he had left and then bent and kissed her father's brow. He was already cold to the touch. Stoically, she left the room, writing a quick note to Ollie to come to town because he was the new Viscount Samuel. She sealed it and took it with her.

The foyer was full of servants, the men having removed their hats, holding them in hand over their hearts. She paused several steps from the bottom, the better to see everyone.

"As you might have heard, we lost Lord Samuel this afternoon. The household will go into mourning, and you shall wear a black armband. His body will be placed in the front parlor. You may say a last goodbye if you wish to. I will send for the new Lord Samuel. My advice to him will be to retain everyone on staff, but I cannot promise you will have a position. It will be up to him."

Since Ollie had yet to wed, Rowena believed he would take any suggestions she gave him. The house already ran efficiently, so she would advise no cuts be made. A housekeeper would need to be hired, however, since she had served in that capacity. Rowena would leave town as soon as possible and return to Dorset.

She gave the letter for Ollie to the butler, and he motioned to a footman who claimed it and left the house. Rowena spoke with the head footman, describing the need to have a servant present at her father's side for at least the next two or three days.

"I can arrange for that, my lady."

The vicar arrived. She had seen him only a handful of days ago as he had overseen the weddings of Lady Tia and Lady Delilah. Now, he would be required to manage the funeral services for Papa.

"My condolences on your loss, Miss Stanhope," he began.

She was known to him because of volunteer work she had done at St. George's.

"I would like the service to be held as soon as possible. The heat, you know."

Papa had complained on several occasions of funerals being held too far past the date of death, especially if they occurred in the heat of summer. He had told Rowena long ago that when his time came, he wished to be buried quickly, with little fuss.

"When your footman delivered the news to me, I took the liberty of consulting the schedule regarding the church. We could hold the service the day after tomorrow at ten o'clock if that pleases you."

"Yes, that will be fine. Is there anything you need from me in order to prepare?"

"No, my lady. I will handle everything at St. George's. My sexton will aid me in this venture. He will even dig the grave. I assume you wish to have Lord Samuel buried here in town. He did so love it here. I know there is a spot next to your mother."

She knew that because she visited it frequently, trying to find a connection with a woman long dead. Growing up, she had wondered why Papa had not buried his wife at Stanfield, but then she realized he wished to be close to her and found comfort from that.

"Yes, that would be his wishes."

The vicar left. Shortly afterward, Aunt Sylvia arrived, Lord and Lady Pebble in tow. She supposed the butler had sent word to them.

"Oh, my dear," her aunt said, taking Rowena into her arms. "This is such a very sad day. Losing Samuel will be hard on us both."

Lord Pebble echoed her aunt's words. "Your father was a decent man, Rowena. He will be sorely missed by us all."

She led them to the drawing room, where Cook sent in some tea and sandwiches for them. Although she sipped on the tea, she could not force down a single bite.

"You must come and live with me now," Aunt Sylvia said.

That was the last thing she wanted to do. Just like her brother, Aunt Sylvia remained in town throughout the year, living in two rooms on the small widow's allowance she had. Too much furniture and too many knickknacks filled those rooms. If Rowena moved there, she knew she would suffocate.

"You could come and stay with us in the country for a while," Lady Pebble suggested. "Town may hold too many sad memories for you. The Season is almost finished as it is."

"I will contact Samuel's solicitor for you," the viscount said. "Surely, your father made arrangements for you in the case of his passing."

"Thank you. I wish to see Papa buried, and then I do plan to return to Stanfield."

"Does Ollie know of your plans?" her aunt asked. "When my husband's cousin took on the title, I was no longer welcome on the estate. Ollie may feel the same way about you."

"I have sent word to him regarding Papa's passing. As far as where I will live, Ollie has previously consented to my use of a cottage at Stanfield once Papa is gone and he takes on the viscountcy." She smiled at Aunt Sylvia. "But I do appreciate your kind offer."

Lady Pebble frowned. "Surely, you could either stay in the main house with your cousin or even remain in this townhouse. Having to live in a cottage?" Her nose wrinkled in disgust.

"No, it is what I wish to do," she insisted. "I am tired of life in town. Tired of the Season. I wish to go to Dorset permanently."

"At least until next Season," Aunt Syliva said. "You still need to find a husband, Niece."

Rowena did not correct her aunt. She had no plans to ever return to town again, but she saw no need to cause a fuss now. When next spring came, she would simply remain at Stanfield.

And continue to do so for the rest of her life.

Chapter Six

Rowena dressed for the day, happy that she had given away her wardrobe of dreary, poorly fitted gowns. She no longer hid behind her gold spectacles, either, though she had kept them as a reminder of her days in town. She was able to do so, thanks to Papa's will.

Two months had passed since her father's death, and she missed being able to speak with him each day. After the funeral, Ollie had arrived in town a few days later, and she had helped smooth his transition at the townhouse. After introducing him to the servants, he had agreed to keep the staff intact. She had hired a competent housekeeper, explaining to Ollie that she had functioned in that role for many years and that the townhouse would need one since she planned to remain in Dorset.

She and Ollie had met with Papa's solicitor, and he had let her cousin know where Ollie stood financially. Rowena already had a good grasp of her cousin's inherited fortune since she had handled Papa's business affairs. The real surprise had been that Rowena had been given immediate access to her dowry. Though she was supposed to gain control of it in three years if she were still unwed, Papa's will stipulated that the entire amount go to her in the event his death preceded that date.

Ollie had accompanied her back to Stanfield, pressing her to live with him in the main house. She had agreed to for the first month, simply because the house had not been opened up in many years. Ollie himself had lived in the cottage designated for the steward of the estate.

Before they left town, she had hired a butler, housekeeper, and cook for Stanfield, along with two maids and two footmen. She trained this staff to the best of her ability and also hired an additional two maids from Mossleigh, the nearby village. Both would serve as scullery maids, which made the new cook happy.

While Ollie had a horse of his own and had cared for it himself, their coachman from town had come with them to serve the new viscount. He had recommended his brother be hired as the groom for their stables. Rowena had even gone with Ollie to purchase two more horses for riding. One, Aurora, had been his gift to her. The horse would be stabled with the others at Stanfield, and she was allowed to come and ride Aurora whenever she chose to do so.

The new staff had helped prepare the cottage she now lived in, and Rowena looked about it, pleased that it was permanently hers, another gift from her generous cousin. She had a girl named Betsy come in twice a week to clean for her, and Betsy took any laundry which needed to be done home with her, returning with it the next time she came.

The one thing Rowena had struggled with was cooking. She had not known how to cook and had not thought of that when she decided to live on her own. She had asked Ollie's new cook for cooking lessons so she might learn the basics and taken everything to heart which the woman had taught her. Unfortunately, her intellect did not extend to the kitchen. These days, her breakfast was a light one, consisting of tea and toast and the occasional poached egg, which was all Rowena seemed to be able to manage.

Fortunately, Cook wanted Rowena cared for and asked Ollie if she might send meals to her cottage. Her cousin had quickly agreed. Cook sent a footman with dinner every single evening at six, and the footman often brought scones and tarts for her to enjoy at teatime the following afternoon. She took tea with Ollie once or twice a week and also had dinner with him at least once a week. This saved her from having to cook herself, for which she was grateful.

After she finished dressing, she ventured downstairs, preparing tea and toast for herself, a copy of the newspapers Ollie had read yesterday waiting on her doorstep this morning. Her cousin had newspapers delivered from town and then passed these down to her, so Rowena still was informed about the happenings in England and beyond. She did skip over the gossip columns, however, no longer caring about the world of Polite Society and what happened with its members.

Once her leisurely breakfast ended and she completed reading the newspapers, she washed the few dishes and set out for the village. Her first stop was the dressmaker's, and Rowena tried on two new gowns, finding both fit her perfectly. Gradually, she was having a new wardrobe made up for herself, but she included no ballgowns, knowing she would never attend a ball again. She did, however, have a few nicer gowns made up for evening wear, knowing she would, on occasion, be invited to dine with other gentry in the neighborhood, including Lord and Lady Pebble, whom she had grown even closer to since Papa's death.

She called at the stationer's and picked up new paper for writing letters, as well as a new set of pencils. Her art supplies had also been delivered to the shop, consisting of a sketchpad and pastels. She had never taken up art before and found she enjoyed walking about the countryside or along the beach, drawing and painting the surrounding landscape. Rowena doubted she would ever be very good at it, but it was something which brought her pleasure.

Returning to the cottage, she picked up the violin she had borrowed from the music room at Stanfield. Ollie told her she was welcome anytime, so occasionally, she dropped in to play the pianoforte since it was impractical to have one at the cottage. She had always played the instrument and decided she would take up the violin, something which could be easily stored within her cozy cottage. She played for an hour, wincing a few times when she hit a sour note. Practice would make her better, and she determined to devote some of each day to her violin.

After that, she indulged in reading for a couple of hours, one of the things she loved most in life. Again, Ollie had told her the Stanfield library was at her disposal. When she went to tea or dinner there, she would return books she had borrowed and collect new ones to read. Her life was a simple one now, one she enjoyed.

And yet, despite her happiness, she was a bit lonely.

Her thoughts strayed to Lord Dyer, as they often did. She never wanted to think of him, but somehow he appeared in them, nonetheless. She believed she had met the true man during their conversation in the Purlington gardens. He had been open about his life, and she had finally forgiven him for not coming to see her. If he had, he might have felt a further obligation to ask her to dance at future balls or visit her. Even though Rowena had been a part of the *ton*, she had never been the part of the world Viscount Dyer inhabited.

She allowed herself to think of that one magical night where she had sat at his cousin's table, laughing freely and enjoying herself more than she ever had with any group of people. She tried not to, but the thought of their kiss came back to her. Rowena did not regret having kissed him. Those kisses was her most precious memory, something unforgettable, which she would think fondly upon until she was on her deathbed.

Knowing it was time to change her gown, she donned a fresh one because she was to have tea with Lord and Lady Pebble this afternoon. Lord Pebble insisted upon sending his carriage for her on these occasions, and it arrived precisely at a quarter till four. She greeted the coachman and allowed the footman to hand her up. Minutes later, they reached the viscount's estate. Pebblestone was larger than Stanfield, and the owners of each estate had been friends going back for generations. She knew Lord Pebble still mourned the death of her father.

The butler escorted her to the drawing room, and Rowena was warmly welcomed by the pair.

"Rowena, my dear. It is so good to see you," Lady Pebble said. "Come and sit. We have much to discuss this afternoon."

The butler returned a few minutes later, announcing Viscount Samuel had arrived.

"I did not know you would be at tea today," she said, greeting Ollie.

"It is good to see you, Cousin," he said, brushing his lips against her cheek.

Lady Pebble poured out for them, and for the first few minutes, they gossiped a bit about the neighborhood. Their hostess seemed to know everything which went on in the surrounding area, and Rowena could always count on the viscountess for the latest news.

Now, the viscountess cleared her throat. "Lord Pebble and I asked you both to come to tea today because we wish to hold a house party at the end of this month." She smiled at Rowena. "I will need your help in this endeavor."

"You are quite organized, my lady," she said. "I doubt you would need help from either of us. Unless you would like to discuss the guest list. I might be able to help you with it."

Lady Pebble smiled. "We think it is time for Lord Samuel to take a wife."

Her cousin blushed as he became the sudden center of attention. "I thought I might consider a bride next Season," he told them.

"That is all well and good," the viscountess continued. "But the Season can be overwhelming, especially for one who has not attended it before. You have been buried in the country all these years, my lord. I thought I might help introduce you into Polite Society by hosting this house party in your honor. Of course, Rowena must attend, as well. It would help round out the numbers. Pebble also has a cousin whose daughter is most shy. She was to have made her come-out this past spring, but she was too anxious to do so and delayed it. I believe she will do better in the company of a smaller group, so I would like to invite her, as well."

Ollie said, "I do know it is time for me to wed. I turned thirty last week and am conscious of the fact I must provide an heir. Yes, my lady. The idea of a house party in my honor appeals to me." He looked at Rowena. "Will you promise to come? I had already planned to seek your advice when I choose a bride. Even though I am older than you, you are much more worldly than I am and experienced in the ways of Polite Society."

"If you insist," she said. "Might I ask if a friend of mine be invited, Lady Pebble?"

"Ah, you must mean Miss Tweedham. I would be happy to have her attend. I would hope the both of you would befriend Pebble's cousin's daughter."

"I would prefer staying at my cottage, however," she told her hostess.

Ollie picked up on her cue. "I, too, could stay at Stanfield. We are just minutes away from Pebblestone, and it would free up bedchambers for your other guests so that no one need to share."

"My thought exactly," Rowena said, actually preferring the idea of escaping a large group of guests and having time to herself at the end of each day.

"As long as you promise to attend all the events each day," Lord Pebble said. "Starting with breakfast each day."

She chuckled. "Since I am the one who has to make my own breakfast each morning, I am more than happy to come and partake of food on your breakfast buffet. Assuming you will serve a buffet each morning."

"Yes," Lady Pebble said. "It is simpler to do so when you have a houseful of guests. Why don't you and I go to my sitting room, Rowena? You have been out a few Seasons now and are familiar with members of Polite Society. Together, we can compose the guest list, balancing it so we have a good mixture of people and even numbers of gentlemen and ladies."

They retreated to the viscountess' sitting room and discussed several names, especially eligible young ladies who might suit with Ollie. It was a mix of those who had attended the Season, along with several locals from the neighborhood surrounding Mossleigh.

Lady Pebble perused the list they had composed. "I believe this set of guests will be perfect. Hopefully, they will all be able to attend. We must have a few other names in mind in case not all are available."

"It is very kind of you to hold this house party in Ollie's honor. This way, he has an opportunity to be in the company of ladies and gentlemen of quality, but the setting will be far different than that of a ball."

"Who knows?" Lady Pebble said. "He might find his bride amongst those on this list."

Selfishly, Rowena hoped that her cousin would be drawn to Miss Tweedham. Of all the friends whom she had left behind in the Literary Ladies Book Society, she missed Miss Tweedham most of all. Her friend had always been excellent company. If Ollie found that Miss Tweedham suited him, it would be wonderful to have her as the new Viscountess Samuel and living nearby. Rowena would enjoy being a doting aunt to their children, much as Aunt Sylvia had been to her.

"I shall write out the invitations and issue them at once," Lady Pebble declared. "Make certain you set aside those dates so that you are free, Rowena. You might even find a husband of your own."

She laughed. "You know that has never been my goal."

The viscountess frowned. "You have told me that for years. I simply do not understand why you do not wish to be a wife and mother."

"I enjoy a simple life, my lady."

A knowing look came into Lady Pebble's eyes. "Even bluestockings need companionship, my dear. You might find some gentleman to your liking amongst this group of gentlemen."

No matter how much she explained her position, Lady Pebble would never understand Rowena's choice to remain on the shelf. Yes, sometimes a yearning for children struck her out of the blue, but she always pushed it aside. She would be an aunt to Ollie's children, and that would be enough. This way, she maintained her liberty. Control over her life and her funds.

Smiling brightly, Rowena said, "I am very much looking forward to this house party, my lady."

Chapter Seven

Con concluded his meeting with Tabor, his steward. They had spent several hours going over the final accounting of the autumn harvest. He thanked Tabor for the fine job the estate manager had done and then retreated to his study.

A little over two and a half months had passed since his father has suddenly passed, and Con missed him dreadfully. He had been close to his father, regularly meeting him in town for dinner or drinks at White's. His father had been very open-minded and kind to all. He never judged anyone harshly, nor did Con ever hear a cruel word come from his father's lips.

He felt at loose ends now, with the harvest completed. Tabor was incredibly efficient and really didn't need Con around. While he had enjoyed getting to know his tenants and learn more about the running of Marleyfield, he feared with the harvest over, he would be bored. He itched to go back to town.

To see Miss Stanhope.

Try as he might, he could not forget the kisses they had shared. Though skilled at kissing, Con usually avoided it because it gave women the wrong idea. Kissing was a very intimate act, almost as intimate as coupling, as far as he was concerned. Over the years, he had learned how to please a woman, but if he kissed her on the lips? She seemed to think that he was much more serious about her than he was. He would kiss napes. Elbows. Knees. Even toes. But kissing a woman the way he did Miss

Stanhope was not something he was accustomed to doing very often.

Closing his eyes, he went back to that night in the Purlington gardens. He could smell the sweetly-scented flowers surrounding them as they sat close together on the bench. Slowly, he relived every kiss he could recall—and the feelings of euphoria kissing Miss Stanhope brought to him. He would never forget the taste of her.

And he yearned to kiss her again.

Nothing held him to Marleyfield now, especially since the harvest had been brought in. True, the mill would be operating many hours a day, but that was something Tabor could look after. Con decided he would journey to town and pay Miss Stanhope a visit. He regretted not writing a note to her, telling her of his father's passing and that he and his mother would be leaving immediately for Marleyfield. It was a small thing, but it had bothered him more than he cared to admit. He had thought to write to her and apologize after arriving at Marleyfield, citing his grief as the reason he had not thought to send her a note or even call in person for a brief visit before departing town.

What if she turned him away? She was no wilting flower. Rather, Miss Stanhope was a strong woman of character. She must have been quite angry when he had not shown up as promised. Hopefully, she would agree to see him and allow him to issue a heartfelt apology.

It was time for tea, so he went to the drawing room, finding Mama already present. Mama had not shed a single tear for Papa, something he had trouble understanding. Then again, they were no love match. He gathered his father had been the catch of Mama's come-out Season, a wealthy earl who was handsome and incredibly good-natured. Mama was smart, stubborn, and used to getting her way. She had been the real power in the marriage, and Papa had simply gone along with whatever she desired. He had told Con once it was easier letting Mama have her way than to stand in her path and be demolished.

As she poured out now, she said, "I think I am going to visit a friend of mine in Sussex. She has been pressing me to come to her. She lost her own husband last winter, and so she did not attend the Season this year because she was in mourning. I shared with her that Marley was now gone, and she thought we might bring one another some comfort."

This was better than he could have imagined. He had been wondering what excuse to give, leaving her alone at Marleyfield while he returned to town.

"Will you be there long?" he asked.

"I wrote to her this morning, agreeing to stay for a few months. You do not need me here, and you know I grow bored after being in the country for a while."

"I was actually thinking of returning to town myself for a bit," he confessed. "I could escort you in our carriage as far as town, and then you could continue on your way."

"In the carriage?" she asked, her gaze daring him to deny her its use.

He was the earl, however, and if he were going to completely exercise his power, he must start now.

"No, Mama. I will have need of my carriage in town. However, I will rent a post-chaise for you to continue on to Sussex. They are sleek and fast and will get you to your destination."

"Everything is in order here?" she pressed.

Knowing she had looked at Tabor's reports only yesterday, he said, "You know they are, Mama. You have kept a close eye on the running of Marleyfield. You do not have to do so in the future."

This was his way of telling her that he was in charge of the country estate. It would be interesting to hear her response.

She sighed. "Your father had no head for figures. No idea what money meant. He was always overly generous with others to a fault. I have had to ride roughshod over everyone in order to have people live up to their full potential."

"Well, I am Marley now," he said lightly. "And I have no

need of you looking over my shoulder."

Mama patted his knee. "You have your father's kind spirit—but you take after me in other ways. I suppose it is time to completely turn the reins over to you, Constantine."

She only addressed him familiarly when they were alone, but she refused to call him Con. Mama addressed all three of her children by their full, given name, though each of them chose to go by a more diminutive form of it.

"I am not a gambler, so I will not be a wastrel as far as the estate goes."

Nodding approvingly, she said, "I know you thought I was too harsh with you, keeping you on such a limited allowance. It taught you the value of a coin, however, didn't it?"

"It did," he agreed. "I knew I did not have enough funds to gamble them away. The thought of gambling holds no appeal to me."

She cupped his cheek. "You are a good man, Constantine. Now, all you have to do is find your countess." She paused. "Perhaps that is the reason you are returning to town?"

"The Season is over and done with," he said brusquely, not wishing to reveal his true reason for returning to town. "The Marriage Mart will not be up and running until next spring."

Mama sighed. "A part of me wishes for you to wed one of the girls who is making her come-out. She would be young and easy to mold."

He frowned. "There will be no molding of my wife, Mama. When I do choose whom to wed, I will wed her for who she is—not who you wish to turn her into."

She chuckled. "I do have a tendency to make others dance to my tune. That makes me think you might wish to look to someone who has been out for a bit. Someone with enough polish to be a countess."

"I will take your advice under consideration, Mama." Trying not to sound too eager, he asked, "Would you be ready to leave tomorrow morning? I would hate to keep your friend waiting."

"I suppose we could do so. I shall have my maid pack. Yes, I can be ready tomorrow morning after I breakfast."

"Do not linger too long over your meal," he advised. "It will take us a good two days to reach town. You should plan to stay overnight there before you continue on to Sussex."

"That is a good idea. You know I hate to stop at inns. Too many do not live up to my specific standards."

"I am glad that is settled. I think I shall go speak with Benchley now and advise him we will leave early tomorrow morning."

Con had inherited Benchley from his father. The valet was thirty, just a few years older than Con himself, and the first time he had employed a valet. His pitiful allowance had not provided enough funds to hire one. He hoped Benchley would be with him for many years. Already, the valet spoiled Con, doing something for him before he even thought about it needing to be done. He liked that Benchley anticipated his every need. Having had a valet for two months now, Con wasn't certain he could ever go back to *not* having one.

He passed Mrs. Seward on his way upstairs and informed the housekeeper that he and his mother would be leaving tomorrow morning.

"Mama will be visiting a friend in Sussex for a few months. I will be in town for an indeterminate amount of time. Of course, I will send word when I am to return."

"I will let Seward know of your plans, my lord, and that of Lady Marley."

"Thank you."

Benchley was not in Con's bedchamber, so he rang for him. When the valet arrived, he said, "I am leaving for town tomorrow morning and will be there indefinitely."

"I will prepare for the journey now, my lord. Is there anything special you wish to take with us, or is it up to my discretion?"

"Pack plenty of everyday clothes. A few pairs of evening clothes, as well. The Season might be over, but there is the chance I could have dinner plans and would need to dress appropriately."

"Very well, my lord."

He returned to his study, once more looking through some of the papers his father had left behind. Con had found his mother going through this very stack of papers shortly after they had returned and buried his father. He had let her know in no uncertain terms that he was the Earl of Marley now and would take care of his own business without any help from her. His rebuff had angered her, but her anger had cooled. In fact, Mama had apologized to him.

Because of that, he had continued to seek her advice on a few business matters. It made her feel needed, and he was not too proud to ask her to advise him. He had even told Tabor to allow her to see any reports she requested, which was how he knew Mama had already poured over the autumn crop totals before he did so today. Hopefully, it would be the last time she did so.

He finished going through the last of them, seeing nothing that needed his immediate attention. It would be advisable to call upon his London solicitor when he reached town, however. Con had spoken with him the day after his father's death and again at the reading of the will shortly before they had left town for Somerset. He took the list of questions he had begun as he read through the papers and would take it to his meeting with the solicitor. This way, if Mama asked, he could tell her that this was one of the chief reasons he journeyed to town now.

The next morning, they set out at half past seven. Usually, Mama slept much later, but she had already told him she planned to sleep in the carriage. She had always hated riding great distances in their carriage and preferred to sleep away as much of the trip as possible.

When she awakened from a long nap, he told her, "At some point, I also plan to visit Dru while I am in town. I am eager to meet little Beau."

His younger sister had not attended the most recent Season

because she was increasing and due to give birth in mid-July. She now had a son, and Con wanted to meet his new nephew. Since Dru and Perry lived in Surrey, it was only a two-hour carriage ride from town to Beauville. Con decided he would wait until his carriage had returned from depositing Mama in Sussex before he attempted the visit. He would write ahead and let Dru know he would be coming.

Their journey to town was uneventful, the roads surprisingly good. Mama stayed overnight at his townhouse, and then she left the next morning in the post-chaise. Con sent a note to his solicitor, letting him know he was in town again, and requesting an appointment at his earliest convenience. He was still at the breakfast table, sipping a second cup of coffee, when a reply came, telling him Mr. Badham could meet with him any time that day.

Immediately, Con left the townhouse, finding a hansom cab after a few blocks. He wanted to give the horses another day of rest before using them. He arrived at the solicitor's office and was welcomed. Over cups of tea, Mr. Badham went into more detail regarding various investments which had been made by Papa and previous Alingtons and explained which were proving profitable and which should be relinquished.

"Of course, you should also speak with your banker regarding these matters, my lord," Badham said.

"I will certainly do so. Thank you for making time for me today, Mr. Badham."

"I am always happy to assist you, my lord. Give my best to Lady Marley."

He left the solicitor's offices. Wishing for his head to be clearer before discussing tedious financial details, he decided to visit with his banker another day. Instead, he hailed a hansom cab and asked the driver to take him to White's. This way, he could see who might be in town. He had a vague idea of what Viscount Samuel looked like. It would be nice to meet Miss Stanhope's father and learn anything he could about her before calling upon her. Since Samuel remained in town throughout the year, there was a strong possibility he would be at White's now.

Con was greeted by Pollard, the man in charge of the gentlemen's club.

"It is good to see you, my lord. May I offer my sympathies in your loss of Lord Marley? Your father was a favorite of many at White's."

His throat tightened. "Thank you, Pollard. Would you have Tommy bring me some coffee?"

"Certainly, my lord."

He walked through the establishment, greeting a few others. Not many were present today, and he did not see Lord Samuel anywhere. He did see Lord Clay, however. They had gone to school together, and he eagerly greeted the earl.

"I did not know you were back in town," Clay said as Tommy arrived and set down a cup of coffee for Con.

"I only arrived last night," he shared, taking a chair. "Marleyfield's autumn harvest has concluded, and I had business with my solicitor. I am surprised to see you here."

Clay shrugged. "Usually, I am in the country this time of year, but I received an invitation to a house party hosted by Lord and Lady Pebble. It will be held at Pebblestone, their country estate in Dorset. I simply stopped in town for a brief respite before traveling the rest of the way to Weymouth."

Pebble. Where had he heard that name?

Then Con recalled that Lord and Lady Pebble lived next to Viscount Samuel's estate. Miss Stanhope had mentioned the pair, saying the childless couple looked upon her as a daughter.

"Do you know who else might be in attendance?" he asked casually, thinking that Lady Pebble would certainly have issued an invitation to Miss Stanhope.

"I haven't a clue," the earl admitted. "But Mama is chattering loudly in my ear these days, telling me it is time I wed."

He recalled Lord Clay's father had died several years ago. "Are you thinking you might find your countess at this house party? I have never attended one before since they are notorious for the number of engagements which occur at them."

"Yes, you have kept clear of the parson's mousetrap," Clay teased. "But now that you hold a title, are you anticipating wedding anytime soon?"

Not wanting to tip his hand, he said, "I am considering doing so."

Since he hadn't learned if Miss Stanhope would be in attendance at this affair, he decided it was time to call upon her, hoping she was still in residence in town. If she weren't, then he would have to somehow obtain an invitation to the house party.

And his best chance lay in Lord Clay.

"Are you engaged for dinner later this evening? If not, perhaps we can meet."

"I am not," Clay told him. "I would like to do so."

They arranged a time and decided to return here to White's for their meal. Then Con excused himself and took a hansom cab to Viscount Samuel's townhouse.

As the butler answered his knock, Con presented him with his card. Actually, it was one of his father's, but he was the Earl of Marley now, so he might as well use them.

"Lord Marley to see Lord Samuel and Miss Stanhope."

"I am afraid they have gone to the country, my lord," the butler apologized. "As far as I know, they will not be returning to town for some months."

This surprised him. Miss Stanhope had told Con she and her father were permanent fixtures in town, rarely going to the country.

But if she were in Dorset, he ventured that she would be at Lord and Lady Pebble's house party.

"Thank you," he said, taking back the card the butler offered him. Even if the butler had kept it and showed it to Miss Stanhope, she would not connect it with him since she had met him while he was using his courtesy title.

Con went to his townhouse, where Benchley had finished

unpacking. He would not tell the servant to pack again until after his conversation with Lord Clay.

He arrived back at White's and met up with his old friend. They enjoyed a long, unrushed dinner and excellent conversation. Over snifters of brandy, however, he turned their talk back to the house party.

"Are you truly interested in attending this house party the Pebbles are giving?"

Clay shrugged. "I suppose so. As I told you, Mama is encouraging me to wed."

"I cannot say why at this point, but I need to be present at it."

"But you have no invitation, Marley. You did not even know about it until I mentioned it." Then understanding dawned in the earl's eyes. "You are interested in someone who might be in attendance. I am right, aren't I?"

"You always were a clever fellow. What do you say, Clay? Will you allow me to be a replacement for you?"

"Hmm," the earl mused. "Mama thinks I will be in Dorset. I suppose I could stay and enjoy what town has to offer instead of heading home again."

Knowing Clay had a love of dice, Con sweetened the pot. He pulled out a handful of guineas which he carried in his pocket. They were a constant reminder to him of his newly-found wealth.

Placing them on the table, he said, "Take these in return for the invitation. May they bring you good luck at the gaming tables."

Quickly, his friend swept the coins off the table and pocketed them. "You are more than happy to take my place, Marley."

"Good. I hope we will both enjoy the time away from our country estates. By the way, how long will this house party run?"

"A week," his friend said. "It starts three days from now. Lord Pebble's estate is called Pebblestone. It is southwest of Weymouth. In Dorset."

It would take two days for Con to reach Weymouth. He could stay at an inn in the town the night before and then travel to Pebblestone the following day. Of course, that would mean putting off his visit to Dru, but he had not written his sister, so she had no idea he was in town.

"Thank you for doing this, Clay. If things go as planned, I will give you all the credit."

Con realized that he was going to the house party not just to see Miss Stanhope. He also wanted to offer for her.

And that surprised him. Very much.

Chapter Eight

Con thought about how he was going to charm his way into a house party which he had not been invited to as Benchley finished tying his cravat.

"There you go, my lord. You are ready to shine at the house party now."

"If I am even admitted to it," he voiced aloud.

The valet frowned. "Why do you say that?"

"I told you when we were in town that we were headed to a house party, Benchley. That much is true. What I left out was the fact that I am not on the guest list and did not receive an invitation."

He watched the reaction appear on his valet's face, beginning with puzzled and changing to concern. "Then why have you decided to show up at it, my lord?"

"That is a very good question. I will only say that there is someone who *is* a guest that I must see. Someone I must apologize to. I wronged her—and wish to set things right between us."

Benchley brightened. "So, it is a lady you seek." He paused, studying his employer. "You seem to be a good man, my lord. Serving you has been an easy transition for me. Although we do not know one another well yet, your father always spoke highly of you. That is the reason I stayed on. Because the previous Lord Marley thought so much of you. If it is meant for this young lady to accept your apology, then I am confident it will happen."

"You have bolstered my spirits, Benchley. For that, I commend you. Now, if you will finish up the packing, we will either be staying at Lord and Lady Pebble's party, or else we shall soon be returning to Marleyfield. Please bring my trunk downstairs when you have finished. I must go and see John now."

He found his coachman at a table downstairs, breakfast before him. John shot to his feet at his employer's appearance.

"The horses are being readied now, my lord."

"Sit, John. Finish your breakfast."

Con joined him at the table, sitting opposite the driver. "If I am to stay at this house party, I will arrange for you to remain at the inn here. Once you have dropped me off—and if I do stay—you can return the horses to the changing station and then have some time to yourself for the next week."

Confusion filled the coachman's face. "You might choose not to stay at the party?"

"I will give you a sign, one way or another. For now, I will make arrangements for you to stay at the inn as well as pay for your meals."

He went in search of the innkeeper and told the man of the possibility of his driver staying for the next week. Con went ahead and paid for that time, telling the innkeeper to keep the money whether or not his coachman returned. The innkeeper thanked him for his generosity, and Con went outside, seeing his carriage was waiting for him.

He needed to arrive early at Pebblestone today in order to plead his case with Lord and Lady Pebble. He did not wish to arrive in the midst of other guests, only to be turned away. Not only would it be most embarrassing, he also did not wish to be the topic of the gossips who would spread the story—and embellish it, of course.

Benchley arrived with his trunk, and it was loaded onto the vehicle. John told Con that he had already inquired about and received instructions to Pebblestone, which was a short, quarter-hour drive from Weymouth. He climbed into his carriage, composing himself. He and Val were known for their charm, and he would be in need of it today if he were to talk himself into this house party.

After several minutes, the vehicle turned up a lane, and Con realized he looked at things differently since he had become the Earl of Marley. Before, he would not have carefully observed the grounds of an estate. Now, he itched to talk to Pebblestone's steward. Learn what crops they grew and how many tenants worked the land. Ask about how the recent harvest had turned out. Val had told Con that he was much the same since he had become the Duke of Millbrooke. Con supposed it was all a part of maturing, taking on different responsibilities that came with their titles.

His carriage turned in front of a rather large house, and he saw Lord and Lady Pebble hurry outside to greet him. They would have been ready for when their guests were scheduled to arrive, but he was a couple of hours early and had most likely caught them unaware.

Climbing from the carriage, he gave the pair his most genial smile, knowing it was one which won over others.

"Lord Dyer?" Lady Pebble asked, obvious confusion in her voice.

"Lady Pebble, Lord Pebble." He bowed to them. "And it is Lord Marley these days. I assumed my earldom a few months ago."

"What . . . are you doing here, Marley?" asked the viscount, clearly confounded.

"I am hoping that the two of you will let me complete a favor which a friend requested of me. You see, I was at White's with Lord Clay when he received urgent news which required his presence elsewhere. He was in a quandary, knowing he had an obligation to attend this house party, but he was needed at his country estate. In desperation, Lord Clay asked if I might be willing to take his place."

Con smiled again, reeling in the viscountess. "I know from my own mother, who is a superb hostess, that numbers matter a great deal when hosting an event, especially one so intimate as a house party. A hostess always aims for the numbers to be balanced. Might you be willing to allow me to replace Lord Clay on your guest list? Of course, if this is not agreeable to you, my lady, I can return to town at once. Perhaps some other gentleman in the neighborhood could then be a last-minute replacement."

Lord Pebble looked perplexed by Con's suggestion, but he saw the gleam in Lady Pebble's eyes. She would know he was a most eligible bachelor. The fact that he now held his father's title made him an even more appealing guest for her house party. It was a well-known fact that ladies who held house parties like to brag on the number of betrothals which resulted. The viscountess would think Con would be seeking a bride now that he was an earl.

At least that is what he was counting on.

"That was most gracious of you to agree to help your friend," she said. "And me."

"Well, Mama did raise me to step in and help others when I can. I would hate to see you stranded with unbalanced numbers."

"I am delighted to entertain you at our house party, Lord Marley."

Her husband picked up on his wife's cue and said, "Yes, my lord. We are grateful you are here."

"My housekeeper will show you to the guest bedchamber Lord Clay was to have." She paused. "In fact, I think you should be given an even better one, my lord."

He beamed at her. "My eternal thinks to you, Lady Pebble. Mama has always spoken highly of you, and I see now why she has done so in the past."

Actually, his mother had never once brought up Lady Pebble's name, but the viscountess did not need to know that.

As his hostess had a brief conversation with her housekeeper, he turned and nodded to his servants. Immediately, Benchley had

Con's trunk taken from the carriage, and John tipped his hat to Con and drove away.

The housekeeper showed him to a large, airy bedchamber, asking if he wished for hot water to be sent to freshen up or help in unpacking.

"No hot water is necessary, but thank you. I will simply allow my valet to unpack for me."

"You may join Lord Pebble in the library whenever you are ready, my lord," the housekeeper told him as she left.

Benchley, who had opened the trunk, began removing clothing from it and said, "You did well, my lord. No hostess wants an uneven number of guests. You are an answer Lady Pebble had not even known to ask for."

He excused himself and headed to the library, where Lord Pebble awaited him.

"I seem to recall reading about your father's passing in the death notices," the viscount said. "May I offer my condolences? He was a most amiable gentleman."

"He very much was so, my lord. Thank you. I miss Papa every day. Not many men have the closeness he and I shared."

They talked of a few banal things. Con wanted to be on his best behavior and not have them regret allowing him to stay in Lord Clay's stead. Then he decided to see what Lord Pebble might have to say about the other guests.

"Since Lord Clay had to rush off, I am woefully unprepared as to who the other guests might be. Could you share some of their names with me, my lord? I am wondering if I might be acquainted with any of them."

The viscount chuckled. "The guest list was the domain of my wife. I do know my cousin's daughter, Miss Lawson, will be arriving shortly. She is a very quiet girl. Barely speaks when she is spoken to. She was due to make her come-out this spring and simply fell apart at the thought of doing so, begging my cousin to allow her to delay it. Lady Pebble and I thought if she could meet a few members of Polite Society in a smaller group, she might meet with more success."

"It is good you are helping a family member," he praised. "To me, family is everything. And a girl does not always have to make her come-out to be part of a successful match. While my sister Lucy wed Lord Huntsberry after her come-out, my other sister Dru did not debut into Polite Society. While visiting Lucy, Dru met one of Huntsberry's neighbors, and they fell in love. She is now the Countess of Martindale."

"It would be wonderful if Miss Lawson could do the same at this house party," Lord Pebble said. "Not only do I wish my cousin's daughter to find a match amongst the guests here, but I have hopes that Miss Stanhope, a close neighbor, might also do the same. You see, we have no children of our own, and Rowena has been the closest thing we have to a daughter."

Rowena. So that was Miss Stanhope's Christian name.

"I actually have met Miss Stanhope," he said congenially. "In fact, we danced the supper dance together at Lord and Lady Purlington's ball."

The viscount nodded. "That is good to know." Then he frowned. "Miss Stanhope has a notion of never wedding. I cannot say that I agree with it, and that is why Lady Pebble and I are happy that she agreed to attend this house party. We are hoping she will meet someone here and change her mind regarding marriage."

"I know Miss Stanhope's interests can lean to the intellectual. But that does not frighten me off, my lord."

Lord Pebble gave him a warm smile. "That is *very* good to hear, Lord Marley." He rose. "If you will excuse me, I have a few things I must attend to before the rest of our guests arrive."

The viscount quit the room, and Con had an idea that he headed straight for his wife, ready to share the news that their new, uninvited guest not only knew Miss Stanhope, but that he had danced with her.

He went to the bookshelves and perused them, pulling out a copy of *Gulliver's Travels.* It had been the novel Miss Stanhope had discussed so eagerly with Val. Con had since read it again, finding a copy of it in the Marleyfield library, even writing to Val to ask him to explain some of the symbolism found within it. He was glad now that he had read the book because it would give him something to discuss with Miss Stanhope.

Returning the book to the shelf, he took a seat in a chair which overlooked the front drive of the house. The view would allow him to see who was arriving. He now had time to consider why he had gone to such great lengths to convince Lord Clay to step aside in order to allow Con to take his place at this house party.

His preference in women usually tended to small, petite blondes, though he had coupled with women of varying sizes and shades of hair color. Miss Stanhope was very different from the type of woman he usually was attracted to. She was very tall for a woman, only three or four inches beneath his six feet. He had no idea of her figure because of the ill-fitting gowns she wore, and he was eager to explore what was beneath them. She had a beautiful smile and the most expressive eyes he had ever seen.

He wondered why she wore spectacles. Some people donned them because they could not see things at a distance, while others could not read up close without them. Since she had worn them at the Purlington ball, the former must be true. Con supposed that Miss Stanhope wore them so she might see where she was going as well as being able to identify others when they approached her.

The fact she was a bluestocking did not chase him off. In fact, he had been the rare boy who had actually enjoyed school, especially history. Con wondered if that might be a subject Miss Stanhope was drawn to and hoped to learn of her preferences soon.

Con smiled, remembering her confession of having a sweet tooth. It was a small thing to recall about her, but it endeared her to him even more. Oh, how he wished Val was here so he might talk to his cousin about Miss Stanhope. His cousin had been his closest friend throughout his entire life, and he had never thought to see Val in love. Val had done so, falling head over heels for Eden, as she had for him. Con wished to ask how Val had known Eden was the one for him. Had it been at first sight? Was it as they began to get to know one another? Or had it been once they kissed?

All he knew was that he would have the opportunity to be in close quarters with Miss Stanhope for the next seven days. A house party was managed differently than social affairs of the Season. Though Con had never attended one, he had heard other men talking about them. The rules of Polite Society seem to be relaxed at these country parties, and so he hoped to be able to spend time alone with Miss Stanhope.

And kiss her again.

He could not forget what had passed between them. Being absent from her had only magnified the intensity of the memories of their kisses. He did recall he had felt comfortable in her company, and she had seemed the same with him. They had both shared very personal things about themselves, things he would never have considered telling another woman. Also, Miss Stanhope had easily fit in with his family when they had joined them for the supper buffet. Con could see her becoming a part of his family—and his life.

Avoiding house parties had been his rigid rule, simply because so many engagements came out of them. He had not wanted to find a wife before claiming his title, but now that he held the earldom—and saw how happy various members of his family were in their marriages—he wanted the same for himself. Miss Stanhope was different from any other woman he had ever met, and that is why he felt the need to be in her presence and get to know more about her.

Con told himself not to think of looking to make Miss Stanhope his wife, especially since Lord Pebble had told him outright that she had no desire to wed. But if his attraction to her continued, he could very much see himself offering for her by the end of his time at Pebblestone. He had always been a man up for a challenge—and now he faced the challenge of his life—getting a bluestocking who wished to avoid marriage to consider taking the plunge.

With him.

Chapter Nine

Rowena awaited her cousin's carriage to convey her to Lord and Lady Pebble's house party. She thought back over the list of guests who would be coming and hoped she might enjoy their company. She had been thrilled when Lady Pebble agreed to invite not only Miss Tweedham but also Lady Sarah. The viscountess had thought with Lady Sarah's large dowry that she would be a good candidate for their guest list. Her friend yearned to wed. Rowena suspected this house party might be the final chance Lady Sarah would have to meet a gentleman in this type of atmosphere and have a chance to find a husband.

While as much a bluestocking as Rowena, Miss Tweedham also longed for a husband and children. She hoped her friend might be a suitable match for her cousin Ollie or one of the other two gentlemen who were from the nearby neighborhood. Selfishly, she hoped that would happen so they could remain in close proximity to one another and continue their friendship for decades to come.

The other two ladies who would be attending were not known to her. One was Miss Lawson, who was the daughter of one of Lord Pebble's cousins. Supposedly, she was an extremely shy young lady, and Lady Pebble hoped Miss Lawson would thrive in a more intimate setting. The final lady on the guest list was Lady Jewell, a young woman of two and twenty, who had recently returned from India. Her parents still remained there, where her father was some type of government official. Lady Jewell's aunt, a Miss Bailey, had traveled to India in order to chaperone her niece's sea voyage back to England. Lady Pebble was friends with Miss Bailey and thought her house party an ideal setting for Lady Jewell to take in the company of some of the members of Polite Society.

Of the five ladies attending, Lady Jewell's aunt would be the only chaperone present. Lady Sarah, whose parents often neglected her, said that Lord and Lady Pebble would be chaperone enough for their spinster daughter. Miss Tweedham's mother, whom Rowena knew fairly well, said that she would trust in Lord and Lady Pebble, too, since they had plans to visit friends during the house party and would be unable to change them in order to chaperone their daughter. Naturally, the viscount and his wife would be chaperone enough for Miss Lawson since they were her family. Rowena herself did not need a chaperone. In her mind, she was already high on the shelf and only attended the house party to pacify Lady Pebble as well as being able to spend time with her good friends.

She had high hopes for Ollie finding a bride while at Pebblestone. Rowena believed her cousin would greatly appeal to the women in attendance. Ollie was jovial and kind and the most decent man she knew. More importantly, her cousin was actively looking for his viscountess now.

The other gentleman she was acquainted with was Lord Clay. Rowena had encountered Lord Clay at a few events and even partnered with him at a card party during her come-out Season. Though she was a bit concerned that he liked cards a little too much, he was still most amiable. The other three gentlemen were unknown to her. Lady Pebble had insisted that Baron Howell be included. Though he was one of their neighbors, Rowena had never met him since she had grown up in town. Lady Pebble shared that Baron Howell had wed three years ago and then lost his wife in childbirth. He was now father to a two-year-old daughter, and the viscountess thought it high time Lord Howell wed again, not only to give his daughter a mother but to provide the baron with more children.

Lord Cramer was another name unfamiliar to her. Lady Pebble said his father had been a distant cousin of hers. The cousin had passed a little over a year ago. Lord Cramer now held the title, and Lady Pebble said he was a serious man in need of a wife.

The last gentleman on the guest list was an unusual choice on Lady Pebble's part. He was a Mr. Tompkins, who served as a tutor at Oxford. Lady Pebble confided that Mr. Tompkins' father, the Earl of Roland, was in poor health and that it was only a matter of time before Mr. Tompkins found himself claiming the title. Since he had not mixed in Polite Society yet, Lady Pebble felt it her duty to help bring Mr. Tompkins into the fold of the *ton*. The house party would prove to be the perfect way to do so.

Thinking over the gentlemen in attendance, Rowena had high hopes for her friends' chances of finding someone who might interest them. She recalled hearing that house parties were notorious for quick betrothals, and she could understand why. During the Season, there were so many people present at events, and it was not uncommon for a girl to dance with a gentleman only a handful of times and meet him in passing at other events before he offered for her.

A house party, on the other hand, allowed a limited number of men and women to be brought together. Conversation would flow, and Lady Pebble shared that the stiff rules of Polite Society were somewhat relaxed in the country. She understood that was the viscountess' way of telling her it would be acceptable for couples to go off and be with one another without a chaperone lurking about.

Though Rowena herself was not looking for a husband, she was eager to have the company of others over the next week. She did enjoy her life since her father's passing, but there had been several occasions when loneliness had overcome her. After this house party, she vowed to get out more in the community. She could volunteer at the Mossleigh parish church. Even call upon others and invite them to call upon her. While her books meant everything to her, she realized she needed the presence of others every now and then so that she would not succumb to loneliness.

She saw Ollie's carriage approaching and rose from her chair, donning her spectacles. Though she no longer dressed as to be so off-putting to gentlemen, it seemed appropriate to wear her spectacles again. She had sent a trunk to Pebblestone yesterday, filled with clothes. Not that she would be staying at the estate, but Lady Pebble had explained that Rowena must change clothes several times a day. She had asked for her trunk to be placed in Miss Tweedham's bedchamber, which would be larger than most of the other guests, and she would share it with her friend when she needed to change her gown for tea or dinner. As for what other activities she might partake in that required a change of gown, Rowena hadn't a clue. Lady Pebble had worked long hours on a list of activities for her guests to participate in, but the viscountess did not share them with Rowena, telling her that she was a guest and did not need to take part in the planning of the house party itself.

Opening the door to her cottage, she went out to meet the carriage. Ollie bounded from it, giving her a ready smile.

"Are you ready for our adventure, Cousin?" he asked, his eyes sparkling.

"I suppose so. It will be pleasant to meet new acquaintances."

He handed her up and joined her inside the carriage, saying, "I haven't a clue what people might do at a house party. Actually, I have no idea how to behave around other members of Polite Society."

"I know you have devoted years of your life to the stewardship of Stanfield, and Papa appreciated your efforts so much, Ollie. It is time for you to make your presence known in Polite Society, though. I think this house party will be the perfect way to introduce yourself. Frankly, I find the Season a bit overwhelming, with so many others present at events."

"I am hoping to find my wife amongst the ladies invited to Pebblestone," he confided. "The thought of entering a ballroom with hundreds of people and not knowing but a handful of them terrifies me. Do you know any of the guests who are coming, Rowena?"

"Two are actually good friends of mine," she revealed. "Miss Tweedham and Lady Sarah. I can vouch for both their good character. The others are not known to me. Miss Lawson is the daughter of Lord Pebble's cousin, while Lady Jewell has just returned from years abroad in India."

"Might I count on you to give me advice once I have met the four of them? I sometimes become a bit tongue-tied around other ladies. Not that I have had much opportunity to be around them."

"I am happy to talk with you anytime, Ollie. I will give you my impressions of the other two ladies, but in the end, you are the one who will spend the rest of your life with your viscountess. My first suggestion to you would be to find someone you have something in common with. Build a friendship upon that commonality."

He grinned. "See? You are already giving me excellent advice."

They arrived at Pebblestone, and she saw Ollie's was not the only carriage in front of the house. She spied Lord and Lady Pebble talking with two gentlemen. Miss Tweedham and Lady Sarah were also amongst their number.

Ollie handed her down, and Rowena saw servants bustling about, carrying in luggage. Miss Tweedham saw her and smiled widely, giving a wave.

"Come and greet our host and hostess, Ollie. We can also meet some of the guests at the same time. The two ladies are my friends I spoke of."

They joined the circle, and Rowena introduced Ollie to both Lady Sarah and Miss Tweedham. In return, they met Baron Howell and Mr. Tompkins. From looks alone, she found both gentlemen to have a pleasant countenance and hoped they were in attendance not just to socialize but actually look for a bride.

A housekeeper took charge of the gentlemen, saying she would show them to their bedchambers, while Lady Pebble took Lady Sarah in hand. Since Rowena already knew which bedchamber was Miss Tweedham's, she slipped her arm through her friend's, and they went up the stairs together.

"I hope you do not mind briefly sharing your bedchamber with me, Miss Tweedham."

"I am happy to do so, Miss Stanhope. I knew with a large number in attendance, that most likely would be the case."

"I will not be staying overnight at Pebblestone," she explained. "My cottage is less than ten minutes from here. My cousin, Viscount Samuel, is also staying at Stanfield. We wished to free up rooms for the guests at Pebblestone."

"Then why did you mention that we are sharing a room?" her friend asked, clearly puzzled.

"Lady Pebble has told me that ladies change their gowns several times during the day. I did not want to have to be taken home each time that was necessary, so I packed a trunk of clothing and had it sent here yesterday."

By now, they had arrived at the room, and she saw a maid unpacking her friend's trunk.

"So, you will merely change clothes here?"

"Yes, that is correct. The rest of the time, the bedchamber will be yours."

Miss Tweedham took Rowena's hands in hers. "I cannot thank you enough, Miss Stanhope. I know my name is only on this guest list simply because of your influence. Lady Sarah's, as well. We came down together and spoke of your generosity in looking after us."

"I have missed you both terribly," she admitted. "While I am not in search of a husband, I know the two of you would be pleased if you found one amongst the gentlemen invited here."

"I may be a bluestocking as you are, but I very much wish to have a husband and children. This house party gives me my best chance to date to find one. Lady Sarah believes the same."

Hot water arrived, and she and Miss Tweedham talked while her friend washed and changed her gown, wanting to wear something which was not wrinkled from travel.

Once her friend was presentable again, Rowena said, "Let us go to Lady Sarah's bedchamber. It is next door to yours. We can go down to tea together."

A maid answered the knock and admitted them. Lady Sarah was sitting at the dressing table, adjusting the pins in her hair. She rose and came toward them.

"I know Miss Tweedham has already thanked you, Miss Stanhope, but I wish to also show my appreciation, as well. I have attended one other house party, years ago, and they are ever so much fun. You must be responsible for seeing us invited to this one at Pebblestone."

"I do hold some sway over Lady Pebble," she admitted. "She has tried to mother me my entire life. Naturally, I would wish for my two closest friends to be here with me."

"Since you had a bit of a say-so regarding the guestlist, would you share with us which gentlemen will be in attendance?" asked Lady Sarah.

Quickly, Rowena ran through the list of the five gentlemen, sharing the little she knew about each of them.

"I am trying to get everyone straight in my mind," Miss Tweedham said. "So, Baron Howell and Mr. Tompkins reside in the neighborhood."

"Yes, that is correct," she told her friend. "As does my cousin, Lord Samuel. Lord Cramer's country estate is in Wiltshire, while Lord Clay resides in Bedfordshire."

"I am eager to meet all the guests," Lady Sarah said.

"It is time we do so. We are to gather for tea on the terrace. Lady Pebble told me since the afternoon is so pleasant, an outdoor tea would be an excellent way to begin the house party."

They started down the corridor and came across another

young lady leaving her bedchamber. She looked at them and quickly averted her eyes, leaving Rowena to guess it was Miss Lawson.

Wanting to include the diffident young woman, she said, "Why, I believe you must be Miss Lawson, the daughter of Lord Pebble's cousin."

Miss Lawson looked up, her gaze meeting Rowena's. "Yes, my lady." Her eyes fell to the ground again.

Rowena introduced herself and her friends, telling Miss Lawson that she was happy to make her acquaintance.

Suddenly, she saw Miss Lawson's shoulders relax, and the young woman looked up again.

"I find it difficult to speak with anyone I am not acquainted with," Miss Lawson said quietly.

Slipping an arm through Miss Lawson's, she said, "Then you do not have to worry because you are now acquainted with the three of us. It is good to have you here at Pebblestone, Miss Lawson. I think this house party is going to be ever so much fun."

They ventured down the stairs, coming across two other women just ahead of them. Since only two other ladies had been invited, Rowena took charge of the situation.

"Lady Jewell, Miss Bailey. It is a pleasure to make your acquaintance. I am Miss Stanhope and live on Stanfield, the estate next to Pebblestone."

She introduced her three companions, and Lady Jewell gave them a bright smile.

"I am so excited to be here," she told them. "The society in India is quite small. I have known the same people my entire life. Papa and Mama wanted a different life for me, and that is why they sent me back to England." Lady Jewell glanced to her aunt and added, "Aunt Bailey was kind enough to travel to India and serve as my chaperone on the way home. We arrived too late to join in this Season, and that is why we were delighted to receive Lady Pebble's invitation to this house party."

Lady Jewell was both attractive and personable, and Rowena

believed of all the eligible ladies present, Lady Jewell would be certain to secure a betrothal.

"Shall we continue to the terrace?" she asked, shepherding their party down the remaining flight of stairs.

When they stepped outside, she saw Lord and Lady Pebble already present, along with Baron Howell. The other man was a stranger to her. Quickly, introductions were made, and she was able to meet Mr. Tompkins. Rowena thought they would enjoy speaking with one another over the course of the house party because of his work at Oxford and her interest in academic subjects.

Lord Cramer and Ollie joined them, and she noted only Lord Clay was missing from their group. Hopefully, he had arrived by now and would be able to have tea with them.

Teacarts were rolled onto the terrace, and Lady Pebble asked everyone to find a seat at one of the tables which had been placed upon the terrace.

Suddenly, someone was at her elbow and said, "Miss Stanhope, it is a delight to see you again. Let me assist you to a table."

Shock reverberated through Rowena as she turned to face the familiar voice.

And found a smiling Lord Marley next to her.

CHAPTER TEN

Con had watched all the guests arrive, drinking in Miss Stanhope from the moment she stepped from her carriage. He had been pleasantly surprised to find her dressed much more appropriately than she had been during the Season. He didn't know where the change of heart had come in the gowns she wore. Perhaps her friend Miss Tweedham, who was much better garbed, had suggested her friend update her wardrobe some.

Whoever was responsible for the change, however, should be congratulated. For the first time, he could actually tell something about her figure. Miss Stanhope possessed a slender frame, along with a long neck he longed to nibble on. Though not much of her bosom was revealed, he saw it was ample, and his fingers itched to caress her breasts. With her height, her legs had to be long, and Con could imagine her wrapping them about his waist as he thrust into her. The image had caused his cock to begin to stir, and he had pinched himself, willing it to shrink.

He did not recognize any of the other ladies who made an appearance. The only fellow he was barely acquainted with was Lord Cramer, an earl a few years older than Con who kept to himself at White's and did not attend many events during the Season. He thought he recognized another of the guests, but the other three gentlemen were unknown to him.

He had noticed Miss Stanhope exit a carriage with the help of a gentleman who climbed from it before her. Because they were the only two inside with no chaperone, he guessed that he might be the cousin she had referred to, the one who was steward to her father's estate. Con found it interesting, if that were the case, that this cousin had been invited. Of course, with him being a close neighbor and a bachelor of a certain age, Lady Pebble might have included him for that very reason. And since he knew Miss Stanhope to be an only child, this cousin would likely be the one who had inherited her father's title.

He waited until it was time for tea to take place and headed to the drawing room. A footman stopped him, telling Con that tea was being served outdoors on the terrace. He liked the idea of that—but he liked the idea more of sitting next to Miss Stanhope during it.

The footman directed him to where he could access the doors to the terrace. As he went through them, he saw a large group had gathered. He counted, realizing he was the last to arrive. He spied Miss Stanhope, still in the daffodil gown he had seen her in earlier, and quickly moved to her side.

"Miss Stanhope, it is a delight to see you again. Let me assist you to a table."

When she turned, he saw the obvious surprise on her face. That meant she must have been privy to the guest list.

He gently clasped her elbow. "Here. We can sit at this table."

Con guided her to the closest table, and he pulled out her chair. Thankfully, she did not make a fuss and took her seat. Another couple took their places as he did, and it completed their table of four. He recognized Miss Tweedham.

"Ah, Miss Tweedham. It is so good to see you again. I am Lord Marley. You might recall we danced together at the Purlington's ball this past Season."

"You remember that, my lord?" she asked, wonder in her voice.

"Yes, I recall dancing with you and Miss Stanhope that evening."

Then Miss Tweedham said, "But you were Lord Dyer then,

weren't you?"

Con realized his new title had given him away. "Yes, I was. I have since assumed the earldom." Before he could be pressed further, he turned his attention to the other gentleman. "I do not believe we have met, my lord."

The man laughed jovially. "Perhaps it is because I have yet to dip my toe into the treacherous waters of Polite Society." He looked to Miss Stanhope to properly introduce them. "Cousin?"

"This is the Earl of Marley," Miss Stanhope said crisply. "He is cousin to the Duke of Millbrooke. Lord Marley, this is my cousin, Viscount Samuel."

The other man nodded. "It is good to meet you, my lord."

"Likewise," Con said, frowning. "But if you are Lord Samuel . . ." His voice trailed off, and he quickly looked to Miss Stanhope. "Has your father also passed?"

She swallowed. "He has. My cousin has now taken the title and resides at Stanfield. Not as its steward, but as its lord."

"My deepest sympathy to you both," he said, feeling the loss of his own father afresh. It surprised him that Miss Stanhope was even in attendance at this house party instead of in mourning.

"You look puzzled, my lord," she said. "While in my heart, I deeply mourn Papa, he made his wishes clear to me long before he passed. He did not want me to go about dressed in mourning clothes for a year, and so I have honored his request."

"I see," Con said, at a loss for words.

Lady Pebble appeared at their table. "Would you be so good as to pour out for those seated here, Rowena?"

"Certainly, my lady."

A servant rolled a teacart up to their table, and he watched Miss Stanhope do the honors. Since he was closest to her, she passed each saucer and teacup to him, and he directed it to the others before taking one for himself. She finished pouring her own tea and then asked Miss Tweedham what she might wish to eat, preparing her plate for her. She did the same for her cousin.

When it came time to serve him, she coolly said, "You are

close enough to the teacart, Lord Marley. You may choose whatever you wish."

So that was the way it was going to be. He was out of favor with her and would have to work his way back into her good graces. He placed two ham sandwiches and a raisin scone on his plate and turned to the others.

"How do you find your new steward?" he asked Lord Samuel. "It must be a bit odd, hiring the man who replaced you."

"Despite what Cousin Rowena said, I have yet to do so," the viscount confessed. "The autumn harvest was too important to me. Now that it has been gathered, I am ready to interview candidates. At least I will do so after the conclusion of this house party."

Con looked to Miss Stanhope. "Are you still residing in town, or have you joined your cousin in the country?"

"I have moved permanently to the country."

"Miss Stanhope has a cottage of her own," Miss Tweedham said enthusiastically. "I cannot imagine living on my own, but she says she enjoys it."

"That is most interesting," he said. "Would it not be easier to live with Viscount Samuel at Stanfield?"

"That is what I have told her," Lord Samuel said. "But Rowena possesses a stubborn streak, and she asked to reside in a cottage on the property. I have gifted one to her."

"I enjoy the solitude," Miss Stanhope said. "And Ollie has been kind enough to allow me the use of the library and music room at Stanfield. I regularly go there to play the pianoforte and choose new books to read for the coming week."

"Tell Lord Marley about the violin," prompted Miss Tweedham. "You have written to me about playing it."

"Yes," Con encouraged, trying to get her to look at him. "I would love to hear about it—and hear you play the instrument."

She burst into laughter, which sounded like music to his ears. "If you heard me play the violin, my lord, you would think otherwise. While I am fairly accomplished at the pianoforte, I am teaching myself to play the violin. Without a tutor, I have only made gradual progress."

Her gaze finally met his, and he spoke from his heart. "I believe you can do whatever you put your mind to, Miss Stanhope. You brim with confidence, no matter what the topic."

As tea progressed, he and Samuel begin to talk about the recent Stanfield harvest, and Con shared with him his own harvest at Marleyfield. While Miss Tweedham sat silently, merely listening, Miss Stanhope regularly interjected with questions and comments. It was easy to see how knowledgeable she was about her father's—now cousin's—estate.

Lord Samuel pointed out that very fact. "As you might guess, I will be relying upon my cousin. She might not have been raised in the country, but she has a keen intellect and understands farming better than most men I have met."

"You should help Lord Samuel in interviewing the candidates for steward," Con suggested.

Miss Stanhope shook her head. "Ollie has run Stanfield for years now. He does not need my help."

"But I appreciate your insight," her cousin insisted. Then to Con, he asked, "What of your steward?"

"Fortunately, I inherited mine, along with Marleyfield. He has no plans to leave, for which I am thankful. I also took on my father's valet. Benchley, while droll, is very efficient at his position."

"I am also in need of a valet as well as a steward," Lord Samuel said. "This being a viscount is still very new to me. At least I have dressed and shaved myself for years, so I am not completely helpless."

"You sound most accomplished, my lord," Miss Tweedham said, looking at the viscount with starry eyes.

He thought that a match between Miss Tweedham and Lord Samuel would benefit Miss Stanhope. She would have her closest friend nearby.

But Con did not want her remaining here at Stanfield. Already, he was eager to press his suit with her. Simply being around her again at tea today and hearing her lively conversation told him that he would never tire of her as he had so many other women. Being able to appreciate her physical appearance was also nice. Her gown was tailored to her figure, and he wondered again why she was dressing so differently than she had in town. Had it been her father wishing for her to hide herself?

Lady Pebble rang a small bell, causing all conversation to cease. Smiling, she said, "I hope you do not mind. This bell will be my way of gaining your attention during our time together."

"I think it a splendid idea," an attractive, dark-haired woman said.

He looked to Miss Stanhope, who leaned closer and quietly said, "Lady Jewell Bailey. Fresh off the boat from India."

He caught a whiff of roses and realized she now wore scented water or perfume. She had not done so when he had met her. Just another change about her, one he quite liked.

"We are in the country, so country hours will apply," the viscountess continued. "A breakfast buffet will be served between eight and ten each morning in our dining room. In the evenings, we will gather in the drawing room at six o'clock in order to enjoy a drink and conversation before dinner, which will be at seven. After dinner, we will return to the drawing room for other activities."

"What about during the day?" a gentleman he had yet to meet asked.

Lady Pebble smiled. "Are you trying to get out of me my surprises, Baron Howell?"

That was the fellow's name. Con knew he had met him, probably three or four years ago. He recalled Howell had wed at the end of the Season. His presence at this house party informed Con that the baron was, most likely, a widower. Many men lost their wives in childbirth, something which worried him even though he was yet to wed. He wondered if Howell had a child or not.

"Just being thorough, my lady," the baron said, smiling charmingly at his hostess.

"We will participate in various activities each day," Lady Pebble promised. "We are close to the beach, and I am certain you will wish to stroll along its shore and enjoy the salt air. The gentlemen can also go hunting, while the ladies catch up on their correspondence. I do believe Lord Pebble is insisting upon some lawn tennis and lawn bowling."

Lord Samuel looked to Con. "Egads. I have never done either of those."

"Neither have I," he assured the viscount. "That is not something you see in town."

"Well, I plan to participate in both," Miss Stanhope said. Then looking directly at Con, she added, "I also plan to win, no matter what the game."

"Is that a challenge, my lady?" he asked, sensing the air change between them.

She shrugged nonchalantly. "If you believe it is, my lord, then it must be."

"Oh, you do not wish to go up against Miss Stanhope, Lord Marley," warned Miss Tweedham. "When she puts her mind to something, she is unstoppable."

"I have heard from Lord Merriman, who wed my cousin, that Miss Stanhope is a talented card player. We shall have to see if her skills extend to lawn games."

He turned his attention back to Lady Pebble, who was mentioning a few other activities. Con had every intention of participating in whatever Miss Stanhope chose to do.

And find an opportunity to kiss her again at the earliest possible moment.

CHAPTER ELEVEN

After Lady Pebble had addressed them, she suggested the ladies depart in order to give the gentlemen some time to themselves. They left the terrace as a group, all the young ladies chatting happily.

Except for Rowena.

Why was Lord Dyer here? No, Lord Marley now. For a moment, she felt a bit of sympathy for him, knowing he had lost his father as she had.

She listened as she heard the different ladies talk about what they would don for dinner that evening. This was the reason Lady Pebble had allowed the ladies to leave, which would give them ample time to dress for dinner. Since she had no talent in dressing hair and hadn't a lady's maid of her own, Rowena never took long to get ready for any event, while she knew others present at the house party would take an hour or two to do so.

"Go ahead to the room, Miss Tweedham," she said brightly. "I must speak with Lady Pebble for a moment."

Her friend didn't question her as Rowena veered from the group and fell behind so that she might speak to Lady Pebble in private.

The viscountess reached her. "How are you enjoying the house party so far, my dear?"

She did not immediately go to the heart of the matter she wished settled. Instead, Rowena said, "I cannot thank you enough, my lady, for inviting my two closest friends. They are both grateful and looking forward to the next week. We have already befriended Miss Lawson, and I believe she will do quite well in this smaller setting."

"I noticed her speaking with Lady Sarah earlier. She seemed more animated than I have ever seen her before. For that, I am grateful." The viscountess paused. "Her father was sorely disappointed that she did not make her come-out this past Season. He fears she will never land a husband because of her extreme shyness."

"Rest assured, I will keep my eye on her. If she seems left out, I will draw her into whatever circle I am a part of."

"Thank you, my dear. You are too kind."

"Lady Jewell seems most interesting, as well," she continued. "I have a strong suspicion that she will leave this house party betrothed. With her looks and pleasant manner, the gentlemen present will all be vying for her attention."

Lady Pebble smiled. "That is the aim of a good house party. A hostess likes to see when a match—or more—can be made amongst her guests. But what of you, Rowena? Have you enjoyed meeting the gentlemen present? I noticed that Lord Marley was at your table for tea."

"I did not realize Lord Marley was invited to Pebblestone," she said, not elaborating, but hoping Lady Pebble would. Knowing how the viscountess had a tendency to gossip, Rowena hoped she would receive an answer as to why Lord Marley had made an appearance.

"He was not on my original guest list," the viscountess confirmed. "In fact, he is a substitute for Lord Clay, who was called back to his country estate on urgent business. Lord Marley happen to be with Lord Clay at the time and was pressed into accepting the invitation on Lord Clay's behalf."

"So, that was how the earl came to be at Pebblestone," she mused aloud.

"Marley is quite the eligible bachelor now," Lady Pebble said, obviously pleased. "He has always cut a fine figure at *ton* affairs, but he had never become serious about marriage until now."

An unsettling feeling blanketed her. "You believe he is here to look for his countess?"

"I believe so," the viscountess confirmed. "He told me of your acquaintance when I mentioned you would be one of the female guests. Perhaps that is why he wished to sit at your table during tea."

She frowned. "Our meeting was very brief. We danced together only once this past Season. I thought nothing of it—or him—since then."

Lady Pebble placed a hand on Rowena's arm. "I hope you will give Lord Marley a chance, my dear. All the gentlemen here deserve one."

Rowena saw the hope in the viscountess' eyes and did not wish to dash it.

"I am certain a betrothal will come from your house party, my lady. Whether it is me or someone else remains to be seen. If you will excuse me, I must get ready for dinner."

She hurried back to the bedchamber, knowing Lord and Lady Pebble gave this house party as much for her as they did for Ollie or Miss Lawson. Why couldn't they leave her alone? It wasn't fair. She did not fit into the mold that Polite Society put most women in. She was perfectly content living the life she had chosen for herself. She would be cordial to all the gentlemen at the party—even Lord Marley—but she had no intention of accepting an offer from any of them. *If* one came, that is.

In their bedchamber, Miss Tweedham was talking over with a maid what to wear this evening.

"There you are, Miss Stanhope. Annie here is Lady Sarah's maid, and she has offered to share Annie with us for the duration of the house party."

"That is very kind of Lady Sarah."

"I am here to assist you in any way possible, Miss Stanhope," the maid said. "Of course, I'll need to see to Lady Sarah first since she is my employer, but Lady Sarah is a generous sort. She knew neither of you had a maid, only each other. I'm happy to help when I can."

After much debate, Miss Tweedham and the maid decided on the gown for that night.

"I do want to make a good impression at dinner this evening," her friend shared. Then smiling shyly, she added, "Lord Samuel is very nice."

Rowena relaxed. "I am glad you think so. He has always been a special favorite of mine." She did not say aloud that she thought Ollie and Miss Tweedham would suit. That would be for the two of them to discover, but she hoped that would be the case.

Annie said to her, "Choose the gown you wish to wear this evening, my lady. I will return now to Lady Sarah and help her, but I will return to assist the both of you."

"No need to rush, Annie," she told the servant. "Miss Tweedham and I can help one another don our gowns."

The maid nodded. "Then I can assist you with your hair."

They removed their gowns, placing them across the bed, and with each other's assistance, dressed again. Miss Tweedham looked nice in a dark green gown, while Rowena went with one of midnight blue. She was hoping not to attract the attention of any of the gentlemen present, but she still wished to look her best that evening.

Her friend stood back, assessing her. "I am so happy you have chosen to go with a new wardrobe. In town, you dressed . . . a little . . ."

"Frumpily?" Rowena volunteered.

Miss Tweedham sighed. "Yes. I never brought it up to you before. I simply did not understand why you did so when you are a very attractive woman."

She did not wish to go into her reasons and merely said, "My clothes were all three Seasons old or older. After Papa passed, I decided I wanted a fresh start, hence my new wardrobe."

"Well, I think you look very pretty these days, Miss Stanhope."

They chatted about the other guests until Annie returned, Lady Sarah accompanying her. The maid had an idea of how she wished to dress Miss Tweedham's hair and worked on it a good quarter hour.

When the servant finished, Miss Tweedham exclaimed, "Oh, this is very flattering, Annie. Thank you so much."

Lady Sarah said, "I could not agree more, Miss Tweedham. You should wear your hair this way more often."

"I can do so while Annie is here to help me, but I am not skilled at dressing hair."

Rowena heard the forlornness in her friend's voice. Lady Tweedham had told her daughter that until she was betrothed, she did not need a lady's maid of her own. Personally, she thought it petty since many girls making their come-out received a lady's maid at that time.

"Perhaps Annie might teach you how to create this style," she suggested.

Miss Tweedham brightened. "Oh, that would be wonderful. Would you mind doing so, Annie?"

"I'd be happy to, my lady," the servant replied. She looked to Rowena now. "And what would you like done with your hair, my lady?"

Having also never had a lady's maid, she replied, "I will keep with my simple chignon. I prefer wearing it for all occasions." Wanting a few moments to herself, she added, "Why don't the two of you go downstairs? I will join you shortly."

Her friends and Annie left the room, and Rowena sat at the dressing table, studying her image in the small hand mirror which Miss Tweedham had brought with her. She noticed the color in her cheeks, and she knew that Lord Marley had put it there. She reflected on their kisses again, wishing she could forget them. Instead, she began daydreaming about them.

Then suddenly, she realized she should be downstairs. She had no idea how long she had been woolgathering and hurried down the corridor to the drawing room, slipping in quietly so as not to attract notice. The room was full, and Lord Marley stepped forward to meet her.

"I thought you were not going to make an appearance, Miss Stanhope."

"Perhaps I am taking a page from your book, my lord, and arriving last," she said coolly.

Rowena did not bother to excuse herself, simply abandoning Lord Marley and making her way toward Mr. Tompkins. Of all the guests present, he was the one she was most interested in getting to know.

He was accepting a drink from a footman, and she did the same, lifting a glass of wine from the offered tray.

"Miss Stanhope," he greeted.

"Good evening, Mr. Tompkins. I have been most eager to make your acquaintance."

He looked puzzled. "And why would you wish to talk with an Oxford tutor, my lady?"

"Perhaps because I am jealous that is what you do. I hope you do not think me odd, but I wish I could also be a tutor, as you are." She hesitated and added. "Or even a don."

Mr. Tompkins looked at her with new eyes. "I find that most interesting. You realize, of course, that women are not given the opportunity to serve as either a tutor or don at Oxford."

"I do. Still, I am interested in many academic subjects. What is your specialty?"

"The sciences, especially natural science. It is a difficult topic for many to grasp, but I enjoy the work I do with the young lords who come to study at university."

"Lady Pebble tells me that when you are not at Oxford, you live in our neighborhood."

A shadow crossed his face. "Yes. My father is the Earl of Rowland. His health is fading fast. In fact, while I usually only come home between university terms, I have taken a leave from my work and am in Dorset for the foreseeable future in order to help care for Papa."

Sympathy for his situation filled her. "You will not be going back to Oxford, will you, Mr. Barnes?"

"I doubt it. The door to my teaching days has closed. Once Papa is gone, I will step into my new role."

"I did not mean to upset you in any way."

He mustered a smile. "You have not, my lady. I agreed to come to Lady Pebble's house party simply because she has always showed Papa great kindness over the years. Papa also encouraged me to attend. If I am needed at home, I can be summoned quickly."

"Would you tell me about a typical day in your life at Oxford?" she asked, wanting to change the subject.

"With pleasure."

For the next several minutes, she listened to Mr. Tompkins speak, wising she could have been born a man and able to pursue a university degree at Oxford or Cambridge and an academic career.

Then Lady Pebble's bell tinkled, bringing all conversation to a halt.

"It is time to go into dinner," their hostess said. "If you gentlemen will be so kind as to escort the ladies into the dining room, there are cards placed at each setting. While you may sit wherever you choose at breakfast each morning, at dinner I will make certain you are constantly seated with different guests so that you might get to know one another better."

Mr. Tompkins offered her his arm. "Shall we?"

They went into dinner, and she saw Ollie taking a seat of honor to Lady Pebble's right. Glancing down the table, she saw Miss Lawson was seated on Lord Pebble's right. She did hope both her cousin and Miss Tweedham might make a match during the house party. Unfortunately, she found Lord Marley seated to Lady Pebble's left.

And she was placed on his left.

She bid Mr. Tompkins farewell for now, and they promised to pick up their conversation again at a later time. A footman seated her, and Lord Marley turned to her.

"What a coincidence that we are seated beside one another, Miss Stanhope."

"If I had not been watching you, I would believe you had slipped from the drawing room and changed the arrangements of the name cards so that we might find ourselves beside one another."

"I am flattered that you were watching me," he told her.

She winced inwardly, not wanting to show any sign of weakness around this man. "What I meant to say is that I did not witness any guests leaving the drawing room."

"It is a clever idea," he noted. "I shall keep it in mind."

As the soup course was being served, Lady Pebble rang her bell again. She looked down the table at her husband expectantly, and Lord Pebble rose to his feet.

"My viscountess and I would like to formally welcome you to our table and this house party, which is being given in honor of our good neighbor, Lord Samuel. The viscount faithfully served as his uncle's estate manager for several years and has now come into the title. We hope that all of you here might get to know Lord Samuel and recognize his good qualities. Please enjoy your meal."

Rowena made certain she did not speak a single word to Lord Marley throughout dinner. She sat across from Lady Sarah and next to Lord Cramer and spent much of her time engaged with them, as well as conversing with Lady Pebble. She sensed Lord Marley's amusement at her not initiating any conversation with him and did her best to ignore him.

"I think it is time to leave the gentlemen to their brandy and cigars," the viscountess announced. "We shall see them in the drawing room soon."

She was not fond of the scent of cigars and decided to speak up.

"Must you gentlemen always smoke those nasty cigars? The smell clings to you and can be quite unpleasant to be around."

A few gasps sounded around the table, and Rowena knew she had overstepped. Instead of apologizing, she pressed on, boldly asking, "Shall we take a vote regarding the matter? Raise your hand if you do not wish the gentlemen to smoke."

She hoped her two friends would follow her lead and looked to Lady Sarah, who had turned bright red. Glancing about, she saw the other ladies looking at her with everything from astonishment to disdain.

Surprisingly, it was Lord Marley who came to her rescue.

"I think, as a gentleman, I would not wish to offend any lady present. I shall refrain from partaking in smoking cigars while at Pebblestone. I hope my fellow gentlemen will follow my lead."

Ollie was the first to speak. "I have never smoked, so I am happy to do so, my lord."

Mr. Tompkins said, "I hope I do not offend anyone, but I also find it a nasty habit. I, too, will not smoke during this house party."

That left only two other gentlemen, and Baron Howell spoke first.

"I gave up cigars when my daughter told me I was stinky. Mary is two and already opinionated," he shared.

Everyone at the table laughed, and then Lord Cramer said, "I am happy to make Miss Stanhope—and the other ladies comfortable. I, too, will smoke no cigars during my time at Pebblestone."

Rowena smiled at those gathered around the table. "I apologize if my request proved abrupt, but I do appreciate your cooperation."

"Shall we retire to the drawing room, ladies?" Lady Pebble asked, giving Rowena a look which caused her cheeks to flush.

She rose, and Lord Marley touched her arm, bringing about an odd sensation.

"You were right to speak up, Miss Stanhope. Do not let Lady Pebble be too hard on you."

Her gaze met his. "Thank you, my lord, for smoothing over my faux pas."

Rowena left the dining room, trying to avoid Lady Pebble as they headed toward the drawing room.

Lady Sarah caught up to her, slipping her arm through Rowena's. "My, you were so brave, Miss Stanhope. I have never liked the scent of cigars. My sense of smell is quite sensitive, and I always dread when gentlemen join the ladies in the drawing room after they have been at their cigars. I apologize for not being more supportive of you, but I wish to anger no one here."

She patted her friend's hand. "I understand. You seek a match at this house party. I will not stand in your way. In fact, I will try to aid you as much as I can."

"Oh, thank you, Miss Stanhope. I have not been invited to a house party in ages. No one thinks of me anymore. It is as if I am invisible amongst the *ton*."

They reached the drawing room, and she said, "There are some very nice gentlemen who are guests, my lady. Let us hope one of them will be for you."

The ladies took seats, and as expected, Lady Pebble came to sit next to Rowena.

"You quite startled me with that outburst, my dear."

"It will not happen again, my lady," she promised.

"See that is true," the viscountess said sharply, her disapproval obvious.

Having drawn her hostess' disfavor, she tried to make amends.

"Shall I play the pianoforte for you, my lady?"

Lady Pebble considered it a moment. "Wait until the gentlemen have arrived. You may do so then."

The group spoke of safe topics until the gentlemen, led by Lord Pebble, joined them.

Then Lady Pebble turned to her. "Would you care to play the pianoforte for us, Miss Stanhope?"

"I would be happy to do so, my lady," she replied.

As she crossed the room, she heard Lord Marley say, "I will turn the pages for Miss Stanhope."

How was she to play with him standing next to her? It had been difficult enough trying to eat her dinner with him so close, their elbows even grazing a few times. This would be much worse, however.

She seated herself, glancing at the pages before her and seeing it was a piece she recognized.

"I can turn my own pages," she told the earl when he came to stand next to her. Too close.

"I know," he said smugly. "But you will look churlish if you deny me now."

"You have me between a rock and a hard place, my lord."

He chuckled. "You are not comparing Odysseus' plight to your own, are you?"

His words surprised her. She had referred to Homer's work, where Odysseus had to travel through a dangerous place on his journey, facing the Charybdis, a perilous whirlpool as well as a cliff-dwelling monster which loved to dine upon men. The hero had maneuvered through the challenges and continued safely on his way.

Rowena would soldier on for now, but she would need to draw Lord Marley aside and tell him to stop seeking her out.

Because if he didn't, she might cave—and kiss him.

Chapter Twelve

Con knew Miss Stanhope had been irritated with him, especially since she had ignored him throughout dinner. He shouldn't have provoked her by teasing her when she mentioned the possibility of him trading the name cards which Lady Pebble had placed on the table.

He had redeemed himself, however, when he spoke up for her regarding the issue of the men smoking cigars as they lingered over their after-dinner brandy. She made a valid point. He himself had caught the scent of cigar smoke on his clothes, as well as his skin and hair, while seated in drawing rooms. While it was a pleasant experience to light a cigar and puff upon it as he sipped his brandy and visited with other gentlemen, the aftereffects were most unpleasant. It had not been difficult to support her on this issue, and it was good the other men present agreed to abandon the habit for the entirety of the house party.

Her fingers now rested against the ivories, ready to play, and he caught the rose scent from before. Standing by her side, he had a delightful view of her breasts as he glanced down, the rounded globes calling out to him. Deliberately, he drew his gaze from them to the page of music. If he were to turn the page when necessary, he better do so. If he didn't, Miss Stanhope was bound to know what had drawn his attention away and scold him thoroughly. Actually, he would not mind her doing so. When angry, it brought color to her cheeks, making her very enticing.

Still, he followed along as she began to play. She had mentioned being adequate at the instrument, but he thought she played the pianoforte beautifully. It made him curious to hear her play the violin, despite the fact she said she was not accomplished in doing so. She had taken it up after her father's death, and that had to have occurred sometime in the past two-and-a-half months. No one could be expected to play brilliantly after so short a time, especially since she had no music tutor to guide her.

She finished playing, and polite applause sounded from the house party's guests. Rising, she exited from the other side of where he stood.

"Thank you. I must also allow the other ladies to entertain you, as well."

This was the part Con dreaded. Not every lady could play the pianoforte well, and it could be painful listening to them do so. Of the five young ladies present, he guessed at least two of them were terrible at it.

He offered his arm to her, and she was polite enough to take it. He guided them to an available settee for two and thought progress had been made when she actually allowed him to take a seat beside her.

"Who else would care to entertain us?" Lady Pebble asked, glancing about.

"I will," a quiet voice said, determination in her tone.

It was Miss Lawson who had volunteered. Con had spoken to the shy young woman in the drawing room before dinner and realized it took a great deal of courage on her part to do so.

Springing to his feet, he asked, "Might I turn the pages for you, as well, Miss Lawson?"

Her cheeks pinkened. "No, my lord. I shall play from memory."

Con seated himself again, his leg brushing against Miss Stanhope's gown. Actually, against her leg, truth be told. The settee was narrower than he'd first thought it. He was glad to see Miss Stanhope did not pull away. Then again, she would not be the kind of woman who backed down from anything.

It made her all the more appealing to him.

From the first keys struck, it was obvious Miss Lawson was incredibly talented. The guests sat in awe for the next several minutes and when she finished, they burst into applause. For her part, Miss Lawson stood, giving a shy smile, and returned to her seat.

"Marvelous, my dear," praised Lord Pebble.

He had learned that Miss Lawson was a relative of Lord Pebble's, but even Con could see the viscount had had no idea how well she played.

"You play beautifully," Lord Cramer commented, his interest in the young lady obvious. "Might we take a turn about the room, Miss Lawson? I would enjoy hearing more about your music. And you."

Other conversations began breaking out, but he had led them to a settee apart from the other guests.

"I suppose you seated us here to isolate me from the others," Miss Stanhope said grumpily.

"Perhaps it was because I wanted you all to myself," he said flirtatiously.

Seeing her frown, Con changed tactics.

"I wished to seat us apart from others because I have an apology to offer you, my lady. We made plans for me to—"

"No apology is necessary, my lord. You are not in my debt in any regard. Besides, we barely know one another."

His gaze was steady upon her. "I would like that to change."

"I would not," she said crisply.

"I still wish to give you my most sincere apology." When she started to speak again, he raised a finger. "Please allow me to finish it."

She sighed, looking put out, but kept silent.

"I was to call upon you the afternoon after the Purlington ball," he began. "I meant to do so. I even planned to send flowers to you."

Her brows arched in surprise, but she said nothing.

Gathering his courage, he told her, "The reason I did not call upon you was very personal. When I arrived home from the ball, one of my father's footmen came to tell me that he had collapsed. I rushed home. The doctor was already there. Papa was in pain. To this day, I know not what caused his death. Only that it happened moments after I arrived."

Con paused, swallowing, the memory of that night still raw within his soul. "I still had so much to say to him. He was such a good man. Beloved by his children and a wonderful uncle to all my cousins."

Suddenly, her hand covered his. "I am so sorry. That must have been difficult." She removed it quickly, most likely not wishing for anyone else present to see the intimate gesture.

He blinked back the tears which had formed in his eyes. "It was. Then I had so much to do. People to meet with. Decisions which had to be promptly made. We left town that next day, taking Papa home to Marleyfield. He loved the place so much. We buried him in the Swanford cemetery. I will admit that it took days for my head to clear."

Gazing deeply into her eyes, he added, "When the fog lifted, I realized that I had not gone to see you. Not even thought to write a note to you, explaining my absence from town. You went to *ton* events and must have noted my absence, and I was in anguish, worried about your feelings. I thought to write to you. To explain myself. To offer up my heartfelt apology." He hesitated. "I chose not to do so. For that, I am ashamed."

"You needn't be," she said, her tone comforting. She removed her hand from his. "I, too, understand all that is involved with the death of a loved one. When Papa died, I had to plan his funeral. Notify so many others. Send the death notice to the newspapers. Meet with Ollie and help him make the transition from steward to viscount. Because of this, I do understand how you had to focus on what was at hand. Calling upon me was unimportant in the midst of such a life-altering event, my lord."

He had to ask. "When did Lord Samuel pass, my lady?"

"The afternoon you were to visit," she said dully, and his heart ached. Not only had he neglected to even her send a note, but she had dealt with such heartache over losing her father.

This time, it was Con who placed his hand over hers. "I regret not coming to see you. I am sorry I never wrote to you."

"It does not matter, my lord. I understand—and accept your apology. I, too, must apologize. I have behaved poorly in your company. That is unlike me. I hope you will also accept my apology."

He squeezed her fingers. "I do."

Then he removed his hand before it became awkward. He glanced about, hoping no one had seen them touching. Even within a house party, gossip could spread like wildfire. He would not want Miss Stanhope's reputation to suffer because of a careless moment.

"Your cousin seems a good fellow."

"He will make for a wonderful viscount," she agreed. "Ollie is very thoughtful regarding his tenants. He recently turned thirty. He is ready to settle into his title—and marriage."

"I recall Lord Pebble mentioning this house party was given in Lord Samuel's honor."

"Yes. He hopes to be betrothed by its end."

"And what of you, Miss Stanhope? Do you have a similar aim?"

"Not at all," she said brusquely. "I have no wish to ever wed. I am happy with the quiet life I now lead."

"You are dressing much better," he told her.

She removed her spectacles and slipped a handkerchief from her sleeve, polishing them.

"Is it appropriate for a gentleman to mention a lady's wardrobe?" she asked.

"It is—if they are friends."

Miss Stanhope asked, "Are we, my lord? Friends?"

"I would like to think we are," he said. "In all honesty, I have never spoken so openly to a woman in my life. I felt a kinship that evening in the garden with you. A closeness. I hope you will consider us to be friends."

"I will. As long as there is no kissing involved."

Her words jolted him. "Have you thought of our kisses as much as I have?" he asked, yearning in his voice.

"I think that an inappropriate topic of conversation, Lord Marley," she said stiffly.

He wanted to believe that she had thought about them as much as he had and said, "I have not been able to forget them. I do not *want* to forget them."

"Well, I do," she said. "If we are to have any kind of friendship between us, then we must pretend that it did not happen."

"I cannot do so, my lady," he said softly. "I still think of kissing you each day. I even do so in my dreams."

A deep blush filled her face. "It is not a topic I care to discuss, my lord."

She started to rise, but he took her arm, gently tugging so that she sat again.

"I will not bring them up again. Unless you do first," he told her.

"Thank you," she said, gazing out over the room, deliberately avoiding his gaze.

"Which of the ladies present to you believe might make for a good wife for your cousin?" he asked, simply wanting to remain in her company, not truly caring what they spoke about.

"My answer will sound biased, but I think my friend Miss Tweedham would be a good match for Ollie. She has also shown an interest in him, and I intend to encourage him to give her careful consideration. If it is not Miss Tweedham, I think Miss Lawson might also make him happy. Ollie is so jovial. I believe he could draw Miss Lawson from her shell."

He smiled. "You are as much of a matchmaker as Lady Pebble is."

She turned, meeting his gaze. "I like to see others happy,

especially those who mean a great deal to me."

"My sisters both made love matches," he shared. "Lucy fell in love with the Marquess of Huntsberry during her come-out Season. Their daughter Elziabeth is six months old. And when my sister Dru went to visit Lucy in the country, she fell in love with one of their neighbors. She is now wed to the Earl of Martindale, and their son Beau is a little over two months old. I had planned to visit them and meet my nephew for the first time, but this house party came up."

She smiled wryly. "You mean the house party you were not invited to."

"True," he agreed. "Fortunately, I was available and able to balance the numbers." He paused, gazing intently at her. "It was fortuitous that you are also in attendance."

"If I did not know better, my lord, I would think you somehow manipulated things in order to be here at Pebblestone. With me."

It surprised him how astute she was.

"Do you believe in fate, Miss Stanhope? I think it led me here so that I might see you in person and be able to apologize. Especially since you say you are not planning on returning to the Season. I might never have seen you again if not for Lord Clay being called away."

Con knew he lied to her. He should admit that he had convinced Lord Clay to pass on the house party in order for Con to take his place. But Miss Stanhope still didn't quite trust him.

And he needed her to do so. Badly.

"Fate. Coincidence. It goes by several names," she said airily. She glanced about. "I see others are taking their leave. I will do so, as well."

He rose and offered her his hand. When she took it, it felt so right. A warm feeling washed over him.

"Goodnight, my lady."

Con watched her leave, wondering why this particular woman had claimed a piece of his heart.

All he knew was somehow, some way, he was going to convince this woman to become his countess.

Chapter Thirteen

Though she had not returned to her cottage until almost ten o'clock last night, Rowena was up early, as usual. It was nice not to have to go out to the well and draw water to boil for her tea, as well as collect enough to wash her dishes. She looked forward to a typical English breakfast, one which she would eat and not have to cook.

She took care with her appearance that morning. She told herself it was not because of Lord Marley.

And knew she was lying to herself.

The former Viscount Dyer seemed even more handsome to her than that night when he had approached her at the Purlington ball. Perhaps it was the more confident air he had about him. While he had been everything from amusing to interesting the night they had met, she thought he was settling into his title well.

Rowena only wished that the urge to kiss him would vanish.

It was going to be difficult to be around him for the next week. Then again, Lady Pebble had already revealed that she would mix up the guests at each dinner, so she doubted Lord Marley would be a dinner partner of hers for several days to come. Rowena herself could make certain she joined small groups which did not include him. If he called her out, her excuse would be that she was trying to get to know everyone who had been invited to the Pebbles' house party. The truth was that she saw others as a buffer to protect her from Lord Marley.

Most importantly, she must protect her heart.

She did not fancy she was in love with the earl. Far from it. She told herself it was merely the physical attraction to him which was so bloody inconvenient. Worry filled her, knowing if she did spend too much time in his company, her heart would begin to overrule her mind, and she would find herself in a pickle. Under no circumstances did she ever wish to fall in love, especially with a charmer such as Lord Marley.

Once again, she waited by the window for Ollie's carriage, which arrived promptly at a quarter till eight. Rowena went outside and allowed her cousin to hand her up.

As she sat across from him, she asked, "What were your first impressions of the female guests? Did any one of them stand out to you?"

He shrugged, looking a bit self-conscious. "I am not certain I should be discussing my situation with you after all, Cousin."

"Why not?" she asked indignantly. "I thought you sought my advice."

"I do not wish to place you in an awkward situation, Rowena."

She studied him a moment. "Are you fearful that I would share any feelings you reveal to me to my friends?"

"No. Yes. Perhaps."

"Let me give you my solemn word. You are family, Ollie. My first obligation is always to you. I can carry on conversations with my friends and not have you be a part of them. Do you trust me to do so?"

"Yes. I do." He sighed. "I quite like Miss Tweedham. She is clever and interesting. I plan to make certain that I can spend more time in her company. As for Lady Sarah, she also seemed quite pleasant. We had a nice time discussing gardening before we went in to dinner."

"What of our time in the drawing room last night? Did you speak to either of the other two ladies?"

"Only Lady Jewell. My, does she have some interesting stories to tell," he declared. "I have yet to really talk with Miss Lawson, however. I feel I owe it to myself to get to know each of the four eligible ladies. At the moment, however, I am leaning toward pursuing Miss Tweedham."

"I have known her for several years now, Ollie, and I can tell you that she has such a good heart. She is also intelligent and patient."

"All those qualities would make for a good viscountess," he mused. "I will continue to get to know all the ladies, however. It is only fair to do so. I fear I will have much to ponder once I do."

Rowena reached for his hand and squeezed it. "Do not feel as if you have to offer for anyone by the end of this house party. While they are known for engagements occurring, do not be in a rush. If you are not certain in a week's time, do not leap to a decision simply for the sake of making one. You could always exchange letters with any lady you are interested in and then spend time with her at next spring's Season before you make up your mind."

"You are right. As always. I just do not wish to miss out and have one I prefer snatched up by someone else at the house party."

"We can watch how things unfold over the next few days. See if any couples pair off from the rest of the group. You will also have more time around the various ladies, and that will help you, as well."

They entered the house and were taken immediately to the breakfast room. A quick count told her only Miss Bailey was not present.

"I see we are an early group," Rowena said, greeting the others and heading for the buffet, where Ollie already was.

"I think our guests are simply eager to begin a new day with one another," Lord Pebble said, smiling at Miss Lawson. "Now that all the young people are here, what will they be doing today, my dear?" he asked his wife.

"After breakfast, I think a stroll along the beach is in order," the viscountess said. "The weather is pleasant this morning. There is nothing like the salt air."

"Are there shells?" asked Lady Sarah. "I have never been to the beach before, but I have seen shells which others have brought back."

"Yes, my lady," Ollie said. "They will be easy to spot. The sand along the beach can be a bit hard to navigate, but as you approach the water's edge, it is more packed down and easy to maneuver along. A majority of shells will be found along that sand, the water washing them up to the shore's edge."

"I walk the beach regularly with my daughter," Baron Howell said. "I can help you find seashells, Lady Sarah. We might even save a few for Mary, as well as the ones you might wish to collect."

"I would appreciate your escort, Lord Howell."

Rowena thought it interesting how the baron had jumped into the conversation. Ollie had certainly lost that round if he was interested in Lady Sarah. She glanced at her friend, who was still talking with Lord Howell. Her face was alight with interest. For the first time since she had known Lady Sarah, Rowena thought her not plain at all. It was amazing how a bit of attention from one gentleman had helped in this transformation of her friend.

"That will take a couple of hours," Lady Pebble continued. "After you return to Pebblestone, Lord Pebble has promised to lead the gentlemen on a hunt. The ladies can gather in my parlor and catch up on their correspondence."

She had no one to write to, other than Aunt Sylvia, and she had posted a letter to her aunt only yesterday, informing her of the house party she planned to attend. Her two closest friends and only other living relative were at this house party. Besides, writing letters were meant for cold, rainy days by the fire. With this end of September still nice, being outside was her preference. While she had no plans to join the gentlemen on the hunt, Rowena determined she would take a ride on Aurora. Ollie had both their horses taken to Pebblestone the day before the house party began, knowing that riding would likely be one of the activities the viscountess would recommend they indulge in.

For now, she would keep her plans to herself, however.

Once breakfast had concluded, the ladies went to freshen up and claim their bonnets. Rowena had brought several and chose a straw one with sky blue ribbons, tying them into a bow beneath her chin.

Miss Tweedham grinned. "Your taste in bonnets has also greatly improved."

"It is our local millinery's work. If we have time to go into Mossleigh, we must visit her shop. She has several bonnets already made up, and she will also create one for you if you wish."

Her friend's eyes brightened. "Yes, we simply must do so. I find it hard to resist an attractive bonnet."

They met the rest of their party in the foyer. All ten of them were going down to the beach. Miss Bailey was nowhere in sight, and Lord and Lady Pebble had wished them well at breakfast, so Rowena knew their hosts would not be going either. She found she liked these relaxed rules of house parties held in the country.

She made a point of skirting around Lord Marley and joining Lady Jewell, Lord Cramer, and Mr. Tompkins. The four of them walked together to the beach, and she found herself next to Lord Cramer when they reached it.

"Are you fond of collecting seashells, Miss Stanhope?" he asked.

"I have never done so, my lord. Although I was born but a stone's throw from here, I have spent most of my time in town. My late father preferred town to country."

"I am the opposite," he admitted. "I feel when the Season comes along, I must drag myself to town. I only bother attending a few events."

She looked up at him, thinking his auburn hair and green eyes an interesting combination. "Why do you prefer the country? I know I do and plan to make Dorset my permanent home, but I would be interested in your opinion."

Though he had seemed taciturn before now, he opened up to her. Rowena found he was a serious, solemn man with a bent toward learning. The time in his company was most pleasant.

"I have a superb estate manager, which frees me up to focus on intellectual pursuits. I am interested in astronomy. Biology. Literature."

"Mr. Tompkins is a science tutor at Oxford," she said. "Have you had a chance to visit with him?"

"No, I have not. I will do so."

They walked along the beach, stopping to pick up a shell every now and then. She loved inhaling the sea air, catching the taste of salt upon her lips. She and Lord Cramer talked a bit about Dante's work as they went, and she enjoyed his interpretation of parts of the poet's *The Divine Comedy*. They even argued playfully about how Dante had portrayed fortune-tellers, and she found she liked the earl very much.

When it came time to turn around and head back to Pebblestone, she encouraged him to walk with Mr. Tompkins.

"I do not wish to abandon you, Miss Stanhope."

"You will not be doing so. I shall walk with Lady Jewell," she proclaimed, slipping her arm through the other woman's.

She was glad she did so. Lady Jewell kept Rowena entertained with stories of growing up in India the entire way back. Lady Jewell had a way with words, painting a picture with them, showing Rowena a world she had never been exposed to before.

When they reached the main house, she said, "I do not know when I have ever laughed so much, my lady. You not only have amusing tales, but you are a master storyteller. You know how to craft a story and then deliver it with maximum impact."

"I have thought of writing them down," Lady Jewell said. "Before I get too busy and forget them. India is still fresh in my mind, in vivid color."

"Do so," she encouraged. "It would be something you could pass down in your family. Your children—and even grandchildren—could read about the adventures you had in the magical place called India."

"I will do so," Lady Jewell said. "Thank you for your encouragement, Miss Stanhope."

At the butler's direction, they returned to the breakfast room. Cakes and scones had been laid out, and footmen poured them cups of tea.

Lady Pebble greeted them. "I thought you might need something to fortify yourselves before the afternoon. Lord Pebble is down at the stables now, seeing that your horses are saddled, gentlemen."

Once they had drunk their tea, the gentlemen left, eager to get to the hunt. Lady Pebble said the ladies could write their letters in her sitting room or even the library. Rowena slipped back to the bedchamber and changed into her riding habit and went to the stables. The men were just riding off, and she waved at them as they passed her.

"Would you saddle Aurora for me?" she asked the head groom.

"Right away, my lady."

Soon, she had mounted Aurora and set out, already having a destination in mind. It surprised her when another rider joined her, and she saw it was Lord Marley. Pulling on the reins, she brought Aurora to a halt.

"What are you doing here?" she demanded.

"I could ask the same of you, my lady," he replied, giving her a lazy smile that made her toes curl.

"You should be hunting with the others."

He shrugged. "I have never been one who was enchanted by running down a helpless fox."

"You seemed eager enough to join the others."

"I was eager to ride. I had already decided to break away from the hunt." He paused. "Much as you have done from the letter-writing ladies. Where might you be riding this afternoon?"

She decided it might be wise to have his company. She still

was new to these parts, and he was pleasant to be around.

"There is a local landmark new to the area which I wish to see. Just north of Weymouth."

"Then I will accompany you," he determined, not giving her any choice.

She had already asked directions from Betsy, who had been the one to tell her about it.

"Follow me."

He did, not asking where they were going or what exactly they would see. She appreciated that.

After three quarters of an hour, Rowena slowed her horse and said, "There. In the distance. Carved upon that hill. Do you see it?"

He lifted a hand, shading his eyes. "I do. It is a rider on a horse. But who is it?"

"It is called the White Horse of Osmington. A local, James Hamilton, cut it into the chalk hillside only a few months ago. It is a tribute to the king."

"King George?" he asked.

"Yes. The Duke of Gloucester built a country house near here. He calls it Gloucester Lodge. The area caught King George's attention, and he has summered here for almost fifteen years now. It is said he has even used one of the bathing machines and ventured out into the sea."

Marley chuckled. "A brave man, our king."

She spurred on Aurora, and they began drawing nearer toward the white chalk tribute cut into the high hill. When they were closer, she brought her mount to a halt again in order to study the picture of a man riding a horse, thinking it looked quite like the king. She had seen him once at a ball he and the queen had attended.

"The locals are quite proud of the artwork. It is two hundred and eighty feet long. Three hundred and twenty-three feet high."

"Is that limestone?" he asked.

"You have a good eye, my lord."

"Ah, a compliment from Miss Stanhope. I can die happily now," he teased. He studied the hill. "This is unique since it is an example of both leucippotomy and gigantotomy."

Surprise filled her. She knew leucippotomy was the art of carving horses, while gigantotomy was the art of carving humans. Both were a part of the ancient craft of creating figures on the side of a hill. These terms were not ones laymen tossed about. It took a highly educated person to know what they were, much less how to use them.

"You are more learned that you let on," she observed.

"I have never tried to hide my academic leanings. History has always been my favorite subject, especially ancient history. I suppose part of it is a result of the names in my family."

"Do explain yourself," she encouraged. "History is also a passion of mine."

"My given name is Constantine, but I go by Con. My mother, her brother, and their cousin were fascinated by ancient history, especially that of Rome and Byzantium. They made a pact when they were children, deciding to name any offspring they had with the names of emperors and empresses. My sisters are Lucilla, who is Lucy, and Livia Drusilla, who is affectionately known as Dru. There are ten cousins in all."

"And you all have these historical names?"

"We do. My Worthington cousins are Valentinian, Ariadne, Cornelia, and Thermantia. Only Ariadne uses her Christan name. The others are Val, Lia, and Tia."

"How fascinating," she said. "That would leave three more cousins, though, if I am not mistaken."

"The Fulton branch. My cousin Lucius died as a boy in a carriage accident, along with my uncle. My cousin Hadrian became the Earl of Traywick at only ten years of age. He asked to be known as Tray from that point on. His sisters retain their empress' names. They are Verina and Justina. Neither has made her come-out yet, and Tray only recently graduated from university. Soon, the Fulton cousins will take their places in Polite Society."

"You have a fascinating family history, Lord Marley."

"Most of us are interested in history because of our names. Me, in particular. Do you lean toward history, my lady?"

"I do enjoy it, especially ancient history. I find modern history dull. Too many wars for my taste, especially this current one with Bonaparte. The Little Corporal has made a mess of Europe, hasn't he?"

"Truer words were never spoken." He gazed out again at the monument and its rider. "I know it is best seen from a distance, but let us ride a bit closer. I would not mind seeing the hill itself."

They rode as close as they could come, dismounting and leading their horses up the hill, touching the carving with their hands.

"Fascinating," the earl proclaimed. "I wonder what the king will think of it."

Rowena did not know what King George III would make of this tribute to him.

What she did know was her opinion of Lord Marley was gradually changing again.

For the better.

Chapter Fourteen

T HE DAY'S ACTIVITIES included a picnic at noon. Con, attending his first house party, decided that eating was a large part of the day and was mindful of not overindulging. He did like the more intimate atmosphere a house party offered, though. Events of the Season were often large affairs, and he gravitated to those he knew well, which had always included Val and members of their families. It was nice to get to know others outside his usual sphere.

Lord Samuel was a jolly fellow and entertaining to be around. He did not have the town polish on him, mainly because he had never been to town. He had spent his entire twenties serving as Stanfield's steward. Con believed the viscount should take a bride from amongst the guests at the house party because Samuel would be entirely lost in the crush of guests at *ton* events.

Baron Howell was another gentleman that Con had enjoyed getting to know better. He had guessed correctly that the baron's wife had been lost in childbirth. Howell had confided in Con that he hoped to find a wife at this house party, wanting a mother for his daughter, but also wishing for companionship for himself. He liked the baron's affable manner. Howell was friendly and rational, and Con believed he cared for his daughter a great deal because he mentioned her frequently. He had even asked Lady Pebble if he might send for Mary and her nursery governess so that Mary might enjoy the picnic with them today.

Mr. Tompkins had been an interesting choice as a guest. He possessed no title and was an Oxford tutor. Lord Pebble had confided to Con, though, that Tompkins' father was not likely to see the end of this year, which would make Tompkins an earl. He wondered if the ladies present knew of this. Most likely, they did. A house party was a microcosm of the entirety of Polite Society, and any information about the gentlemen present would be traded amongst the ladies.

He had yet to penetrate Lord Cramer's walls, however. Cramer seemed very intelligent. In fact, Con had listened to a discussion between Cramer and Tompkins and found it hard to follow because of its complexity. He wondered if the earl would be able to set aside his erudite ways, especially if he hoped to find a match at this house party.

Glancing out the window, he saw servants toting chairs and tables to the back lawn in preparation for the picnic.

"It looks as if the picnic will begin soon," he announced, turning away from the window.

"Oh, I do wish it were being held on the beach," Lady Jewell said. "Perhaps it could move there instead. I think it would be wonderful to look out on the water as we dine."

"That would be a bit impractical," Miss Stanhope told her. "The beach is a good half a mile from where the house sits. It would be difficult to get both food and furniture to it. And then we would sink in the sand."

"Oh, I had not thought of that," Lady Jewell said, pouting slightly.

Con thought her a true beauty, but as most ladies, Lady Jewell did not take into consideration what servants went through in order to make things pleasing for a household.

"What we could do on another day is have Cook prepare baskets of food for us," Miss Stanhope continued. "The gentlemen could carry those baskets down to the beach, and we could have a picnic that way."

"But what would we sit upon?" Miss Lawson fretted.

"Why, we could take blankets with us and spread them out," Miss Stanhope told her. "That way, we would not get sand in our clothes.

Con liked how nothing seemed to ruffle Miss Stanhope.

Except his kiss.

He meant what he had told her. He would not bring up kissing again unless she were the one to do so first. He only hoped that she would before the end of the house party. If he didn't make any inroads with her by the end of this week, he would be out of luck in pressing his suit. It wasn't as if he could woo her next Season because she would not be attending it. That gave him pause.

Was Miss Stanhope the right woman to be his countess?

If she wished to avoid the Season, it would go against everything he wanted. Con had agreed to a pact with his cousins, established by Ariadne. Long ago, the ten cousins had been brought to town only once when they were children, all at the same time. They had immensely enjoyed being together. Ariadne had suggested as adults that they should all come to town for the Season each spring, bringing their children with them, something members of Polite Society simply did not do. Ariadne said the Season would be for attending a few social events, but more importantly, it would be a time for family to come together. The cousins could enjoy each other's company, and their children would enjoy being brought up surrounded by family.

If Miss Stanhope did not want to come to town, how was he to go to the Season each year without her? Would she even agree to let their children come with him, leaving her behind at Marleyfield?

Con shook his head, knowing he was getting ahead of himself. He determined that if Miss Stanhope were his countess, she would want to be with him, no matter where they were. Con believed in love—and he thought he was in love with her. She had been so amiable that night they had joined Val's table and seamlessly fit in. Perhaps Miss Stanhope was opposed to the

Season because the *ton* had not been welcoming to her. If wed to him, however, she would have a large, loving family who would always greet her with open arms.

But could she love him?

That was the question. And he needed that answer. Soon. Either she would prove open to marriage—and love—or Con would need to move on before his heart became too invested. Already, the thought of a life without Miss Stanhope in it seemed too much to bear.

Lady Pebble appeared in the library. "We can go outside now. Ladies, you will want to retrieve your bonnets and possibly your spencers. It is a bit cool today but not unreasonably so."

The men had forgone wearing hats during the house party, and that remained the case now. He accompanied the others, led by Lord Pebble, and they went out onto the terrace and then down to the sprawling lawn. Several tables had been set up, covered in starched, white tablecloths, set with china and silverware. A long table had also been set out, and several servants stood behind it, ready to serve them.

He passed one table and noted no name cards were present. Lady Pebble had assigned seats at tea and dinner yesterday, and Con had been far from Miss Stanhope. Today's picnic presented him with the possibility to eat with her.

Mr. Tompkins joined him, also glancing at the tables and smiling. "I see the seating will be open for our picnic."

"Do you have a particular lady you wish to sit with?" he asked.

"Miss Lawson," the tutor said. "I am finding her most interesting."

Deciding to finally share his own feelings, he revealed, "I am hoping to sit with Miss Stanhope."

Tompkins grinned. "Then we shall simply have to maneuver them our way, my lord."

The ladies appeared, and Con found his heart speed up at the sight of Miss Stanhope. She wasn't the great beauty Lady Jewell was, but to him, she was very beautiful. She carried herself with grace. She was intelligent and looked after others, letting him know her heart was in the right place. He could see her as a mother figure to all his tenants at Marleyfield. Most importantly, he could picture her with a babe in her arms and others tugging at her skirts. The image brought a smile to his face.

He and Tompkins moved toward the women. It helped that Miss Stanhope and Miss Lawson happened to be walking next to one another as they arrived on the lawn.

Mr. Tompkins said, "Miss Stanhope, Miss Lawson, please come join Lord Marley and me."

Miss Lawson blushed profusely at the suggestion, while Miss Stanhope curtly nodded her approval. Together, the four took a table. A footman asked if they cared for tea or coffee and said that wine was also available. Both ladies asked for tea, and he and Tompkins went along with the same. The footman told them to go ahead and make their way through the buffet, and he would see the tea delivered to their table.

Mr. Tompkins took Miss Lawson's elbow in hand, guiding her to the buffet.

"He is interested in her," Miss Stanhope said.

"He is," Con confirmed. "He asked if I would join him at this table."

"And I was also asked because I was standing with Miss Lawson," she observed.

"Yes, but I would have wished for you to join me at whatever table I sat," he said, thinking she would appreciate his honesty.

"You know I am not interested in marriage, my lord," she reminded him as they reached the buffet.

"I am not clear on exactly why," he told her. "Yes, you have talked of having your freedom, but would you not have more as a married lady? You would no longer need a chaperone to go anywhere. Your income would be assured."

"I do not use a chaperone now since I am already on the shelf," she replied blithely. "And thanks to Papa's generosity, my income is assured and under my control. I do not have to beg for pin money. I will never have to wait upon a husband and get nothing in return."

"Servants usually wait upon husbands, and you are discounting the love and affection that a husband could bring you."

"I do not believe in love," she said flatly.

"Well, I do," he said stubbornly, taking the plate a footman offered and handing it to her, then accepting one for himself. "I plan to wed for love. I will give my countess plenty of affection. I will consider her my best friend. And she can keep any dowry she has to be used as she likes."

Con asked for several items to be placed on his plate as they continued down the line.

"Then you are different from most titled lords," Miss Stanhope said crisply.

He turned, facing her, his gaze penetrating her. "That is what I am trying to tell you." He stared at her a long moment before looking away.

They reached the sweets, and he chose a pear tart and a slice each of apple pie and chocolate cake. His plate was too full already, and a maid placed the three items on a separate plate, handing it to him.

Looking to Miss Stanhope, he said, "I have sweets for the both of us if you would not mind sharing."

She gazed at him a long moment. "Thank you."

They returned to their table, where the discussion was animated. He had heard that Miss Lawson was shy, but she seemed to be perfectly comfortable in their party of four. It was apparent that she also seemed to hang upon every word Mr. Tompkins uttered, and the tutor did the same whenever she spoke.

Con turned to Miss Stanhope. "I think we are witnessing the first match being made," he said quietly.

She smiled. "I agree. Lord and Lady Pebble will be so pleased, especially because it means Miss Lawson will remain in the neighborhood."

He didn't know if she smiled at him or the fact that Mr. Tompkins and Miss Lawson seemed inching toward a betrothal. He would like to think it might be both, but Miss Stanhope was one who kept him guessing.

"Bloody hell," he muttered under his breath.

"Did you say something, my lord?" she asked sweetly.

"Not a thing," he replied, tamping down his frustration.

At least the food was tasty, especially the sweets. He glanced about and saw others were now talking, empty plates being cleared. Lady Pebble's bell tinkled, gaining everyone's attention.

"We will begin our lawn games soon," she informed the group. "The servants will be setting up bowls, as well as battledore and shuttlecock."

A loud groan came from Lord Samuel, and the viscount volunteered, "I have never played a lawn game, so I will concede now."

"Nonsense," his cousin answered. "You cannot give up before even starting. Give all of us the pleasure of beating you, Ollie."

Everyone laughed at Miss Stanhope's remark, and the cousins grinned at one another. Lady Pebble came by each table, dividing them up between the two activities.

Glancing at Miss Lawson, the viscountess declared, "You and Mr. Tompkins will be a team. Miss Stanhope, you and Lord Marley can be another one. I will assign you first to battledore and shuttlecock, and you will play one another. Your game will be held over there," she said, pointing to the far south side of the lawn.

The two couples left their table, going to the designated area. A footman handed each of them a small racket, and both gentlemen received a feathered shuttlecock.

"What do we do?" asked Miss Lawson, clearly never having played before.

Con explained, "In my schooldays, the way we played was whoever kept the shuttlecock going the longest would win."

The footman said, "Lady Pebble said that whichever team

outlasted the other would receive a point. The team to first reach ten points wins."

"Could we practice a bit first?" asked Mr. Tompkins. "I have not held a racket in years."

The footman agreed and told both couples where to stand. Con tossed his shuttlecock into the air and hit it toward Miss Stanhope. She returned it, and they kept it going for a half-dozen hits before she swung and missed it.

"This grass is slippery," she said. "My foot almost slid out from under me." She paused, obviously thinking. "Wait a moment."

Placing her racket on the ground, Miss Stanhope sat upon the ground. Then to Con's surprise, she removed her slippers. Hiking up her gown, he got a view of shapely calves and long, long legs. Then he realized what she was about to do.

"You cannot remove your stockings," he sputtered.

She smiled, a wicked gleam in her eyes. Slowly, she peeled the stocking down her leg, over her ankle, and removed it from her foot. Now her leg and foot were enticingly bare, causing his mouth to go dry.

"Why, I believe I just did so, my lord. Do you think it gives me an unfair advantage over you?" To emphasize her point, she wriggled her toes.

"Not at all, Miss Stanhope," he said evenly, sounding as if he had recovered, but he was far from it. His eyes remained fastened upon the curve of her calves as she removed the other stocking.

Then she stood, her gown falling, her legs covered once more. Still, those bare feet proved to be tantalizing.

Glancing to the other couple, she said, "Have you practiced enough? I believe we are ready to begin."

CHAPTER FIFTEEN

ROWENA HAD NEVER done anything remotely athletic beyond the athleticism needed to ride a horse. Plenty of men and women could do that. Playing battledore and shuttlecock was a new, delightful experience, though. She had to keep her eye on the shuttlecock at all times, moving back and forth, getting under it and swinging her racket up at an angle to reach Lord Marley or hitting it overhanded while it was still high in the air and returning it to him.

It was a thrill to move with bare feet across the soft grass. She had never set foot outside without wearing her shoes and stockings. Being barefooted was incredibly liberating, and she knew she would go outside her small cottage every now and then and leave her slippers and stockings behind.

She grew more experienced as play went on, getting the feathered shuttlecock to her partner better. They scored several points, keeping their shuttlecock in play longer each time than their opponents. With the other pair scoreless, sympathy filled her, and she looked to Lord Marley. They seemed to communicate silently, and he deliberately missed his next return, allowing the other team to score their first point. While she did not wish to throw their match, Rowena did want her new friend and Mr. Tompkins to score a few points.

Lord Marley and Rowena won their match, ten to three, and they graciously received congratulations from their opponents.

The losing pair was sent off to play bowls, and Lord Howell and Lady Sarah took the spot next to them, with the baron's daughter Mary accompanying them. Rowena had never seen her friend looking happier. She thought if a match could occur between these two, allowing Lady Sarah to be an instant mother, it would be a very good thing for all three involved.

"Are you without slippers and stockings?" Lady Sarah asked, looking bewildered.

"Yes. Playing in bare feet is my advantage. I am certain it gave me an advantage over Miss Lawson."

With a boldness that surprised Rowena, Lady Sarah said, "Then I shall play the same way."

She sat on the ground, Mary running to sit next to her. Together, both lady and child removed their shoes and stockings, much to the delight of Mary. The pair brushed their feet along the grass, giggling together. Then Mary threw her arms about Lady Sarah and kissed her cheek.

Looking to the baron, she saw happiness radiating from him as he said, "I have not heard Mary laugh nearly enough. She has done so all day in Lady Sarah's company." He paused. "She makes me laugh, as well."

Rowena said, "I have been friends with Lady Sarah for four years now. She is kind and loving."

Lord Howell met her gaze. "I think she will be good for both of us."

Joy filled her, knowing her friend would achieve her dream of becoming a wife. "When will you offer for her?"

"Soon."

"You will be better for having Lady Sarah in your life," Lord Marley said. "Mary will also benefit."

Blast. Why was Lord Marley so . . . so . . . well, Rowena could not come up with a word to describe him. The charming, thoughtful man who had revealed so much to her in the gardens that night kept appearing, causing Rowena to doubt herself and the decisions she had made regarding her life.

And marriage.

What if he meant what he said? That he would allow his wife to have her freedom. To control her own dowry. Or was that simply talk, something that he used in flirtation, which would not be close to reality. Part of her believed he would say whatever it took to get her to kiss him again, yet another part thought he was being utterly genuine. She thought back to his closeness with his cousin, the duke, and how happy Millbrooke and his duchess had seemed that night at the Purlington ball. Did the duchess have the same kind of freedom that Rowena had always longed for? Was she in love with her husband? It certainly seemed that way.

Lord Marley had spoken of love. She did not love him and found it impossible to believe that he loved her. Yet sometimes, she caught him looking at her, something in his eyes that seemed to tell her otherwise.

Lady Sarah had now picked up her racket, and Rowena said, "You may practice for two minutes and get used to how hard a stroke needs to be in order for you to return the shuttlecock to your partner."

She turned to see if Lord Marley wished to practice again, but he had left her. She spied him crouched next to Mary, talking with her. Her throat swelled as she watched the pair. He looked so right next to the small girl, smiling at her, showing her his racket, smoothing her hair. When he stood, Rowena averted her eyes, not wanting him to see what was in them.

"Are you ready for play?" asked Lord Howell.

"Ready to win, my lord," she cheekily replied.

This time, the game was much closer. She and Lord Marley still took the victory, ten to seven, but they had been tied several times during the match before pulling away near the end.

"We are better at balls," Lady Sarah said, with Mary shouting, "Balls! Balls!"

"Congratulations," Lord Howell told them. "Let us see if you can hold off the other two pairs."

Since they had won, they remained where they were, facing

Ollie and Lady Jewell next. Despite his worries about never having played any lawn games, her cousin proved to be almost their equal. Lady Jewell said she frequently played games in India, and her experience showed. They went into the final point, tied at nine all. Rowena felt the pressure, fearing she would be the one who might cost them the game.

Instead, she made a diving save when one of Lord Marley's strokes went wild, hitting it high in the air in order to give him time to recover. That proved to be the difference, and they won their third straight game. She watched Ollie carefully to see how he was around Lady Jewell, but he did not seem to treat Lady Jewell differently from how he treated Rowena herself. He wondered if the same would have been true if Miss Tweedham had been partnered with him.

Last, they faced her friend and Lord Cramer. While the earl moved with grace, poor Miss Tweedham was hopeless, constantly missing the shuttlecock with her racket. Thankfully, Lord Cramer treated her with kindness when they lost.

"I was awful at that," Miss Tweedham said. "I apologize, my lord. You should have chosen a better partner to play with."

"It is all in good fun," Lord Cramer said.

"It isn't always about winning," Lord Marley added. "Most of the time, it is about playing the game itself and enjoying it as you do so." He glanced to her. "And enjoying the company with you."

Rowena felt her cheeks heat but said, "Yes, it is all about the fun. You had never been to a house party before. You had never played battledore and shuttlecock either. Now, you have done both."

Miss Tweedham grinned. "Yes, I have. And I was much better at balls."

"She was," Lord Cramer shared. "The two of you should try your hand at it now since you have beaten everyone else at this game."

She handed her racket to a nearby footman. Lord Marley did

the same, taking her hand and placing it in the crook of his arm as he escorted her back to where they had picnicked and where the balls competition occurred. The entire way, Rowena was aware of his scent, a mix of bergamot and sweat from playing their game. Instead of being repelled, she found it . . . intoxicating.

"You used your racket with ease," he complimented.

"I have not hidden the fact that I am highly competitive. Fortunately, I felt at one with my racket and found our games stimulating."

"I find our conversations stimulating, Miss Stanhope, as well as your gameplay."

She found herself blushing again, something she had never really done in the past. Then again, no attractive earls had plied her with compliments up until now.

Much less kissed her.

Forget his kiss, she told herself.

But that was like telling a duck to forget how to take to water. The more Rowena tried to forget how Lord Marley's kisses made her feel, the more she remembered them.

Mary came toddling toward them when she spied them, and Lord Marley swept her up in his arms, twirling her about and then setting her atop his shoulders. The girl plunged her fingers into his hair to hold on. For a moment, Rowena wished she could do the same and feel the soft waves.

"You are a natural with children, my lord," Baron Howell observed.

"I have always liked children," the earl shared. "I am the proud uncle to a niece and nephew. I have yet to meet my nephew, however. He was born in July. I hope to visit with him soon. Two of my cousins also have children, a girl and a boy, and I enjoy spending time with them."

Curious, she turned to him. "I find it surprising to hear this, my lord. Experience has taught me that men and women in Polite Society rarely spend time with their own children, much less others' children."

His enigmatic look gave her pause. "Ah, Miss Stanhope, I and others in my family are exceptions to that rule. In fact, my cousins Ariadne and Val and my sister Lucy all brought their children to town with them this spring for the Season."

"Are you speaking in jest?" she demanded, not one to take to teasing.

"Not at all, my lady. Ariadne is the one who suggested this to the other cousins in the family. We all agreed when we had children of our own, we would bring them to the Season. Leaving a child at home in the country for months is cruel, especially if you love them and they love you. Ariadne and Julian did attend some events this year, but they also made plenty of time to see family. We ten cousins enjoy one another's company and want our children to also enjoy their cousins' company."

"That is . . . most unusual."

A determined look crossed his features. "When I wed, I will always go to town in the spring. Not because I am keen on attending balls or routs, but because I will want to see my cousins and their children—and allow my children time with their extended family. The bonds of family run strong between the Alingtons, Worthingtons, and Fultons. As more of us wed, we are spread far and wide across England. The Season is the perfect excuse to gather and spend time with one another each year." He paused. "My countess must understand this."

"I see."

That decided her. Even if she admitted her attraction to Lord Marley and kissed him again, she would never wish to go through with a marriage to him. Not that he ever would offer for her, but if he did, she would not be able to accept. She had spent a lifetime in town and never wanted to see it again. As a bluestocking, she had never truly been accepted by those of the *ton*, her only friends being the eccentrics and misfits who were also not a good fit into Polite Society. Lord Marley—and his extended family—were very much a part of that society. She would be miserable if she tried to return to it.

Ollie approached them, handing each of them a ball. "The field is ready for play," her cousin told them.

Rowena was determined to concentrate on the game at hand and do her best to enjoy what remained of the house party.

And not wish for things that could never come to pass.

Chapter Sixteen

Benchley finished dressing Con after his bath. He could not imagine how long it had taken the Pebblestone staff to heat water for so many guests, but Lady Pebble had said that everyone would have an opportunity to bathe after their vigorous play at lawn games. Because of that, and the fact they had eaten their fill at the picnic, no afternoon tea had been served.

It was still half an hour before they were to gather in the drawing room before dinner, and he decided to visit the library. Being around books had always soothed him.

When he arrived, Lord Samuel was present. Con decided to cross the Rubicon with Miss Stanhope's cousin, knowing there would be no going back after he spoke his mind.

"Lord Samuel. Might I have a word?" he asked.

"Of course, my lord." Then the viscount's brow furrowed. "This wouldn't be about Miss Tweedham, would it? Are you interested in her?"

"Easy, Samuel," he said, taking a seat in a chair to the viscount's left. "I have no designs upon Miss Tweedham—but it certainly sounds as if you are interested in her."

He thought it better to speak to Lord Samuel about his interests before Con revealed his own.

"I apologize. I did not mean to sound panicked."

"You care for Miss Tweedham," he said, hoping to ease the other man into conversation.

"Quite a bit," the viscount admitted. "I believe she also has feelings for me. I know you once danced together, though, and I was worried that you believed you might have staked your claim."

"No," he said, chuckling. "I will admit that I only asked Miss Tweedham to dance because I asked your cousin to do so first. It seemed rude not to invite her friend to do so as well, since she stood right there."

Lord Samuel visibly relaxed. "Then you have saved me a conversation with you. I was going to seek you out this evening and spell out my feelings for Miss Tweedham. I did not want it to be a competition between the two of us for her affections."

"What would you have done if I confessed a *tendre* for Miss Tweedham?" he asked idly.

The viscount grinned. "Then I might have needed to kill you."

They both laughed, easy in one another's company. Because of that, he felt hope rise within him. If Lord Samuel liked him, then he might help Con in wooing Miss Stanhope.

"I came to this house party specifically because your cousin would be in attendance," he revealed. "I actually paid Lord Clay in order to take his place."

"You paid off Clay . . . all to see Rowena?"

"Yes. Like you, I wish to share my true feelings with her. In fact, I have done more than hint at them, but she is as prickly as a pear. She either ignores me—or avoids me."

"Yet I saw you partner at the lawn games this afternoon."

"That could not be helped. She would never be impolite, and that is what it would have taken for her to dump me and find a new partner." He hesitated and then decided to take the plunge. "I think I might just be in love with her."

Lord Samuel broke out in a huge smile. "That would be wonderful, my lord. Rowena needs love in her life. My uncle depended upon her, but he never truly showed her any love. Rowena is the most capable woman I know, but she has a tendency to keep others at bay."

"She has indicated to me that she will remain in the country permanently. That she will never wed."

"I think my cousin has armed herself in battle gear like a knight of old. If you can get through the walls which she has erected around her, Lord Marley, you will never find a more loyal, loving woman."

"Thank you for listening to me."

"Do you have a plan to win over Rowena?"

He shook his head. "I am making it up as I go along."

"If the time is right and the moment would not seem forced, I will put in a good word for you," Lord Samuel promised.

"I appreciate that. More than I can say."

Baron Howell entered, and the three of them discussed the neighborhood a bit.

"Did you return your daughter to your home?" he asked.

"Yes, I took Mary and her nursery governess back to Meadowbrook. It was hard to leave Mary again, but I am hoping the time is right to find a new mother for her."

"She seemed to take to Lady Sarah."

"Very much so." Lord Howell smiled. "As have I."

Con was glad to hear that. He knew Lady Sarah had been out for many years. The baron would be a good husband to her. Though Lady Sarah had a huge dowry, it had not tempted any men in Polite Society. He hoped these two would find happiness together.

"We should go to the drawing room," he told the other two.

He did not attempt to seek out Miss Stanhope, but he always knew where she was in the room and whom she spoke with. She seemed at ease with others here, and he wondered why she had not been successful at finding a husband. Then again, if fate had brought them together, then it had been waiting for his arrival in her life.

Dinner was the usual affair. Much to his disappointment, Miss Stanhope was seated at the far end of the table. He did enjoy his conversation with Lady Jewell, however. She began telling him a story about India, and soon the whole table had quietened, listening in.

When she finished, Con said, "You have a way with words, my lady. You are a true storyteller. You know how to draw in your audience."

"Thank you, my lord," Lady Jewell replied, batting her lashes coquettishly at him.

That was not what he wanted to happen. He had not flirted with a single woman at the house party. Except for Miss Stanhope, that is. Then he saw Lord Cramer glaring at him and found that interesting. The earl was quiet and brooding. Lady Jewell was talkative and outgoing. He had not seen Lord Cramer's interest coming. He turned his gaze and kept it on Lord Cramer until the other man met it. Con shook his head subtly, hoping Cramer received his message that Con had no interest in the woman.

Lady Pebble's bell rang out now, and he turned his attention to his hostess.

"Tonight, we shall play whist in the library. Two tables will be in play, and that means four couples will compete at a time. One couple will need to sit out each hand. I will allow you to choose your partners as we make our way to the library."

Con did the quick math in his head and decided he need do nothing. As guests left the drawing room, they paired up exactly as he had predicted. Lord Samuel moved immediately to Miss Tweedham's side. Lord Howell did the same with Lady Sarah. Lord Cramer's wide strides placed him next to Lady Jewell in seconds.

The only couple he took a chance on now were Mr. Tompkins and Miss Lawson. They, too, gravitated toward one another, leaving him a clear path to Miss Stanhope.

Offering her his arm, he said, "I see we are to become partners by default."

She looked about them as they walked. "You are right. While

I knew Ollie seemed to be developing feelings for Miss Tweedham, and I hoped that Lord Howell was doing the same for Lady Sarah, I had no idea the others were forming as couples."

"Hopefully, you do not mind being part of the pair who will claim victory at cards this evening."

Clucking her tongue, she said, "My, you seem quite certain of yourself, my lord."

"I am certain that I have wound up with the best card player in the room, Miss Stanhope."

"If you listen carefully and do everything I say, I believe we will have more than a fair chance to win."

They arrived in the library, and she took him aside, outlining her strategies. Con had to admit they were solid.

"I understand my role, Miss Stanhope. I will follow your lead."

"Do so until I tap my foot against yours," she advised. "That will be if I think anyone has caught on to our method of play. If that is the case, I want to turn the tables on them."

"I look forward to play this evening," he told her, yearning for more than cards to be at play. Lips. Teeth. Tongues. Those were a few of the things Con wanted to use in love play with her. He would not let her down, though. When the time called for it, he had a knack for being able to focus.

They actually sat out the first round, with two of the couples at one table and two at another. While Lord and Lady Pebble spoke with Miss Bailey, he and Miss Stanhope concentrated on the players and analyzed the kind of games they played.

"Lady Jewell gives away when she is ready to take a trick," he said. "Watch her carefully. She licks her lips each time."

After two tricks, Miss Stanhope said, "I agree. And look at Lord Howell. One eyebrow shoots up when a card is played in a suit of which he has none."

They continued evaluating their future opponents. Studying them paid off. Not only were they able to beat all four couples, they did so soundly.

When play for the night ended, Lord Cramer said, "Lord Samuel, you did not tell us that your cousin was so clever at cards."

"I did not know that myself," the viscount admitted. "We have never had an occasion to play together. In fact, we have only seen each other rarely since I have been at Stanfield and she and my uncle resided in town."

"Miss Stanhope is known for her card play in town," Con volunteered. "She regularly wins at whist. If she were allowed into the gaming hells of London, she would no doubt emerge victorious from them, as well."

"Gaming hells are no place for a woman, much less a lady of good breeding," Lady Pebble declared. "I have sent for the teacarts if anyone is thirsty or hungry."

"I think Lady Sarah and I are going to take a brief stroll outside," Lord Howell said.

"A good idea," agreed Lord Cramer, who looked at Lady Jewell. "Would you care to get a bit of fresh air, my lady?"

One by one, all the couples exited the library, leaving Con with Miss Stanhope with their hosts and Miss Bailey. Miss Bailey said she would retire for the evening.

With four couples traipsing about outside on the lawn and in the gardens, he did not wish to run into any of them and had an idea.

"Perhaps you might consider playing the pianoforte for me, Miss Stanhope."

"Now?"

"Yes, now, my lady. I would like to hear a bit of music."

"The drawing room is available, Rowena, dear," Lady Pebble said. "You may play for Lord Marley there."

They said goodnight to Lord and Lady Pebble and left the library. She said nothing on their way to the drawing room. Once they reached it, however, it was another matter.

"You do not have to pretend that you wish to hear me play the pianoforte, Lord Marley. Just because the other couples have paired off, I do not expect you to do the same with me. You are welcome to do whatever you wish."

"Whatever?" he asked huskily, closing the doors behind him to ensure their privacy.

He turned, facing her, seeing the color high on her cheeks. She looked at him, yearning in her eyes. He took a step toward her. They were almost touching now. He refused to bring up kissing, though. Con needed to know it was what *she* wanted. He already knew he most certainly did.

She wet her lips, causing desire to shoot through him fast as lightning. Being such an innocent, she had no idea how much her gesture weakened his resolve. He fought the urge to reach out. To touch her. To brush his lips against hers.

Then she surprised him. "I believe I want to kiss you again, Lord Marley."

CHAPTER SEVENTEEN

*T*EMPTATION WON OUT.

Rowena knew Lord Marley was a man of his word. He had promised he would not bring up kissing her again. That she would have to be the one who spoke of it first.

Who asked for it . . .

She had always believed herself to be a strong person, stoic, thinking always with her head and never her heart. She had banished all emotion from her life, living rationally and simply. She had run her father's household with precision. Pursued intellectual topics which interested her. Led the Literary Ladies Book Society. But she realized now that she had cut herself off from feeling anything. Perhaps she had done so because she believed there was no one out there for her. Over time, Rowena convinced herself that she did not want, nor did she need, a man in her life. That children were for others to bear and raise.

Now, her emotions were conflicting within her. She not only wished for a strong, emotional connection with a man, but she felt stirrings within her body that told her she also desired something physical in her life. And not with just any man.

Lord Marley was the *only* man she would let in for a brief glimpse as to who she really was.

Rowena knew she did this not because she expected him to offer for her after he kissed her. He was what others would consider far out of her league. Before, as Lord Dyer, he had been charming and handsome. Now, holding an earldom and wealth, he would be the ideal husband for a good number of ladies who sought a husband in Polite Society. She would not infringe upon his bright future. She only wanted him for now. For a little while.

Besides, what harm could a few kisses bring?

Looking at him, she said, "I believe I want to kiss you again, Lord Marley."

She couldn't help but chuckle at the surprise registering on his face. Shrugging, she asked, "So, you did not think I would bring up kissing, much less ask you to kiss me, did you?"

His magnificent amethyst eyes darkened with what she guessed was desire. "We will not waste time talking, Rowena."

This time, she was the one surprised that he addressed her by her given name. She knew marriages where a couple never used their Christian names with one another.

Suddenly, she was in his arms. His mouth crashed down upon hers. Her lips would be bruised tomorrow, but tomorrow would have to wait. She was only interested in now.

He kissed her hard, as a man who crawled through a desert, begging God for a single sip of water to quench his thirst. He was that man—and she was glad to be his oasis.

Since he had already taught her something of kissing, Rowena opened her mouth, encouraging him to ravish it. That was all the invitation he needed, and his tongue swept inside, taking command. But she was no longer a naive, inexperienced flower, not knowing what to do. This time, she kissed him back from the start, with everything she could give.

She heard sounds coming from them both, little squeaks and sighs from her, low moans and groans from him. They kissed for what seemed like an eternity, and she would gladly have stayed in his arms that way forever, kissing him and letting him kiss her, but he had other things in mind.

She did not know when he had turned her, but he stepped into her, pushing her back against what she guessed was the door to the drawing room. His mouth stayed on hers, ravaging it, as his hands glided down her arms, capturing her wrists. He then pressed his full body against hers, raising her arms until they were high above her head, pinning them to the door. He caught them in one hand, leaving him with a free one. It came to cradle her cheek.

Her body came to life. Her breasts grew heavy, her nipples aching for his touch. She felt odd, not being in control of her hands, but she also liked the hardness of his muscular chest against her softness. Then she felt something lower, something very hard, between them, and guessed it was his manhood. She squirmed against him, wanting to touch it.

His mouth left hers, and she gave a cry of distress.

"Hush, love," he said so softly that she wasn't certain whether he had spoken or not.

His lips trailed down her throat, finding her pulse, which beat wildly out of control. He licked it, causing it to jump. Then he nipped her throat with his teeth, startling her. His tongue licked the place, soothing the love bite.

He continued to kiss her neck, and Rowena had never known how sensitive it truly was. She wriggled against him, wishing she could wrap her arms about him. He lifted his head, a chuckle sounding in his throat. Their gazes met.

"Are you going to stop kissing me?" she asked, almost indignant.

A slow smile spread across his face. "I have only just begun, love."

His mouth returned to hers, the kisses gentle now. The tips of his fingers lightly grazed her throat, gliding downward, tracing her collarbones. His touch caused her body to tremble in need. She had never felt like this before, and a cry escaped from her. He shushed her again, one hand slipping inside her bodice, lifting out her breast. She should be shocked, but she wanted his lips on it more than anything she had ever wanted.

He bent, his tongue circling her nipple, coming ever so close to touching it. The place between her legs tightened and then pulsated. Her body had become that of a stranger's, reacting unfamiliarly, but she believed he did know it—and knew exactly what she needed next.

Slowly, his tongue teased her nipple before he lifted his head, blowing softly, a delicious sensation rippling through her at the cool breeze. Then his mouth moved to her breast, feasting upon it. He released her hands, and they fell limply to her sides as his hand began to caress her other breast. He drank his fill of one and then moved to the other, causing whimpers to escape from her. Deep sensations ran through her. She knew she should be doing something for him, too, but hadn't a clue what. Selfishly, she thrust her fingers into his hair and held his head close against her breast as he continued to nip and lave it.

She felt her knees began to buckle, knowing she only stood because his body held up hers. Again, he anticipated her needs and swept her off her feet, carrying her to a settee they had shared the first night of the house party. He sat, her in his lap, and once more, his tongue mated with hers, new sensations traveling through her.

Rowena wrapped her arms about his neck, wanting more from him, but not knowing how to ask for it. As they kissed, though, his hand stroked her calf, the heat of his fingers penetrating the layers of clothing she wore. He then brushed against her ankle, his fingers massaging it, moving up her stocking-clad calf now. She willed him to keep going, to move higher. To touch her very essence.

Once again, he moved exactly where she needed him to go. He reached her thigh and went even higher. Then his finger stroked the seam of her sex, and she murmured, "Yes."

Breaking the kiss, he gazed deeply into her eyes. "Do you like that? Do you want more of it?" he asked, his voice low and rough.

"Yes," she whispered. "Very much."

"Then you will certainly like this," he added, repeating the same caress, causing her to suck in a quick breath.

Without warning, he pushed a finger deeply inside her, curling it, stroking her. She gave a small cry, partly in surprise and partly in sheer delight, as her back arched.

"You are going to enjoy this, Rowena," he told her. "Your body is going to do things it never has done before. And I want you to remember when this is over and you are lying in your bed tonight, thinking of us together, you will know that *I* am he one who made you feel this way. Promise me."

"Yes," she managed. "I . . . promise."

"Shall I continue?"

"Yes," she said, urgency in her voice. "Touch me. Now."

Magic happened, his finger dancing inside her, another one joining it. He whispered to her that he searched for her pearl, calling it the pearl of pleasure. Within seconds, he had located it. Circling it. Pressing against it. Causing her to cry out.

Then something began building within her. Something taking hold of her. Something out of her control.

"I am frightened," she told him. "Of what is coming."

"You have nothing to fear, love. Because you are with me."

His words calmed her, allowing her to enjoy not only the coming storm—but the storm itself when it erupted. It came from nowhere—and yet it was the result of everything building up to this very moment. It was as if pure joy mixed with sunshine and then washed over her. She cried his name. Her hips moved, adding to the pleasure, and she wanted the wild sensations to never end.

Slowly, the pleasure subsided, however, leaving her feeling weak as a kitten.

He removed his hand from under her skirts, and she watched as he brought his fingers to his mouth, licking them.

"Ah, your juices are sweeter than I had even dreamed they might be."

She should have been shocked by his action, but it somehow pleased her. *He* pleased her.

He eased her breasts back into her bodice, taking care to straighten it. Then he stood, placing her on her feet, smoothing her gown.

"What was that?" she asked.

"Is it your intellectual curiosity searching for an answer—or a woman seeking an answer from a man who has just pleasured her?"

Her face grew hot, and she knew it now flamed. "Perhaps a bit of both," she said primly, causing him to laugh.

"The French call it *la petite mort*."

"The little death," she translated. "I can understand why."

"We English are not quite the romantics the French are. We call it an orgasm. It is something that ripples through your body, giving you immense pleasure."

Rowena thought a moment. "Is it just women who experience this . . . orgasm you speak of, or is it also something men can feel? If so, I must return the favor."

He looked at her and then burst out laughing. She frowned, causing him to smooth her hair.

"I do not mean to make fun of your innocence, Rowena. Yes, men can also feel an orgasm, but we are not going to worry about that tonight." Mischief in his eyes, he added, "We shall save that for another encounter."

She huffed. "What if I do not wish for any more of these . . . . encounters?"

He shrugged. "Then we will not participate in them. You are the one who gives consent, Rowena. Always remember that. Never let a man force anything upon you that you do not wish."

Already, she was more than willing to have him touch her intimately again, and she wanted to do the same for him. Give him the immense pleasure which he had shared with her. At this point, she was not willing to concede that to him, however.

"I should be going. Ollie will be looking for me."

"Will he be?" Lord Marley mused. "I suppose he will." He sighed. "How I wish you were staying here at Pebblestone. If you were, I would come tap upon your door tonight. Crawl into your bed and hold you close. Touch you wherever you wished me to."

The thought caused her to shiver.

Her head chose this moment to overrule her heart, however, and Rowena told him, "There will be no next time, Lord Marley. I was merely wishing to add to my experiences. To have insight . . . as to what passes between a man and a woman." Then she paused, swallowing. "We did not . . . make a baby just now, did we?"

He framed her face with his long fingers. "No, Rowena. We did not. That would require my slipping my cock inside you and spilling my seed."

"I have had no one to speak of these things about, my lord. Certainly not my aunt Sylvia, much less Lady Pebble."

"I am happy to answer any questions you might have, Rowena."

"Please do not get used to calling me that, my lord."

"Might I do so when we're alone together? Would you call me Con?"

She wanted to tell him that she could not trust being alone with him again, but she heard herself say, "Yes, Con. I will do so."

"Would you sit at the pianoforte and play something for me now? Your cousin will be coming soon enough. Lady Pebble will direct him here. I wish for him to find us not as we were but as we should be."

She moved to the instrument and sat before it. He followed, standing next to it and facing her, one hand resting upon it. She played one piece for him, and then in the middle of the next one, Ollie came through the door, and she lifted her fingers from the keys, mid-song. Rowena hoped by now that her color had faded though she could still feel her lips being somewhat swollen. Then again, Ollie's looked as if he had been doing a bit of kissing himself.

"There you are, Rowena. It is time for us to leave for the evening."

Rising, she looked at Lord Marley, who said, "Thank you for playing for me, Miss Stanhope. I enjoyed our time together a great deal."

He winked at her, and she almost burst out laughing. It would be hard to explain to Ollie, however, what was so funny, and so she stifled her laughter.

"We will see you again tomorrow, Lord Marley," her cousin told the earl.

They went downstairs where Ollie's carriage waited for them. He handed her up, and they were both pensive on the way home, not a word exchanged between them. Rowena went inside her cottage and undressed, donning her night rail, and climbing into bed. Once there, she thought exactly of what Lord Marley had done to her body. How he had played it as she played her violin, bending it to his will.

She knew, no matter how much time passed, she would never forget what had happened between them that night.

Chapter Eighteen

It was hard for Rowena to rise that morning. She had been restless, not getting much sleep. She washed and dressed, donning her spectacles, and then waited for Ollie's carriage to show up. Closing her eyes, she was taken back to the drawing room last night. She fought against the memories but finally gave in to them.

How was she going to be in Lord Marley's company for the remainder of the house party and maintain her sanity?

As a gentleman, she knew he would make no further move, even as she longed for him to do so. She could not rid herself of the notion that she was not good enough for him, though. Polite Society had taught her that. It had judged her—and found her sorely lacking. Lord Marley was a man who thrived in the company of others. Where she no longer had an interest in going to town, he had been very frank, telling her how important his family was to him and that he would make a point of attending each Season, simply because he wanted to spend time with his various relatives and their children.

She heard Ollie's carriage arriving and opened her eyes. Rising from the chair, she went out to the vehicle. Where she felt sluggish and thought she must appear tired, her cousin had bright eyes and a ready smile.

"Good morning, Rowena," he said, handing her up into the carriage. "Is it not the most glorious day?"

"I have not been up long enough to establish whether it is or not," she teased, pushing aside her gloom. "You, on the other hand, are in a grand mood."

He grew serious. "I have decided to offer for Miss Tweedham," he confided.

"Oh, Ollie! That truly is the most wonderful news. I am so very happy for the two of you."

"Some may think it a bit too soon, but I simply know in my heart that she is the one for me. I cannot believe she has attended the Season without one gentleman recognizing her worth."

"It will be delightful to have my closest friend so nearby, wed to my cousin."

He hesitated a moment and then asked, "Won't you change your mind, Rowena, and move to the main house with us?"

"That is the last thing I would do," she declared. "Especially now. The two of you will need your privacy. You will be the viscount and viscountess, and you will be raising your family there. I would only get in the way." She offered him a smile. "I promise to visit often, however. I do have one favor to ask of you, though."

"Name it, Cousin. You have done so much for me through the years, and now you have brought the woman into my life whom I will wed. I can deny you nothing."

"Although we are not brother and sister, I feel as close to you as I would a brother. Would you allow your children to call me Aunt Rowena? Or perhaps Aunt Ro. Rowena might be a mouthful for a little one to say."

He reached out and took her hand, squeezing it. "Of course. That would make me—and Miss Tweedham—very happy."

"Do you have an idea when you might speak to her regarding your future together? I will keep your secret as long as you wish, but I am eager to celebrate the betrothal with you."

"I am not certain. I want it to be the right moment. I also believe your friend Lady Sarah might also be receiving an offer of marriage, as well."

"From Baron Howell?" she asked eagerly, and Ollie nodded. "I have seen them together. She seemed very happy yesterday, with Mary being present."

"Lord Howell spoke to me of this yesterday. I think he might offer for her as soon as today."

"Lady Pebble will be crowing, seeing that two betrothals came from her house party."

"What of you, Rowena? Do you believe Lord Marley might think to offer for you?"

Her cheeks heated. "No, Ollie. That will not be the case."

"Are you certain?" he pressed.

Panic filled her. "Why? Has he said something to you?"

"I only know that he thinks very highly of you."

She brushed off the words. "That is because I am acquainted with his cousin, Lady Merriman. She asked him to dance with me once, and he obliged her. I assure you, Ollie, there is nothing between us."

"If you say so," he said cryptically, causing her to wonder if Lord Marley had spoken to her cousin or not.

Rowena had no time to question him further because they arrived at Pebblestone and went into breakfast.

As they dined, Lady Pebble told the group that after breakfast, they would have the opportunity to walk into Mossleigh and visit the shops in the village. A ride was scheduled for that afternoon.

Lord Marley spoke up. "Perhaps we might visit Lord Cramer's and Lord Howell's estates while we ride through the neighborhood. Since I am so new to my title, I am learning about estate management. I would enjoy seeing each of your properties, gentlemen, if you do not object."

The others agreed to the earl's proposal.

"Instead of returning to Pebblestone for tea, we could take it at my house," the baron volunteered. Looking to Lord Pebble, he asked, "Might I send one of your footmen to Meadowbrook with a message so that my Cook will know to expect a large party for tea later today?"

The viscount agreed, and Lord Howell slipped away to write his note.

When he returned, they readied themselves to walk into Mossleigh. The village was about a mile and a half from Pebblestone. They started out as one large group, but couples gradually paired off, leaving Rowena in Lord Marley's company once again.

"Have you been into Mossleigh before, my lady?"

"Several times now since I have returned to live in Dorset. Before then, I can only recall one visit to the village. Remember, I was raised in town."

"Are you liking the change from town to country?" he inquired. "I would think it might be a bit of an adjustment for you."

"Not in the least, my lord. The few times I came to Dorset, I felt as if I were home. Where I was meant to be. Papa and I actually visited a few friends in the country over the years, and it was the same every time we left the city. I suppose I am a country girl at heart."

"I wish you could see Marleyfield," he said, his tone wistful. "Although I was raised there, I was often away at school. Then after I left university, I chose to take rooms with Val in town."

"Why did you do so? Were you not welcomed at Marleyfield?"

"My father enjoyed dabbling at being a country lord. He and I were close and saw each other frequently whenever he and Mama came to town for the Season."

He paused, looking contemplative before he continued.

"I think what kept me away was Mama. My mother is someone who is, shall we say, quite strong in her opinions."

Even though Rowena had not been introduced to Lady Marley, she knew that to be the case. There were few women in Polite Society as outspoken and opinionated as his mother.

"I hate admitting this now because it makes it seem as if Papa were weak. He simply found it easier to keep the peace by giving into Mama on everything. She is the who truly ran Marleyfield and did not want my help. I had thought I would spend a majority of my year in the country once my schooldays were behind me, but when I saw how things would be, I quickly moved to town. Val was in a similar situation. His father did not want a son around, usurping his authority before Val held the dukedom. That is why we gravitated toward town and remained there year-round."

"Did you find yourself unprepared regarding your responsibilities?" she asked. "I would think having had nothing to do with managing an estate and suddenly being responsible for one would prove to be difficult."

"A little," he admitted. "Though I have a gem of a steward in Mr. Tabor. He has taken me about Marleyfield on numerous occasions, explaining all I need to know. I have met my tenants and can call all by name now. The records kept under his supervision have been very thorough, and I have reviewed them extensively, familiarizing myself with everything about Marleyfield. I was happy to participate in the autumn harvest."

His gaze met hers. "I also informed Mama that the time had come for her to relinquish her hold. She knows now not to be examining ledgers and giving Mr. Tabor orders. That I am the one who will make all decisions regarding Marleyfield."

"You were brave to stand up to her. Not everyone in your position would have done so, my lord."

"I believe Mama admired me for taking a stand. I suppose I have more of her in me than I suspected."

The group came together again as they reached the village. It was small and could easily be seen in a short span of time. At Rowena's suggestion, they decided to meet up at the local bakeshop in an hour.

"I can certainly recommend the toffee sticky buns," she told them. "They are not to be missed."

Once more, they coupled off, going in different directions. She and Lord Marley visited several of the shops, and she stopped at the milliner's, looking at bonnets.

"Try that one on," he said, pointing to one. "I think it would suit you."

She untied the bonnet she wore and set it aside. He handed her the new one, a woven straw bonnet with a short, round crown and a graceful, oval brim which would frame her face in a flattering way. It had a lilac ribbon which could easily be detached and replaced with a ribbon of a different color. Rowena placed it atop her head, tying the ribbons in a bow beneath her chin. He looked at her admiringly.

"Yes, that will do nicely. Might I purchase it for you?"

"No," she said, a little too sharply. Softening her tone, she added, "It is not advisable for a gentleman to buy such a personal item for a lady."

Sadness filled his eyes. "I understand. It suits you, you know. You are most attractive wearing it, Miss Stanhope."

Rowena purchased the bonnet. Not that she needed it, but when she wore it, she would think of Lord Marley and how he had found her attractive in it. While the milliner wrapped it for her, they strolled about the shop. She noticed a smudge on her spectacles. She removed them, and Lord Marley quickly whipped out a handkerchief.

"Allow me," he said, and she passed the spectacles to him.

He held them up to the light, taking the handkerchief to wipe the smudge. Then he frowned. Bringing them closer to his own eyes, he stared through the lens, moving his head slowly as he viewed the other hats on display.

Lowering them, he said, "You do not need to wear spectacles, do you?"

Guilt flushed her cheeks. "No, my lord. I do not."

"Then why do you insist upon never been seen without them?" he demanded. "Do you choose to hide behind them?"

She nodded. "They were a part of the armor I donned each time I dressed for a *ton* event. I had already been rejected too many times. The spectacles—and the way I dressed—were to protect me from further hurt. If you are not noticed, then you cannot be hurt," she explained, knowing how pathetic that made her sound.

"You are no longer in town, Miss Stanhope. You have changed your manner of dress to a more flattering one. Why not also give up the spectacles?"

Heat filled her cheeks. "I actually had before this house party began. Because I would be around several strangers, I chose to wear them again." Shrugging, she added, "They seemed like an old friend."

He folded them, placing them into the inside pocket of his coat. Even though she longed to abandon using the spectacles, Rowena's protest died in her throat when he reached and took her hand.

Gazing deeply into her eyes, he said, "Please do not wear them again, Miss Stanhope. Shine—and let the world see who you truly are."

He then released her hand before the small gesture could be seen.

The milliner said, "Here you go, Miss Stanhope. Thank you for your business."

She turned to accept the parcel, but Lord Marley took it instead.

"Let me carry it for you," he said, leading her from the shop.

Since they had visited everywhere in the village, she told him they should head to the bakeshop now. Rowena kept swallowing, trying to force down the lump which had lodged in her throat.

The four other couples had already arrived before them, and Miss Tweedham said, "We have already ordered tea and sticky buns for all."

"Thank you, my lady," Lord Marley said. "That was most thoughtful of you."

No one mentioned the fact that Rowena was no longer wearing her spectacles, and no one commented when she kept silent during their time in the bakeshop.

Their group left Mossleigh, and the ladies gravitated toward one another, each sharing what purchases she had made in the village as they strolled back toward Pebblestone. She walked arm-in-arm with Miss Tweedham, knowing that her cousin would soon offer for her friend. Rowena was glad she knew of the happy news ahead of time because at this moment, her spirits had sunk lower than at any other time since her father's death.

They arrived at Pebblestone, and the ladies went to freshen up and deposit their purchases in their bedchambers. When they returned downstairs, they were met by Lord Pebble, who instructed them to go to the stables.

"Horses will be readied for you so that you might enjoy your afternoon ride," the viscount said. "Remember, you will be taking tea at Lord Howell's today."

At the mention of the baron's name, she noted that Lady Sarah blushed. She stepped toward her friend and asked, "Are you enjoying the house party, Lady Sarah?"

"Very much so, Miss Stanhope. I am also eager to see Lord Cramer's and Lord Howell's estates. I do hope we will get to see Mary when we call at Meadowbrook."

"She is a delightful child," Rowena said, her friend quickly agreeing.

They went out to the stables, and she saw that Aurora had been saddled for her. A groom helped her to mount, and soon they cantered along the lane to Lord Cramer's estate. The earl proudly showed his property to them, answering several questions from Lord Marley. She could tell Lord Marley was serious about assuming his duties and learning all he could to make Marleyfield thrive. After an hour, they rode more of the countryside, and she couldn't help but enjoy her time on horseback. Aurora was a dream to ride, and Rowena did so several times a week.

They reached Baron Howell's estate, and he showed them around as Lord Cramer had. Once they had seen his property, which was smaller than that of Lord Cramer's or Pebblestone, he said, "Let us leave our horses in the stables. My grooms will water them while we are at tea."

Once they had an opportunity to freshen up, they went to the drawing room. Lord Howell's cook had outdone herself, with an array of sandwiches and sweets alike. Since they were all so hungry from their long ride, everyone ate well. The baron had asked for Mary to be brought down to the drawing room, and she had insisted upon sitting in Lady Sarah's lap. Rowena studied her friend and knew she would be a good mother to this child and any other offspring she and Lord Howell might have.

"Shall we be going?" Mr. Tompkins asked.

"Wait. I have one more thing to share," Lord Howell said. He crooked his finger at Mary, and she climbed from Lady Sarah's lap and came to him.

"Remember the present?" he asked. When his daughter nodded, he added, "Go and bring it to me."

Mary scurried across the room, picking up something off a table and bringing it back. She handed it to her father. Everyone present leaned closer, trying to see what it was.

Then the baron took his daughter's hand, and they both went to stand before Lady Sarah. He took to one knee. Rowena heard a few gasps.

"Lady Sarah, you know that I became a widower over two years ago. While Mary and I have done our best to move forward, we both realize something is lacking at Meadowbrook."

Lady Sarah smiled at the pair, obviously knowing what would come next.

Lord Howell smiled. "What is missing is a woman's touch. Mary is in need of a mother. Meadowbrook has need of a baroness to look after it. Above all, I wish for a companion to share my life and, hopefully, more children. Mary and I would like to ask if you might honor us and become my wife and her mother."

Lady Sarah's eyes misted with tears. "Yes, my lord. It is most definitely yes." She looked to Mary. "I will be happy to help raise you and love you, Mary, my dear."

The baron opened the small box his daughter had brought to him. "I wanted you to see this, my lady. It will be your wedding ring. It has been in my family for five generations. Five Howell brides have worn it."

"I will wear it with pride, my lord," Lady Sarah said, her voice breaking.

Mary began jumping up and down with joy. Lady Sarah was swamped with embraces from the other women, while Lord Howell received congratulations from the men.

"I have already spoken with Lord and Lady Pebble," Lord Howell shared. "They are happy to allow you to stay at Pebblestone for the next three weeks while the banns are being read. We can wed in the Mossleigh church unless you would prefer to do so in your home parish."

Lady Sarah radiated happiness now. "Our home will be here, my lord. I would prefer for our wedding to take place here, as well. I do want to send word to my parents to let them know."

Rowena only hoped that Lady Sarah's parents would journey to Dorset for the ceremony.

"Now, you can leave for Pebblestone," Lord Howell told the group. "I wish to remain at Meadowbrook and show Lady Sarah more of the house since it will soon be her home. We will dine here and then join you in the drawing room at Pebblestone later this evening."

Their party, smaller now, returned to the stables and rode back to Pebblestone. All the way there, Rowena thought of how her two good friends would now live in the neighborhood. She would be able to see them any time she liked. Yet a curtain of melancholy had dropped over her. Though she would always have Lady Sarah and Miss Tweedham as friends, their paths in life would diverge drastically now. They would become wives and mothers, while Rowena would be left alone.

She dismounted from Aurora and heard, "A penny for your thoughts."

Turning, she found Lord Marley next to her. Tamping down

her sadness, she smiled brightly.

"Isn't it wonderful about Lady Sarah and Lord Howell?" he asked.

"Yes, it is very good news indeed."

Rowena hurried away, joining Miss Lawson and linking arms with her as they returned to the house.

Because Lord Marley was the last person she wished to be with now.

Chapter Nineteen

As Benchley dressed him for the evening, Con reflected upon the proposal they had all witnessed that afternoon. He had seen the joy on both Lord Howell's and Lady Sarah's faces. He wanted that for himself.

With Rowena...

He thought now the dominoes might begin to fall with this betrothal. From what Lord Samuel had shared with him, Con believed his new friend would soon ask Miss Tweedham to be his wife. Whether the other two gentlemen attending the house party decided to make offers of marriage was yet to be seen. He wanted to do so himself desperately, but instinct told him Rowena would turn him down.

Perhaps she was so practical and intellectual that the aspect of love did not enter her sphere of thinking. If he appealed to her more rational nature, he might have a better chance in securing a positive response from her.

But would his loving her be enough for a successful marriage?

"You seem quite pensive this evening, my lord," his valet noted.

"I am thinking over how Lord Howell asked Lady Sarah to be his wife at tea today."

Benchley beamed. "That is very good news indeed. It will be celebrated in the servants' hall. Lord Howell's valet is a jovial sort, and Lady Sarah's maid has had high hopes for her mistress to make a match at this house party." Hesitating a moment, the valet then asked, "Might I inquire how things fare for you, my lord? I know you came to this house party specifically for one particular lady. Is it Miss Stanhope?"

"It is," he confirmed. Shaking his head, he added, "I haven't a clue where I stand with her."

"I would think it would be simple enough, my lord. Speak to her from your heart."

"I appreciate your advice, Benchley, but Miss Stanhope is quite the intellectual. Her head would make any decision regarding her future. Not her heart."

The valet smiled mysteriously. "Then perhaps that is something you need to change, my lord."

Not only was Benchley's advice what Con needed to hear, but it made Con wonder what the valet had experienced in his past to share that nugget of wisdom.

Benchley finished tying Con's cravat and helped him slip into his coat. Since it was still early, he made his way down to the library, where he found Viscount Samuel pacing, mumbling to himself.

"Forgive me, my lord. I do not mean to interrupt you."

"No, do not leave, Marley. Stay. I could use a friend to talk with now."

They took a seat opposite one another, and Con asked, "Is this about Miss Tweedham? Are you ready to offer for her?"

"I am. I want to do so, and yet I am terrified. My future will be decided in a single moment. What if she says no?"

"I have watched the two of you together, my lord, and I believe Miss Tweedham will respond in the affirmative."

"I do not think I can do what Howell did. Ask her in front of an entire group of people."

"Most gentlemen do so in private," he agreed. "I think Lord Howell simply knew his own mind. His daughter is quite important to him, and he wished to have her a part of the proceedings. It was convenient to make his offer with us taking tea at Meadowbrook. All the parts came together."

"They already looked like a family, didn't they?" asked the viscount.

"They truly did. I am happy for them. Lady Sarah will be an excellent mother to Mary."

"You do not think anyone else is interested in Miss Tweedham, do you?" Lord Samuel asked, worry on his face.

"No. Everyone has seen the two of you together. No gentleman would speak before you do," he assured Samuel.

"You are good to reassure me, my lord. I wish I could do the same for you. I brought up your name to Rowena."

His heart skipped a beat. "And?"

"I do not think she understands the depth of your feelings. In fact, my cousin seemed quite dismissive of the idea that you might even be interested in her."

Con blamed the *ton*. Rowena had been out three Seasons without any offers. Members of Polite Society did not take kindly to anyone—especially a woman—who marched to a different step than others. Being a bluestocking, Rowena had met with disapproval from the beginning. He realized the *ton* had poisoned her, making her think little of herself because they cruelly did so. He would need to help rebuild her confidence in herself before he could even think to speak his mind to her and let her know the depth of his feelings.

But could he do so in the little time left at Pebblestone?

"We should go to the drawing room," he told Lord Samuel. Placing a hand on the viscount's shoulder, he squeezed it reassuringly. "You will know when the time is right to speak with Miss Tweedham. I have faith in you."

"Thank you," Lord Samuel said sincerely. "I appreciate our new friendship."

They joined the others who had already gathered in the drawing room. Rowena was not amongst their number, but she did come in a few minutes later with Miss Tweedham, whose eyes immediately sought Lord Samuel. His friend headed toward the pair, and Con moved toward them as well, hoping to bolster the viscount's confidence.

"Good evening, ladies," he greeted. "I wonder what is planned for this evening's entertainment."

"I would not mind hearing Miss Lawson play again," Miss Tweedham said. "And you, too, Miss Stanhope."

"I cannot compare to Miss Lawson. She could play professionally, while the best I can do is hope to entertain a few guests in a country drawing room."

Con did not like how she seemed to put herself down and spoke up.

"While Miss Lawson plays with skill, you also have an affinity for the pianoforte," he insisted. "I think you play beautifully and would enjoy hearing you do so again."

A blush spilled across her cheeks at his compliment. "Perhaps sometime during the remainder of the house party, I will be asked to play again."

Their conversation turned to the ride they had participated in this afternoon and the two estates they had seen. Lord Samuel mentioned a few things he and his steward had begun on his estate, and Con listened eagerly, always looking for something new to try at Marleyfield.

They were called in to dinner, and he found himself seated next to Miss Lawson. He had watched her timidity change over the course of the last few days. She was no longer a turtle who remained inside her shell, only popping out upon occasion.

"It seems this house party has done wonders for you, Miss Lawson," he observed.

"I have always been painfully shy, Lord Marley, so much so that I asked to postpone my come-out this past Season. The thought of being surrounded by dozens—if not hundreds—of others was simply too much to fathom. I am a simple country girl who has no experience in life and cannot make conversation easily."

"I beg to differ. I think anyone present at the table this evening would say you are a fine conversationalist, Miss Lawson."

"I have Miss Stanhope to thank. She approached me that very first day, making me feel so welcome. She introduced me to others and let me know she was my friend from the beginning. Because of that, it liberated me from the shadows I had kept to. I owe Miss Stanhope a great deal."

"Miss Stanhope always thinks of others. I am glad she was able to help you ease into Polite Society."

"It might have been different if I had siblings, but I have been alone most of my life. My mother passed when I was very young, and I do not recall anything about her. Papa is kind but distant. My governess has been my constant companion. She was the one who taught me how to play the pianoforte."

"You do so beautifully, my lady. We have spoken of how we hope to hear you play again."

Dinner concluded, and Lady Pebble told them there would be dancing this evening. That seemed to perk up everyone at the table, and Con couldn't help but glance down to Miss Stanhope, thinking of their single dance together. Her gaze met his, and he believed she thought of the same thing. At least now they had an opportunity to dance together again.

They adjourned to the drawing room, where servants had pushed back the furniture to the walls, allowing ample room for them to dance.

Then Miss Tweedham said, "We might try to dance some on the terrace. We could open the doors and still hear the music outside."

"Is it too cold to do so?" Lady Pebble asked.

"We shall see," Lord Pebble responded, opening a pair of French doors and stepping outside. He returned, saying, "The evening air is a bit cool, but dancing is such an active pastime. I think everyone would be comfortable dancing outside."

"Why don't we begin inside and warm up a bit?" Miss Lawson suggested. "Then we might move to the terrace."

Just then, Lady Sarah and Baron Howell entered the drawing

room, and all thoughts of dancing were paused. The couple was roundly congratulated by all present, including Lord and Lady Pebble, who were seeing the couple for the first time since their betrothal occurred.

Lady Pebble pressed her cheek to Lady Sarah's. "Oh, my dear, Lord Pebble and I are delighted to hear of your engagement. When might the wedding take place?"

Lady Sarah looked to her fiancé, who said, "I have already sent word to the vicar to begin the reading of the banns on Sunday. Lady Sarah and I will wed in the Mossleigh parish church in three weeks after the banns are completed."

Viscount Samuel blurted out, "I wish to wed there, as well. With Miss Tweedham." He turned to her and clasped her hands in his. "I know I am mucking this up badly, but I can stay silent no longer. Miss Tweedham, you would make me the happiest of men if you would agree to wed me."

Con had never seen a more genuine smile than the one Miss Tweedham bestowed upon Lord Samuel.

"Yes, my lord. Yes. I would be honored to become your wife."

"I do not mean to rush you, my lady," the viscount told his new fiancée. "And we do not have to wed at Mossleigh. The ceremony can take place whenever you wish. Wherever you wish. I am simply humbled that you have agreed to become my wife."

More congratulations were offered, and Lord Pebble signaled to his butler. Soon, champagne flutes were passed out to the guests, and Lady Pebble's eternal bell tinkled again.

They grew quiet as Lord Pebble said, "I am most pleased to celebrate the two betrothals which have occurred at our house party. It will be wonderful to add Lady Sarah and Miss Tweedham as neighbors. Here is to a long and happy marriage for both these couples."

The group raised their flutes, and Con downed his champagne quickly. He thought if Miss Stanhope saw how happy her two friends were that she, too, might be willing to risk a chance at happiness herself.

"Let us dance!" exclaimed Lady Pebble. "And who knows? More betrothals may be yet to come."

"I shall play for the dancing," Miss Stanhope volunteered, causing his spirits to sink.

Thankfully, Miss Bailey stepped in. "You young people should be the ones dancing, Miss Stanhope. I am more than happy to play while everyone dances."

The two betrothed couples headed out onto the terrace, and Con went to Miss Stanhope.

"Would you do me the honor of dancing with me, my lady?"

She gave him a strained smile, no enthusiasm evident. "Yes, my lord."

He took her hand and placed it on his sleeve, feeling her tremble slightly. He escorted them out the doors. Moments later, Miss Bailey began to play. Everyone's spirits seemed lighthearted as they danced.

Except for his and Miss Stanhope's.

And Con hadn't a clue how to change things between them.

Chapter Twenty

Rowena got very little sleep and had to drag herself from bed the next morning. She made the decision not to attend the house party today. While she was happy for her friends and their recent betrothals, she was tired of being around other people. She longed for solitude. It was easier to think that than admit the truth.

She could no longer be around Lord Marley.

Did he have feelings for her?

That was difficult to discern. He seemed to be two different men—the charming rogue who dazzled Polite Society versus the sensitive gentleman who opened up to her during that night in the gardens. The first would not be capable of being a suitor to her simply because she was not someone he could possibly be attracted to. As for the second version of Lord Marley, she doubted that man existed anymore. While he had been struggling financially and only in possession of a courtesy title the night of the Purlington ball, he now had come into his earldom and had no worries about money. The *ton* would expect him to wed someone equal to him in looks and rank, not some bluestocking who scarcely was worth their attention.

Perhaps he did like her company a bit. She certainly enjoyed his. Then again, she could think of no instances where a gentleman and lady became friends. That is all she could ever be with Lord Marley. Rowena liked him. She definitely enjoyed kissing him. But after this house party, they would never see one another again since she had no plans to return to town. He would go home to Marleyfield and make his annual pilgrimage to London for the Season. With his looks, title, and wealth, it was only a matter of time before he wed and had children.

She remained in her night rail and added her dressing gown atop it, waiting for Ollie's carriage to approach. When it did, her cousin left the vehicle and came to knock upon Rowena's door since she was not waiting for him outside.

Opening the door, he frowned. "Are you unwell, Cousin?"

"I awoke in the middle of the night with a terrible megrim," she lied. "I could not go back to sleep because the pain was so great."

"Should I summon the doctor? I can have him here within half an hour."

"No, Ollie. I simply need to spend the day in bed. I could use the rest. Hopefully, I might even be able to nap and catch up on my sleep. Please give my apologies to Lord and Lady Pebble and the other guests."

He brushed his lips against her brow. "You will be missed. I will tell the others of your megrim. I will call upon you this evening when I return to Stanfield."

"No, I might be sleeping by then and would not wish to be disturbed. I shall try to return to the house party tomorrow."

"Send word to me if you have need of anything," he told her, returning to his carriage.

Rowena wanted to ask how she was to send word since she had no servants with her. Betsy was not due to come and clean until sometime tomorrow. It did not matter. She would not need Ollie for anything.

Returning to the window, she watched his carriage pull away. Gloom enveloped her. She forced herself to go out to the well and draw some water to put on a kettle for tea. Fortunately, she had caught on quickly as to how to create a fire. Since there was a chill in the air this morning, she built one now in the hearth.

Once her tea had steeped, she sat by the fire, a book in her lap. She found she could not concentrate, though, and drifted off.

Something disturbed her sleep. The sound was in the distance. Constant. Insistent. It pulled her from sleep.

Suddenly, she was yanked to her feet.

"Are you all right? I knocked on your door, but you did not respond. Samuel said you had a megrim. You look terrible."

Lord Marley's eyes roamed her face. Rowena blinked rapidly several times, pulling herself from her dreams and returning to reality.

"I was asleep. I did not sleep much last night."

"Because of the megrim."

"Yes. Because of the megrim."

She became aware of his hands clasping her elbows. Of the heat radiating from his body. Of the masculine scent emanating from him. Something stirred within her.

"Thank goodness you are not seriously ill," he said, enveloping his arms about her.

Rowena's cheek pressed against his chest. Her ear was directly over his pounding heart. Her own arms wrapped around his waist. One hand began to smooth her hair, the gesture hypnotic, lulling her into closing her eyes again. She thought she could stay this way forever. She was awake enough now. It was as if her body sprang to life, being against his. Need poured through her. For his kiss. His touch.

Knowing this might be the last opportunity she would have to be alone with him, she decided to ask something of him. Since she was destined to be forever on the shelf, Rowena wanted a part of him for herself. For her memories. Something she could live off for all the years to come.

She tilted her head, looking up at him. Those magnificent, amethyst eyes gazed back down at her.

"Show me what it is like. Between a man and a woman."

He startled. Frowned. "Where is this coming from?"

"I want to know, Con." Deliberately, she used his given name as he had asked her to do. "I feel my body going taut as a string on my violin. Something tells me that you will know how to play my body, the same way I play that instrument."

She felt his body stiffen. "What are you asking of me, Rowena?"

Showing a courage she never knew she had, she said, "I want you to take me to bed."

A slow smile spread across his handsome face. She lifted a hand, cupping his cheek, her thumb slowly stroking it.

"You know what you are asking me? You know what this means."

Rowena knew she would no longer be a virgin. She would possess carnal knowledge.

"I do."

His lips touched hers, the kiss achingly tender. It was a kiss she would never forget.

He released her, striding toward the open door and closing it. Then he returned, his arms going about her again. His kiss was gentle at first, but soon the passion flared between them, and his kisses became more demanding. She reveled in them.

In him.

One hand now clasped her nape, holding her steady, his arm braced against her back. The kisses were long. Drugging. Heated. And they conveyed just how much he wanted her.

Rowena knew if a dozen ladies of the *ton* had been lined up beside her, Con would have chosen each of them before ever considering her as a romantic partner. But he was here with her now, only her, and she had his full attention.

She intended to make the most of this experience.

It was her turn to respond to the challenge Con issued, and she began kissing him back, their tongues now warring with one another. Her hands moved up and down his rock-solid back. For a few stolen moments, he was hers. No one else's. The thought drove her wild, and she kissed him with abandon. Her hands dropped to his buttocks, kneading them, enjoying the groans which came from him. He mimicked her actions, his own, large hands grasping her derriere and squeezing.

Hot desire shot through her.

"I want more," she urged. "Your mouth on my breasts. Like before."

"With pleasure."

The gleam in his eyes caused her to tremble. He unknotted the belt of her dressing gown and pushed it from her shoulders. Then he reached down and captured the edge of her night rail. In one, swift motion, he removed it, tossing it aside. She now stood bare in front of him, his eyes roaming her body.

"To think you hid this from everyone," he said softly, his gaze admiring.

He cupped her breasts, the pads of his thumbs brushing back and forth across her nipples, causing them to stand out. His gaze never left hers, though, and she saw his eyes continue to darken in need.

Before she knew it, he had swept her from her feet and carried her to the only bedchamber in the cottage. She had yet to make the bed, thinking she would return and try to sleep. He placed her upon the mattress.

"Watch," he commanded, and she did as he slowly removed his coat. His waistcoat was next. He unbuttoned it and shrugged from it before untying his cravat. Pulling it from his neck, he tossed it in her direction. The silk landed on her belly, and she grasped it in one hand, dragging it up between the valley of her breasts. She caught his scent on it, and the place between her legs tightened in response.

He watched her, and she continued to playfully move the cravat up and down. He licked his lips, lifting his shirt over his head and dropping it on the ground.

"You little minx," he said, his voice a growl.

Moving like lightning, he sprang quickly to her, snatching the cravat from her. He grabbed her wrists and wrapped the cravat around them several times, binding them together. Her core now pounded hard, throbbing in need. He pulled her wrists above her head, tying the cravat's ends to one of the bedposts. She was not uncomfortable, only restrained.

A wicked smile crossed his sensual lips. "You are exactly where I want you, Rowena."

Just the husky tone caused her to tremble. It held danger—and desire.

He moved between her legs, his hands gliding up and down her thighs.

"So smooth. Like silk."

Then he lifted her legs so that the backs of her knees rested on his shoulders, with her calves and feet hanging down his back. His head bent, going between her legs. Instinctively, she knew where he headed and whimpered.

He lifted his head. "I have yet to touch you, love."

She made another sound, and he raked a finger along the seam of her sex. He held it up.

"Look. Your juices already flow for me. You *want* me. Don't you, Rowena?"

"Yes," she whispered.

"I did not hear you."

"Yes!" she cried.

That was all it took. His head dropped again, and he licked his tongue along the entire seam of her sex. She gasped, need filling her. The next few minutes were shocking—yet oh, so fulfilling. He pushed his tongue inside her, lapping at her, feasting on her. His lips, his teeth, his tongue all worked together to drive her to the brink of madness.

And then the little death rocked her hard. Rowena cried his name, again and again, bucking against him as wave after wave of pleasure filled her. When it ended, she lay limp, so weak she could not even open her eyes.

He untied the cravat from the bedpost. Circled it until her wrists were freed. Then he kissed the palm of each hand tenderly. She opened her eyes to find him gazing at her with a look she had never seen on his face.

And was too frightened to ask what it meant.

"Are you certain you wish for us to couple?" he asked softly. "To see what it is like when we come together?"

"It couldn't possibly be better than that," she managed to say. "But I am ready to find out."

"Then we will make love now." He hesitated. "You may feel a touch of pain. That cannot be helped. It is fleeting and only happens the one time, when you first couple with a man."

"I am prepared," she told him, wondering what lay ahead, not certain she was ready, but putting on a brave face for him.

He quickly removed the rest of his clothes, and she was in awe of his body. The long, muscular legs and muscled chest, with a light matting of dark hair upon it. The broad shoulders, so firm as she held them. He spent a long time touching her. Kissing various parts of her body. Her eyelids. Her shoulders. The backs of her knees. His fingers danced along her body, making it hum with need.

Then he climbed atop her, keeping his weight off her as he braced himself on hands and knees.

"Wrap your legs about my waist," he told her.

She did as he asked, anticipation flooding her, mingled with a little fear of the unknown. But she was with Con and knew he would take good care of her.

He stroked her with his fingers for a few minutes and then placed his swollen cock against her. Before she knew it, he had thrust deeply inside her.

His hands cupped her cheeks. "You are so beautiful, Rowena. So very, very beautiful."

As he kissed her, his hands left her face. He also pulled almost entirely from her but then thrust into her once more, filling her. Soon, a rhythm had been established between them, and they danced a dance to music only the two of them could hear. She knew when her orgasm was about to strike, and she called out to him as it did. For his part, he thrust once more and gyrated against her. She could feel his hot seed spilling within her. Hoping there was no babe created—yet accepting if it had occurred, she would be fine with that.

This time, he collapsed atop her, his mouth nuzzling her neck, a feeling of closeness unlike anything she had ever experienced. This feeling that lingered was almost as nice as the actual love play itself. He pulled out from her and rolled to his side.

Smoothing her hair, he said, "I hope that satisfied your curiosity."

"I could not have dreamed it was like that," she admitted. "It was wonderful, though."

He pressed a soft kiss against her lips. "You are wonderful, love. Everything about you is special."

Con nudged her so that she rolled away from him onto her side, then he pulled her back against his chest. His arm came about her. He dropped a kiss upon her shoulder.

"Sleep. You need it."

"Will you leave?"

"I will be here when you awaken," he promised.

Reluctantly, Rowena closed her eyes, telling herself she would not miss out on anything. That he would stay with her.

What she did feel was that she was fully a woman now. Before too much time passed, she would write about this experience if she could find the words. For now, she simply wished to lie in Con's arms and savor the moment. Without knowing it, she dropped off to sleep.

Chapter Twenty-One

Con's thoughts drifted as he held Rowena snugly to him. He finally knew the bliss which his sisters and cousins felt with their spouses. Soon, Rowena would be the Countess of Marley. He would show off his new countess with pride.

The only family she had that he was aware of was Viscount Samuel. Naturally, she would wish for him to be present at their wedding. Or perhaps there were distant relatives he did not know about yet. He seemed to recall that she had mentioned an aunt, but he did not know where she lived or how close Rowena was to her. What he did know was that he wanted to wed this remarkable woman as soon as possible. He felt he had already wasted enough time and was eager to capture every moment he possibly could with her, a bright future ahead of them.

Still, she might actually want the banns read and a wedding which took place within a church. Rowena no longer had any ties to town, so she might wish for the ceremony to be held in Mossleigh. Most likely, she would also wish to see her two friends wed, as well. Con almost woke her so that they might plan for their rest of their lives.

He would not do that, however. For now, the world was held at bay. It was just the two of them in her cozy cottage, no others intruding.

She began to stir, and he waited for her to fully awaken, hoping she would not be too sore after their lovemaking because he wished to couple with her again. Con inhaled deeply, catching the faint scent of roses which clung to her skin and hair.

Then she looked over her shoulder, and he brushed a kiss upon her cheek. She began turning her body toward him, their lips meeting in a hungry kiss. He could sense the passion running through her and knew she was made for lovemaking. He had heard cases of other gentlemen wedding, ones who barely touched their wives, only doing so because they needed an heir off them. It would not be like that between the two of them. They would learn from one another what pleased the other. He would teach her—and Rowena would teach him, as well.

Just as his lips had roamed over her body earlier, hers now did the same to him. Her tongue teased his nipple, bringing a surge of hot desire tearing through him.

He caught her chin, raising it, their gazes meeting.

"You do know that you are playing with fire, my lady."

"I find I am drawn to fire, my lord," she said saucily, causing them both to laugh.

He let her explore his body until he could take it no longer, knowing he was ready to spend at any moment. Lifting her by her waist, Con settled her above him, slowly lowering her onto his enlarged cock. Her eyes widened in surprise—and then delight—as she took him in.

"You set the pace, love," he told her. "You are the one in charge now."

"I find I rather like this position," she purred as she began to move against him.

He groaned, holding lightly on to her waist, allowing her free rein. At first, she moved slowly, getting her bearings, and then, she confidently rode him. When Con came, it was an explosion, a greater fulfillment than he had ever reached before with any other woman.

Rowena laughed with sheer joy, collapsing atop him, kissing his chest and nibbling her way up it to his neck.

He groaned and asked, "Who knew how sensitive my neck

could be?"

Her lips finally reached his, and they kissed deeply. If she were already so skilled after two rounds of love play, what would she be like in a month? A year?

Con looked forward to finding out.

She eased off him and turned to her side, resting her head in her hand, her elbow propped up on the pillow.

"My sincere thanks to you, Con."

"For what?" he asked, reaching out and brushing his fingers lovingly along her cheek.

"For giving me this incredible experience. Something I never thought I would ever participate in."

He chuckled low. "Well, we will be participating frequently, I hope. May we talk of when our wedding might take place?"

She jerked away, sitting upright. "What? A wedding? There is to be no wedding," she said, shaking her head.

A sick feeling washed over him. "Rowena," he said calmly. "You do realize we will wed now. After what we have done."

"No," she protested, climbing from the bed.

He did the same, placing his hands on her bare shoulders. "I have always given you the choice. When you asked for us to couple, I asked you if you knew what it meant. You said you did."

"Of course, I knew what it meant," she said sharply. "It meant I would no longer be a virgin. That I would have lain with a man. Made love with him."

"True," he said. "But it also meant that we would wed."

"I did not consent to a marriage with you, Con," she insisted, angrily shaking his hands from her shoulders. She reached for her dressing gown and quickly slipped into it, knotting the belt as she glared up at him.

"Rowena, I never would have agreed to make love to you if I did not think we would then wed. Surely, you understand that."

"What I understand is that I do not wish to wed. You—or anyone else. I thought I had made myself perfectly clear regarding this. That you know I had no plans to ever wed."

Confused, he asked, "Then why did we engage in lovemaking? And do not tell me it was to satisfy your intellectual curiosity."

"I did not believe I would ever have an opportunity to couple with a man," she explained. "Then you gave me the chance to do so. While I enjoyed it a great deal, I am not going to marry you, Con. I must ask you to leave now."

"Leave? I am not leaving until we settle this matter between us. If you want the banns read as Lady Sarah and Miss Tweedham want done, I am perfectly willing to wait those three weeks. My personal preference would be to purchase a bishop's license—or even go to London and seek a special license there. But we *will* marry, Rowena. There is no question about that."

Con watched her jaw set stubbornly.

"In order for a couple to wed, both must agree to do so. I will not agree to a marriage of any kind, be it in the Mossleigh parish church or running away to Gretna Green with you, my lord."

"Oh, so we are now back to 'my lord' and not 'Con.' How could you be so intimate with me and deny a marriage between us?"

He took her hands in his, holding fast when she tried to pull away. "Did you not feel the magic between us, Rowena? We could have that every day of our lives. I want you as my countess. I will have no other *but* you."

"You will change your mind, Lord Marley. You will go to next Season as an earl, something you have never done before. Women will fall at your feet, fawning over you and fighting for you to make one of them your wife."

Gritting his teeth, he said, "I do not wish for any of them. *You* are my choice, Rowena."

"My choice is not to wed at all," she said firmly. "I am going to have to ask you to leave now, my lord. Go back to the house party."

Stunned, Con gathered up his clothing and quickly dressed. Heading to the door, he looked at her. Her arms were protectively crossed in front of her, her golden-brown hair spilling about her wildly.

"This is far from being over," he said. "You will come to your senses."

"I have made my decision. It is final."

He tossed the one weapon he had left at her. "What if we just made a babe, Rowena? What if you are now with child? My child. Would you have a bastard? Raise a child without its father? You know how cruel others in the *ton* can be because you have been affected by the gossip in Polite Society. Would you subject our child to such a dismal future?"

His arrow had hit the mark. Her mouth trembled.

"We will address that—if we need to," she said brusquely. "For now, I wish you to leave."

He knew there would be no reasoning with her now, so Con left the cottage, childishly slamming the door behind him. He went to the horse he had left tied in front of her cottage. Mounting it, he rode swiftly back to Pebblestone. When he reached the stables, he handed off the reins to a groom and stormed back to the house. It was quiet, which let him know the others still were at the beach. Lady Jewell had continued to ask for a picnic by the water, and Lady Pebble finally told them this morning at breakfast that would be the case. The viscountess warned them that they would have to sit upon blankets and eat from hampers provided by her cook, but everyone seemed pleased by the idea of dining at the water's edge.

He had made his excuses, not wanting anyone to know he was going to check on Rowena.

Con returned to his bedchamber, pacing furiously, his mind swirling as he recalled their final words.

How could she refuse him?

He was an earl of the realm. Charming. Handsome. Wealthy. Affable. It was ridiculous for Rowena to turn down his suit when he could give her the world. Did she do so out of some misplaced sense of pride?

And then it struck him.

He had not once mentioned the fact that he loved her. That should have been the first thing that came from his lips, not demanding she dance to the tune he set. A rush of emotions swept through him, knowing he had made a huge mistake. Telling Rowena that he loved her had been the most important thing, yet he had neglected to do so. Con wanted to immediately return to her cottage, but he feared she would not open the door to him. He decided to wait until she returned to Pebblestone. He doubted she would do so today or even later this evening. It would be difficult, but he would need to carry on as if nothing had changed—when everything had changed for him.

All Con knew was that if Rowena did not agree to wed him, he would never wed at all.

CHAPTER TWENTY-TWO

ROWENA SAT DRY-EYED, her insides aching.

Had she made the right decision in sending Con away?

She wasn't certain about anything anymore. She had always seen a clear path before her in the past. Her life had been simple. Uncomplicated. She thought it would stay that way after her father's death. But then a handsome lord had stepped into her life, worming his way into her heart.

She made an instant decision, one which she hoped she would never regret. It was foolish to toss away the chance of a life with Con simply out of misplaced pride. Perhaps she was not as attractive as other women, but she had other things she could offer. She was bright. Caring.

And she desperately wanted a life with this man.

Rowena hoped he might give her a second chance—and that he would have no regrets in their marriage.

Her mind made up, she returned to her bedchamber and removed her dressing gown, looking at the rumpled bedclothes, seeing Con in that bed with her. He had opened her eyes to so many things. A world of desire and passion. A place where family stood above all else. She worried she might not be able to hold his interest over a course of a lifetime. Then again, even if she were a stunning beauty, he might become bored with her over time. Rowena had seen how fickle men of Polite Society could be, turning from their wives to a parade of other women.

Her heart told her Con would not be that kind of man.

She admitted to herself that she did love him. And that she hoped he might find it in his heart to love her back, despite her recent rejection of him.

Once she dressed, she brushed her hair, winding it into her usual chignon. She must get to Pebblestone and see if the opportunity to have a life with Con still existed. This was not London, though. She did not have her father's carriage at her disposal, nor could she simply walk a block and summon a hansom cab to take her to her destination. She looked up and saw the skies were threatening rain. She could not chance walking that great a distance, looking like a drowned rat when she arrived. She couldn't even go to Ollie's stables because Aurora and her cousin's horses had been conveyed to Pebblestone for the duration of the house party.

Then she thought about her cousin's carriage. It took them to the house party each morning and returned them home every evening. Surely, during all those hours in between, the coachman returned to Stanfield instead of leaving the team hitched to the coach.

Rowena walked the half-mile from her cottage to Ollie's stables, where the lone groom came out to greet her.

"Lady Rowena, can I help you?"

"Does your brother bring Lord Samuel's carriage back each day after dropping us at Pebblestone?"

"Aye, he does. Are you needed to be taken there, my lady?"

"Yes, please. I was suffering from a megrim this morning and did not accompany Lord Samuel to Pebblestone. I am feeling much better, however, and wish to join the others, if only for dinner."

"Give us a few minutes, my lady, and we'll have the carriage readied for you."

"Thank you. I appreciate it."

A quarter hour later, Rowena found herself on the way to Pebblestone. Her mouth was dry, her palms sweating. Nerves flitted through her. She and Con had parted in anger, and she was uncertain how he would receive her presence. She thought it important, though, to come now. Anger could fester, turning into something ugly. If she had any hopes of a life with Con, she needed to see him as soon as possible and apologize for her previous stubborn stance.

The vehicle rolled up the lane as thunder sounded nearby. The carriage arrived at the house just as it began to sprinkle. She was handed down by a footman and admitted by another one, who told her the guests were gathering in the drawing room. She thanked him and headed toward the staircase. Rowena found herself a bit lightheaded and told herself not to faint. She had never done so in the past, and now would be a dreadful time to do so.

Upon entering the drawing room, she only saw about half the house party's guests present.

Con was not amongst them.

What if he had been so upset by what had passed between them that he had left Pebblestone? The thought filled her with apprehension. It was not as if she could chase after him. She had no means of reaching him unless she bought a ticket on a mail coach. Even though she had gone about town without a chaperone, it could be dangerous for a single woman to travel alone in such a manner. And where would she go? To town—or to his country estate? Rowena knew Marleyfield lay in Dorset, but she had no idea where in the county it was located. Even if she did receive directions to it, what would occur if she showed up unannounced upon his doorstep?

She worried she would not see him again. If he truly had left Pebblestone, would she be brave enough to go to town next spring and confront him at the first event of the Season? They had parted on such ill terms that she doubted he would look favorably upon her if she showed up months after their final conversation.

Her quandary was solved the moment he stepped into the drawing room. Their gazes met instantly, and she saw the surprise in his eyes, knowing he had not expected to see her tonight.

Lady Pebble approached her. "I am relieved that you are well enough to join us this evening for dinner, Rowena. I did not realize you got megrims."

"Only upon rare occasions, my lady."

Miss Tweedham came and slipped her arm through Rowena's. "Lord Samuel and I spoke some about our wedding today. I would like for you to stand up with me, Miss Stanhope. It would mean a great deal to me if you would do so. After all, you are the one responsible for bringing us together."

"I would be honored to stand with you as you speak your vows," she said sincerely. "Have you written to your parents yet about your happy news?"

"I have. I told them that Lord Samuel and I will wed at the Mossleigh parish church. Lady Pebble was kind enough to include her own letter with mine, extending an invitation for my parents to stay at Pebblestone, as well."

"I am so very happy for you, Miss Tweedham. I always wanted a sister, and I feel as if we shall be as sisters from now on."

The entire time they spoke, she surreptitiously watched Con, keeping notice of where he was in the room. Slowly, he seemed to be making his way toward her as he spoke to others.

Lady Sarah joined them. "Oh, Miss Stanhope, I am so glad you are no longer ill."

"I am happy to rejoin the house party. What did I miss?"

"We went to the beach to picnic," Lady Sarah told her. "Lady Jewell even suggested we all slip off our stockings and shoes and frolic in the sand and water."

It caused her to think of going barefoot during the lawn games. "I am sorry I missed doing so. Miss Tweedham and I were discussing her upcoming wedding. Have you and Lord Howell confirmed any plans regarding your ceremony?"

Lady Sarah blushed prettily, and Rowena thought how lighthearted her friend now was ever since she had become betrothed.

"I had an idea which I would like to talk over with Miss Tweedham." Lady Sarah looked to the other woman. "I recalled the recent wedding this past summer held at St. George's. The one where Lady Tia Worthington and Lady Delilah Drake wed at the same time in the same ceremony. Since the banns will be read each Sunday for the both of us and we will be eligible to wed once that is completed, I wondered if you might consider a double ceremony, Miss Tweedham. Of course, if you do not wish to share such a special day, I understand."

"That is an intriguing idea, my lady," Miss Tweedham enthused. "And since we both wish to wed in the local parish church, it would only make sense if we did so. I would need to talk with Lord Samuel about this before I could agree."

"And I would do the same with Lord Howell," Lady Sarah said, her excitement obvious.

"Of course, I am more than happy to host the wedding breakfast for each of you, no matter what is decided," Lady Pebble offered.

The two women thanked the viscountess and excused themselves, going to find their betrotheds to discuss the matter.

"I must tell Lord Pebble of this," Lady Pebble said, beaming. "Mossleigh has never seen a double wedding ceremony in my living memory. Excuse me, Rowena."

Now that she found herself alone, she was even more aware of Con circling about. He came toward her, and she saw the wariness in his eyes.

"I am glad you are recovered, my lady," he said stiffly. "I hope my presence at the house party does not make you uncomfortable. If so, then I will—"

"Do not leave," she pleaded. "Please. Do not go on my account."

He shrugged. "I am not certain why I should stay. The house party is scheduled to end in a few days' time, and the other guests have all paired up, whether they have announced a betrothal or not."

"Con, I must speak with you privately," she said quietly.

His brows arched at the familiar way she addressed him. "Then I am more than happy to speak with you. When would you like to do so? If it is too difficult for us to steal a few moments alone here at Pebblestone this evening, perhaps I could come to your cottage later this evening."

Before she could reply, Rowena saw a footman rush into the room. He headed straight to Mr. Tompkins. The two exchanged a few words, and then the footman exited the room. She realized he was not on the staff at Pebblestone because he wore a different uniform, and concern filled her, knowing Mr. Tompkin's father was gravely ill.

"Do you think it is about Lord Rowland?" she asked Con quietly, and he nodded.

Mr. Tompkins went to speak to Lord and Lady Pebble. The couple nodded solemnly, and then Lord Pebble said, "Mr. Tompkins would like to address our group."

She saw sadness permeate the former tutor's face. Then Rowena felt Con take her hand, threading his fingers through hers. She appreciated the gesture of comfort.

"I have just received word that my father has passed," Mr. Tompkins told them. "I knew his condition was serious and had been unchanged for several weeks. It was Papa who urged me to come to this house party and not constantly sit at his bedside."

Mr. Tompkins swallowed. "He passed peacefully in his sleep less than half an hour ago. There had been no change in his condition. No warning which would have had the staff summon me home."

The new Lord Rowland's gaze fastened upon Miss Lawson. "I wrote to Papa yesterday morning, thanking him for urging me to come to this party at Pebblestone." His features softened, and he smiled gently. "I told Papa of you, Miss Lawson. Of your sweet nature and innate goodness. I wrote that I would offer for you once I became the Earl of Rowland. I am doing so now. I do not know exactly when we might wed if you accept me, but I am asking for you to wait for me. Will you do so, Miss Lawson? Will you become my countess?"

She closed the distance between them, coming to stand before him.

"Yes, my lord. I would be happy to accept your offer of marriage. And I will wait as long as is necessary."

He took her hand and raised it to his lips, kissing it tenderly. "Thank you, my lady." He then gazed about the room. "In a short time, I feel as if I have come to know everyone within this room well. Thank you for your friendship."

Lord Rowland left the drawing room. Con squeezed Rowena's fingers and then released her hand.

Lady Pebble said, "In light of the earl's passing, I believe we should dine and then forgo any entertainment in the drawing room afterward. Shall we go into dinner now?"

Con slipped her hand through the crook of his arm and escorted her to the dining room. Rowena found her name card next to his and was grateful for his nearby presence.

The soup course had only begun when Lord Cramer came to his feet.

"Lady Jewell, may I speak with you privately for a moment?"

Lady Jewell looked surprised by his request but said, "Certainly, my lord."

Lord Cramer pulled out her chair and helped her to her feet. They exited the dining room.

"I wonder what that is about," mused Lady Pebble.

But Rowena knew. Her suspicions were confirmed moments later when the couple reentered the room, holding hands.

Lord Cramer said, "With the passing of Lord Rowland, I did not want to waste another moment. I am happy to announce that Lady Jewell has done me the honor of accepting my offer of marriage. Although this is a sad time and it does not seem fitting to celebrate, I could not let Lady Jewell slip from my grasp."

Con spoke up. "Lord Rowland would be the first to congratulate the two of you. Life is for the living, and you and Lady Jewell will have a good one together. No one begrudges you for speaking up and offering to make Lady Jewell your countess. My heartiest congratulations to you," he told the couple.

Dinner continued, Miss Bailey beaming at her niece throughout it.

"Will you take your new husband to India to meet your parents?" Miss Bailey asked.

Lady Jewell shook her head. "Things are changing in India, Aunt. That is why Mama sent me to England. To start a new life." She looked at her new fiancé. "I think Lord Cramer and I will be happy staying right here in Dorset."

"Will you make it a triple wedding?" Lady Pebble inquired. "That would be a sight to see."

"A triple wedding?" asked Lord Cramer, clearly confused.

"Perhaps I spoke too soon," the viscountess apologized.

Ollie said, "Since the banns are being read the same three Sundays for Miss Tweedham and me, as well as for Lord Howell and Lady Sarah, the ladies have come up with the idea of our holding a joint ceremony."

"Just as Tia and Dilly did," murmured Con in Rowena's ear. His lips brushed against her lobe as he did, sending a thrill rushing through her.

"Yes, we were discussing it before Lord Rowland was called away," Lord Howell said. He looked to Lady Sarah, who nodded. "And it seems as if my fiancée and I have agreed to this."

Miss Tweedham said, "We have decided to wed on the same day after the last calling of the banns. Lady Sarah and I are good friends and will remain so, especially since we will be living close to one another after our marriages." She looked to Lady Jewell. "Do not feel the same obligation, my lady."

Lady Jewell looked adoringly at Lord Cramer. "I only wish we could wed sooner."

"You could purchase a bishop's license," Con volunteered. "There is a small fee associated with it, but it allows you to wed in either the bride's or groom's local parish church without the calling of the banns. The other alternative is to purchase a special license in the office of the Archbishop of Canterbury in London. It gives you the freedom to wed wherever you choose. In a church. A townhome. Whatever you find convenient."

Lord Cramer asked, "What is your wish, my lady?"

"I would prefer a church wedding," Lady Jewell said. "It is what Mama and Papa would want, too. But the idea of the bishop's license is appealing to me. Could you get us one of those, my lord?"

Gallantly, the earl said, "I would ride to the ends of the earth for it, my lady. I can leave tomorrow morning and return by late evening at the earliest or by the next day."

"Please do that," Lady Jewell requested. "I know the house party ends the day after tomorrow. It would be lovely if we could end it by having everyone attend our wedding."

They all agreed it was a wonderful idea. Lord Pebble volunteered to go and speak to the vicar tomorrow morning to arrange for the ceremony to take place the following day. The ladies all decided to forgo tomorrow's ride and would decorate the church. Miss Lawson said she would be happy to provide the music for the ceremony.

Dinner ended, and Con said, "Your cousin is headed your way. I will come to you in an hour."

Rowena nodded. "I will see you then."

Ollie said, "It is good to see you looking healthy again, Rowena. What do you think of this double ceremony?"

"I think I will witness two couples who are very happy to be coming together in marriage," she replied.

"Are you ready to return home?"

"Yes."

She promised Lady Pebble that she would return for breakfast tomorrow.

"Lord Pebble will go see the vicar after we eat," the viscountess said. "Then we should be given access to the church so that we might decorate it for the wedding ceremony. You have a way with flowers, Rowena. You will have to tell our gardeners which blooms to cut, and then we can use them to fill the church. To think that our little house party has had four betrothals coming out of it. Why, I will be the talk of the *ton* come next Season."

"I suppose you will need to hold an annual house party, my lady, since you have done such an excellent job of making matches at this one."

"Selfishly, I am happiest for Miss Lawson," the viscountess shared. "Lord Pebble and I worried about her coming to this house party because of her extreme shyness. To think she will soon be a countess will make her parents very happy."

Rowena and Ollie bid their hosts goodnight and went to his carriage.

"I hope you do not mind that I asked the carriage to bring me to Pebblestone," she told her cousin.

"It was due to return for me. I am glad you made use of it." He paused. "I am sorry that you come out of this house party without a betrothal, Rowena. It must sadden you when you see the other four ladies so very happy."

She was not ready to reveal anything to Ollie yet, especially because she did not know how Con would react to what she had to say to him.

"I am a firm believer in fate, and these four couples were obviously meant to be. I am very happy for you and Miss Tweedham, Ollie. I think you will build a wonderful life together."

He dropped her at her cottage, and Rowena waved goodbye. She entered and knew she had less than an hour before Con appeared.

And decided her own fate.

CHAPTER TWENTY-THREE

ROWENA AND LORD Samuel left Pebblestone immediately after dinner. Con would give them time to arrive home before he would go to the stables to borrow a horse. He went to the library to pass the time until then, and Lord Cramer appeared as Con was perusing the shelves.

"My best wishes again to you and Lady Jewell," he told the earl, a little surprised at the match because Cramer was so taciturn and Lady Jewell the opposite.

"I know to others, we may seem very mismatched," Lord Cramer admitted. "Lady Jewell is vivacious, drawing others to her with ease. I am a serious, solemn sort of fellow, but she has brought out the very best in me. I could not afford to leave this house party without offering for her."

"I think it is important for a couple to balance one another in a relationship," Con told the young man. "Obviously, you both have strong feelings for one another." He smiled. "It is a good thing that you decided to attend this house party."

"I was doing so in hopes that I might find a wife," the earl shared. "I have been to the Season and found it both superficial and overwhelming, especially for a reserved gentleman such as me. I hoped the intimacy a house party offered might help me get to know a handful of young ladies better. Frankly, I liked all the women present, but I was especially drawn to Lady Jewell. It is a good thing since a few of the other gentlemen present also found matches in the other guests."

Lord Cramer hesitated, studying Con for a moment. "I thought perhaps you and Miss Stanhope might make a go of things."

He shrugged. "That remains to be seen. It is not for lack of effort on my part."

The earl brightened. "Then I wish you success in your endeavors, Lord Marley."

Lord Cramer frowned, and Con asked, "What is it?"

"I had intended to ask if you would ride with me tomorrow to see about this bishop's license. You seemed to know what you were talking about, and I wanted to make certain I had it in hand since the wedding is being planned. But if you need time to woo Miss Stanhope, that is more important."

He knew things would be settled later this evening between him and Rowena. If she agreed to wed him, he could miss one day with her. And if she again clarified her position and let him know there was no chance of a betrothal between them, he would be better off not being at Pebblestone tomorrow.

"I shall be happy to accompany you, my lord. What time would you like to depart?"

They arranged to leave by seven o'clock the next morning, and Con told Lord Cramer he would see him then. He left the library and went down to the stables, asking a groom to saddle a horse for him. Thankfully, Lord Pebble's servants were well trained, and the groom did not ask him where he was riding off to so late.

He arrived at Rowena's cottage a quarter hour later, dismounting and tying the horse's reins to the post. Trepidation filled him as he approached the door. He had not let his hopes rise simply because she wished to speak with him in private. If anything, he steeled himself for the worst. Knowing this might be the final time they ever spoke alone, he rapped upon the door.

Immediately, it opened. He saw she still wore the same gown she had worn to dinner. Her eyes betrayed nothing of her feelings as she asked him to come inside. Con did so, and Rowena closed the door behind him.

They both started speaking at once and then stopped, each chuckling, which broke some of the tension in the air. He decided to take the lead because what he had to say was too important to wait.

"Normally, I would bow to a lady and allow her to speak first, but I left something very important unsaid the last time we were together here."

"I am sorry we parted on such an angry note," she said. "That is why I need to—"

"No, let me finish." He took a deep breath. "I have been a confident man all my life, knowing my mind and acting accordingly. I have never been indecisive regarding any matter, much less quick to anger. I am now taking the advice of my valet."

Her brows arched hearing that, and he nodded. "Yes, my valet. Benchley told me to speak my heart—and that is what I wish to do now, Rowena."

Con took a step toward her, gathering her hands in his, bringing them to his lips for a tender kiss.

"I love you," he declared. "That was the most important thing—and one I should have said before all the other hurtful and angry words spilled from me. I do love you, Rowena. I cannot tell you when I started loving you, only that I do. I can see a life for the two of us, one in which we are both lovers and friends, equal partners in our marriage. I know you have said you will never wed, but I hope you will reconsider." He swallowed. "Because if you are not going to marry me, then I, too, will never wed."

"It is you. Or no one."

He had barely spoken the last word when she burst into tears. Her sobs continued, racking her entire body. Con enfolded her in his arms, smoothing her hair, whispering words to soothe her, but she cried all the harder. Finally, he fell silent, simply holding her, for what might be the last time.

Her tears subsided, and she looked up at him. "I, too, love

you, Con. Will all my heart. I want a life with you. Children with you. I want to grow old and gray with you."

Confused, he asked, "Then why so many tears?" He framed her face with his hands and pressed a gentle kiss to her soft lips.

"I have never cried before," she revealed, her body still trembling.

"Never?"

She nodded. "I have always been stoic. Rational. I had to be. Papa was almost like a child, and so I became the parent and always told him what to do. I managed the household. Met regularly with his solicitor and banker regarding his investments. Gave advice to Ollie regarding the running of Stanfield." She sniffed. "I knew Papa was dying because his doctor informed me of it. Because Papa was a simple creature, I kept that from him, wanting him to enjoy his final days without worry. By the time he passed, I had already come to terms with his death, knowing about it in advance and preparing myself for that eventuality."

What she revealed surprised him. He did not think he would have had the maturity to do all she had from such a tender age.

"I have never shed a tear, Con. Ever. I cannot tell you what all these tears were about because I am not certain myself. Perhaps I am feeling a bit of relief that our feelings are the same and that we have a chance to be together."

"I do love you, Rowena. I want to wed you as soon as possible."

She smiled, a radiant smile which warmed him. "I will marry you whenever you wish, Con."

"I know you would like for your cousin to be present at the ceremony. I believe you had mentioned an aunt at one point."

Rowena nodded. "Yes, Aunt Sylvia lives in town. I would also like for Lord and Lady Pebble to attend. They have been as family to me over the years. But what of your family? You have your mother. Your sisters and so many cousins. We must send word to all of them."

He thought a moment and then said, "I am to go with Lord

Cramer tomorrow to purchase a bishop's license for his and Lady Jewell's wedding."

"Oh, I have agreed to stand up with Miss Tweedham when she and Ollie wed in three weeks. Do you think we might wed in the meantime? Between those two weddings?"

Con thought a moment, not certain how Rowena would react to what he had to say.

"I know you are not fond of town, but I believe it would be the best place for the ceremony to take place. Your cousin and Lord and Lady Pebble could come to town. My two sisters and Cousin Ariadne only live about two hours from town, so it would be easy for them to attend the ceremony. It would also give me time to send word to Mama, who is visiting a friend in Sussex, and Val. My other cousins are too far away."

He took her hands in his again. "I hope it wouldn't be too terrible for you if we wed in town."

"I think it sounds convenient for all," she said, causing his heart to sing. "That way, we could have as many of our loved ones present as possible."

"Then I will leave for London after Lord Cramer and Lady Jewell's wedding. I will purchase a special license for us when I arrive as well as go to Surrey to see my sisters and Ariadne. I suspect Ariadne will offer to host our wedding breakfast. She has done so for her siblings and other cousins in the past. It has become almost a ritual."

"I am so looking forward to meeting your family, Con, and making them mine."

He kissed her with enthusiasm. "Oh, they will simply adore you. Tia already does. At least you have met her and Hugo. I am sorry Tia's sister, Lia, and her husband Rupert will not be able to be at the ceremony, but I hope Val and Eden can come to town. You got along well with the two of them."

She gazed up at him in wonder. "Is this truly happening? Or am I dreaming?"

"If you are, love, then I am in those dreams with you. When

you awaken, I will always be there, loving you."

Con took her to bed and made slow, sweet love to her. Afterward, he told her a little about Lucy and Dru and also Marleyfield. Then he kissed her a final time and rose from the bed.

"I must return to Pebblestone. Lord Cramer and I are leaving early tomorrow morning."

He took her hand and brushed his lips against her knuckles. "I am sorry we will not be able to spend time tomorrow together."

"You are helping a friend, Con. Besides, Lady Pebble is going to keep me busy all day. I am to supervise the gardeners about which blooms to cut and then help the others decorate the Mossleigh church for the wedding. We would not have had time together because of that."

"I do not want to take away from Lord Cramer's and Lady Jewell's happiness. Could we wait and share our good news after the wedding takes place?"

"Well, I will have to prevent myself from bursting with the news," she teased. "But I suppose I can keep the secret to myself another two days."

He leaned down and kissed her. "You look comfy where you are. Stay in bed. I will see myself out."

Con rode home, joy soaring through him. He had wondered what would happen when he took Lord Clay's place at the house party. Now, he was filled with good cheer, knowing he had found love. That not only did he love, but he was loved in return by the most wonderful angel who walked this earth.

A FOOTMAN CAME and bent, saying in Con's ear, "Lord Marley, your carriage has arrived. Your valet is seeing to having your trunk placed upon it now."

"Thank you," he said.

Con turned to Rowena, who sat beside him, their fingers entwined beneath the table.

"It is time for me to go."

She gave him a wistful smile. "I will miss you terribly, Con."

Giving her a rakish smile, he said, "Not half as much as I will miss you. Shall we share our good news now?"

They rose, their hands still joined. He saw Lady Pebble was the first to catch sight of that. Her mouth formed an O, and she elbowed her husband. Lord Pebble turned and saw them. He beamed and also rose.

"While it is not yet time to toast our lovely, wedded couple, I believe Lord Marley has something to share with our group."

All eyes fell upon Rowena and him, and Con saw smiles break out on the faces of those present.

"I am sorry to interrupt this wedding breakfast, but my carriage is ready. I am departing for town now, where I shall purchase a special license to wed the love of my life, Miss Stanhope."

He turned to face her and gave her a spontaneous kiss, causing those gathered to break into applause.

"We will marry in town in another week to ten days. It will be easier for Mama and my sisters to meet us there, along with a few of my cousins." He looked at Viscount Samuel. "Although your cousin is of age and does not require your permission to wed, I hope you will give us your blessing and that you will attend the wedding."

"Other than my own upcoming wedding, this is the best possible news, my lord. Yes, I shall be there."

"We will return to Pebblestone in time for the double wedding ceremony," Rowena assured the other guests.

"My work is done here," Lady Pebble proclaimed. "I must be the only hostess who has ever had every single guest invited to a house party become betrothed."

Con looked at the viscountess. "Thank you for asking us all here, my lady." He grinned. "Even if I came under unusual circumstances."

Her eyes met his. "There was no emergency for Lord Clay, was there, my lord?"

Ready to admit the truth, Con said, "No, my lady. I learned that Miss Stanhope would be present at your house party and believed if I did not find a way to attend it, I would lose her."

He looked across the group seated. "Besides finding my countess, I also have gained good friends. Friendships which I believe will last a lifetime."

Looking to the newlyweds, he added, "I am sorry to have interrupted your wedding breakfast, but I did not want to rush off before everyone knew of our engagement."

"I think it quite romantic, Lord Marley," the new Lady Cramer said, beaming at him.

"Naturally, you and Lord Cramer are invited to our wedding, but I figured you might be on your honeymoon and not be able to attend." He looked at the others. "I know two more weddings are yet to come, so if we do not see you at ours, we will come celebrate all our happiness at yours."

Rowena accompanied him outside, tears misting her eyes.

He cradled her cheek. "Do not weep at us parting, love."

"These are tears of happiness, Con," she told him. "And I seem to be just like a watering pot these days, emotional about everything."

He thought of his sisters and cousins and how they had talked about being the same when they were increasing. While he doubted she was with child yet, he would not mind a river of tears coming from her when she was. The thought of Rowena carrying his babe in her belly made him flush with happiness.

Con kissed her. "You may water away, Rowena Stanhope. Let me know the moment you arrive in town."

"I will," she promised.

Climbing into his carriage, he waved at her as his coachman set out. He would be counting the hours until he saw his beloved again.

Chapter Twenty-Four

Upon arriving in London, Con had Benchley send off the letters he had written to his sisters, Ariadne, and Val. He had written to his mother while in Dorset and posted the letter to her from there since she was in Sussex, and it was much closer to Dorset than town. He had told her to rent a post-chaise and return to town immediately if she wanted to see him wed.

He left for Doctors' Commons, seeking the special license which would allow Rowena and him to wed once everyone arrived in town. He assumed they would do so at the Aldridge townhouse, especially if Ariadne volunteered to host the wedding breakfast. It took almost three hours' total to be seen by the Archbishop of Canterbury's assistant, fill out the necessary documents, and pay the substantial fee for the license. It did not matter. He would give his last guinea to see Rowena as his countess.

Once he returned to the townhouse, he asked Adams to assemble the staff. They gathered in the foyer, and he stood a few steps from the bottom in order to be able to see them all.

"I wanted to let you know that I will wed within the week. Make whatever preparations are necessary to welcome my wife."

His staff gave a rousing cheer, which touched Con. He had not been back inside the townhouse since he had left to carry his father's body home to Marleyfield. It still seemed slightly odd that he was now the earl.

Mrs. Adams approached him. "My lord, shall I remove Lady Marley's things from the countess' rooms? Or would you rather wait and have her maid do so?"

"I trust you will do an excellent job," he told the housekeeper. "Move my mother to the blue room."

"Yes, my lord."

He thought Mama would prefer that room, which was the largest of the guest bedchambers. He would prefer her be located in it because it was at the opposite end of the hallway from his own rooms. Con intended to have Rowena sleep in his bed each night, something Val had shared that he and Eden did. Con had liked the idea and knew his bride would approve, as well. This way, they could be as noisy as they wished during lovemaking and not disturb anyone, least of all Mama.

Going to his study, he wrote to Seward, the Marleyfield butler, informing him that he was taking a wife and wanted Mrs. Seward and the staff to prepare for the new countess' arrival, saying they would be coming to Marleyfield in about three to four weeks' time. That would allow Rowena and him to attend the double wedding at Mossleigh before returning to Somerset. He also instructed Seward to prepare the dower house for his mother and decide which servants would be going with her. Knowing she was opinionated—and vocal about her opinions—he did not wish to have the servants' loyalties divided between the new countess and the dowager one. This way, Mama could have the run of the dower house, and Rowena would be in charge of his household.

The next morning after breakfast, he sent word to Mr. Badham that he would like an appointment sometime that day. He received a message to come to the solicitor's offices at one o'clock, and he was on time for his appointment.

Mr. Badham greeted him and led him to his office, where Con informed him, "I am to be married, Mr. Badham. I will need you to draw up the marriage settlements for me. My bride is Miss Stanhope, daughter of the late Viscount Samuel."

"Why, Lord Samuel was a client of mine, as is the new viscount."

"Yes, we discovered this once Miss Stanhope agreed to wed me. Since you will not have to meet with another solicitor, the marriage contracts should be easy enough for you to draw up quickly."

Con handed over a list. "These are my requirements. Please read over it and see if you have any questions for me."

Mr. Badham took several minutes to do so and then said, "You are being most generous, my lord. Are you certain this is what you want?"

"It is—or I would have not set my requests down on paper," he said brusquely. "See that you write these up as I have requested. Miss Stanhope is of legal age and will sign the marriage contracts herself."

The solicitor studied Con a moment. "You must care for Miss Stanhope a great deal, seeing how well she will be taken care of, my lord."

"I love her. I would give my life for her."

Mr. Badham looked taken aback at his bold declaration. "I will see to this at once, Lord Marley. Shall we meet the day after tomorrow to review them? I should have the completed documents by then."

"I will come to your offices once Miss Stanhope has arrived in town. That should be in the next few days."

"Very well, my lord."

Con set out for Surrey at nine o'clock the next morning, planning to stay overnight. He knew his letters had arrived yesterday and hoped that Lucy and Ariadne would be waiting for him when he arrived at Beauville, as he had requested. He had decided to meet with everyone at Beauville so that he might see the estate and steal a few minutes with Beau.

When his carriage pulled into the drive in front of the house, he saw two other carriages standing in place. Dru and Perry stood waiting for him, and his sister flew into his arms the moment he disembarked.

"Oh, Con! I am so happy to see you," Dru exclaimed. "It seems as if it has been forever. Mama wrote and said you would be in town and were coming to visit us, but we received no letter from you until yesterday. And what is this family meeting all about?"

He kissed her cheek. "All in good time, little sister." Turning to Perry, he offered his hand. "I am happy to see you but even more eager to meet my nephew."

Perry chuckled. "You mean the most beautiful babe in all England? The best natured and best eater? The one who—"

Dru punched her husband in the arm. "Hush, now. I cannot help it if Beau is perfect." She slipped her arm through Con's. "Come inside. The others are waiting for you in the drawing room. Penelope and Elizabeth came with their parents, and they are in the nursery now, so you will also get to see them as well."

"I am looking forward to seeing all three of them. And having some tea."

As they entered the foyer, Dru told the butler to have tea sent to the drawing room. They went upstairs, and soon he was embracing and kissing Lucy and Ariadne and shaking hands with Judson and Julian.

"It is so very good to see you all," he told the group. "I know the Season was only a few months ago, but I have missed everyone."

"Please sit," Dru asked, and they took seats, everyone eagerly facing him.

"What is this announcement that you had us gather for?" Lucy asked.

"Why, don't you know?" Ariadne asked, a knowing smile on her lips. "Look at Con. Can't you tell? He is in love."

His sisters started talking at once, throwing questions at him. The three husbands sat, smirking at him.

Ariadne got their attention. "Let Con tell us about Miss Stanhope. Then you can ask him whatever questions you would like."

Surprise filled him, then he realized he should have known that Ariadne would have guessed.

Taking a deep breath, he said, "It is true. My fiancée's name is Miss Stanhope. Ariadne and Julian met her at a ball this past Season. We supped with them, Val and Eden, and Tia and Hugo."

"Miss Stanhope is an excellent conversationalist," Julian said. "Quite bright." He grinned. "And pretty."

Con could not wipe the grin from his face. "That she is. We danced at Tia's request, and I found myself quite drawn to Miss Stanhope. In fact, I had asked if I could call upon her the next afternoon, but—"

"You *never* do that, Con," Lucy interrupted. "That alone tells me Miss Stanhope is special."

"Unfortunately, I had to break my promise to her because we lost Papa so suddenly. By the time Mama and I took him home to Marleyfield and buried him, I realized I had not let Miss Stanhope know the circumstances of why I did not call upon her."

Dru chuckled. "I am surprised she agreed to see you, Con."

"I came to town to do that very thing, but I learned she was in the country. Her father had also recently passed, and she had returned to Stanfield, the family's country estate." He paused. "I also learned she would be attending a nearby house party."

"Oh, a house party is such a good way to truly get to know someone," Ariadne said.

"It is. If you are invited to it, that is."

Lucy gasped. "You showed up without being invited? Con!"

"I took the place of a gentleman who had received an invitation. It took some quick thinking and fast talking on my part, but Lord Clay allowed me to take his spot on the guest list."

"Who was the hostess?" Judson asked.

"Lady Pebble."

Judson nodded. "Ah, I know her husband. Lord Pebble is a good sort."

"Lady Pebble suspected a bit of subterfuge on my part, but

she was gracious enough to allow me to attend, especially after I pointed out to her that the numbers would be skewed with Lord Clay now absent."

"Oh, a hostess always strives for balance," Lucy said. "But you are fortunate she did not send you away, Con."

"Enough of how you got there," Dru said. "Tell us about Miss Stanhope and how you fell in love with her."

"She is far more intelligent than I am. In fact, she has advised her cousin, who served as her father's steward, for many years. I will probably be learning from her about how to run Marleyfield. Rowena is also well read. She is kind to everyone she meets. Others would call her a bluestocking, but I admire the depth of her knowledge."

"And she does love you, too, doesn't she?" Dru asked anxiously.

"It is a love match," he shared.

For the next hour, Con told them about the house party. How the various couples began pairing off. How he and Rowena had won partnering at cards and lawn games.

"She actually took off her slippers and stockings to play battledore and shuttlecock?" Ariadne asked. "Oh, I thought I liked her before, but now I truly think she is an original."

"She had decided not to wed," he told them. "The *ton* has mistreated her."

"For being a bluestocking?" asked Lucy anxiously.

"Yes. What is important is that neither of us could deny our feelings for one another. I have already purchased a special license, and I have sent word to Mama to come to town as quickly as possible."

"What of Val and Eden?" asked Julian. "They are close enough to make it to town for a wedding."

"I did write to them and ask them to come if they could. I know the other cousins are too far away, and I am in a hurry to wed Rowena."

"Love does that to a man," Perry said, and the other husbands nodded in agreement.

"Well, all of us will certainly pack and come to town to be a part of your special day," Ariadne said. "I hope you will also allow Julian and me to give the wedding breakfast."

"I was counting on it," Con told her. "It is tradition for those who wed in town."

"Are there any particular foods you wish served?" she asked.

"I will leave that to your discretion, but Rowena is terribly fond of sweets."

"Leave it to Cook and me," his cousin assured him. "You will not be disappointed."

"Will you leave town and go straight to Marleyfield, or will you take a honeymoon?" Dru asked.

"We actually have a double wedding ceremony to attend in Dorset."

Con explained how each of the couples at the house party had become betrothed and that they had already witnessed Lord Cramer and Lady Jewell's wedding before he departed for town.

"Rowena's cousin and Miss Tweedham are having the banns read at the local church, as well as Baron Howell and Lady Sarah. They plan to wed on the Sunday of the last reading, so we have decided to stay in town for a week or more after our own wedding and then travel down to Dorset for that ceremony. We do not know when Lord Rowland and Miss Lawson will wed, due to the recent death of his father."

"Well, it sounds as if it was a most successful house party," Ariadne said. "Lady Pebble must be walking on air because of all the betrothals which occurred during its course."

"May I go to the nursery now?" he asked. "I have yet to meet Beau, and I heard that Elizabeth and Penelope are also at Beauville today."

"I will go with you," Dru volunteered. "Everyone else can stay here."

He accompanied his sister to the top floor, where the nursery was located. Penelope, at nineteen months, was toddling about with self-assurance. Elziabeth, who was seven months, was on her hands and knees, rocking back and forth.

"She is on the verge of crawling," Dru said. She went to the crib and leaned over, caressing the cheek of the babe lying there. "And this is my Beau."

The babe was a couple of weeks younger than his cousin Elizabeth. He stirred then, stretching his arms and legs, yawning widely.

"You may hold him if you wish," Dru said.

Con lifted the babe from his bed and placed Beau's head in the crook of his arm.

"It is Uncle Con, Beau," he told the babe, who looked at him curiously. "We are going to be great friends."

He wound up on the floor with the three children. Beau had learned to sit up and sat next to Con. Elizabeth continued to rock back and forth, still determining whether or not she wanted to move forward. He took turns holding the two little ones, and then he gave a ride to Penelope, allowing her to climb upon his back as he crawled about the nursery on hands and knees.

"You are going to make for an excellent father, Con," his sister predicted, tears misting her eyes. "I cannot wait to see you with children of your own."

He had Penelope climb down, and she went to play with some blocks as he said, "You seem happy, Dru."

She sighed. "I have never been happier, Con. I seem to love Perry more with each passing day. It is marvelous to be only a few minutes away from Lucy and Ariadne." She frowned. "I hate that you will be so far from us, though."

"That is what the Season is for," he reminded her. "For our families to come together and enjoy one another. For our children to spend time together and grow to love and cherish their cousins."

"You are right," she agreed. "We will always have the Season."

He grinned. "I am always right. I am your big brother."

Con leaned over and kissed Dru's brow.

"I cannot wait to meet Rowena. If she stole your heart, she must be very special."

"Oh, she is, Dru. She most certainly is."

Chapter Twenty-Five

Rowena and Ollie arrived in town, and she sent Con a message to let him know. Since it was Ollie's first time in London, she told him she would give him a tour of his residence and also town. The townhouse tour had barely begun when the new housekeeper Rowena had hired approached, telling them that Lord Marley had arrived.

Smiling at her, Ollie said, "Why don't you let Mrs. Jones give me the house tour in your stead? I know how eager you are to see Lord Marley."

"Thank you," she said, hurrying downstairs to the drawing room.

The moment she caught sight of Con, it was as if her heart erupted in song. Rowena found herself in his arms. He kissed her enthusiastically.

"I know it has only been a handful of days, but it has felt like a lifetime apart from you," he told her.

"I feel the same way, Con. I never want to be apart from you again."

"How was your journey to town? Did Lord Samuel accompany you?"

"He did. The housekeeper is now showing him his London residence since he has never seen it before."

"All but Mama has arrived in town as of this morning, and they have gathered now in my drawing room. Would you and your cousin come to meet them?"

Knowing how much his family meant to him, she said, "We would be delighted to."

They collected Ollie and went outside to Con's carriage. He told them it would only be a short drive. When they pulled up at the townhouse, Rowena thought how grand it was.

And soon, it would be one of her homes.

As Con handed her down, he said, "I hope so much of my family being present will not overwhelm the both of you."

"I have already met a few of them. I am looking forward to knowing your sisters most of all." She grinned at him. "And hearing stories of what you were like as a boy."

He laughed. "I am sure they will bend your ear with plenty of those."

He introduced her to Adams, and the butler led them upstairs to the drawing room. When they entered, Rowena was taken aback for a moment by so many smiling, eager faces. She was quickly welcomed by the Duke and Duchess of Millbrooke and Lord and Lady Aldridge, whom she had supped with at the Purlington ball. Then Con introduced her to his two sisters, both younger than he was. Lady Huntsberry was a few inches over five feet, with tawny hair. Lady Martindale was several inches taller than her sister and had the same tawny hair her sister possessed. Both had the amethyst eyes of their brother, and Rowena couldn't help but want a child or two of theirs to also claim the unusual eye color.

The Marquess of Huntsberry and the Earl of Martindale, husbands of Con's two sisters, were also very friendly, and she and Ollie couldn't have received a nicer welcome from the group.

Lady Huntsberry said, "It is as if we are gaining another sister in you, Miss Stanhope."

"Enough of these titles," Lady Aldridge declared. "The cousins in our family have always been informal when we are in private. You must call us by our Christian names. I am Ariadne."

"I am Rowena," she told them. "And my cousin is Ollie. Con

has told me all about the historical names the cousins were given, so I already know what some of your given names—and nicknames—are."

"There are so many of us here," Con said. "I think I would like to give Rowena a chance to get to know the women of the family. Would that be to your liking, love?"

She nodded. "I am already comfortable in everyone's presence," she assured him. "But it would be nice to focus on the ladies."

"Then we gentlemen shall leave you ladies to it," he told her. "We will take Ollie with us and introduce him around at White's since he is new to town."

"Thank you, Con," she said quietly, knowing Ollie would be in good hands with her fiancé and the other members of his family.

Once the men left the drawing room, Ariadne rang for tea, and Rowena got to know her future sisters-in-law, as well as Eden and Ariadne, much better. These women were all kind and made her feel a part of the family. She learned more about the orphanage which Ariadne and Julian owned as well as hearing about how Eden was the former governess to Verina and Justina, two of Con's Fulton cousins. All four women also were fairly new mothers, and they spoke at length about their children. Rowena could see the love and pride they held for their offspring, and they assured her Con would be a wonderful father to their children.

In turn, she talked a little about the Ladies Literary Book Society she had created, and Lucy thought they should continue it every Season when they came to town.

"A family book society," Eden said, laughing. "What a marvelous idea. The former governess in me is all in favor of this."

"I hear that each of you will bring your children to town when the Season is in progress," Rowena said.

"It was Ariadne's idea," Eden told her. "We all love our children so much. I cannot imagine leaving William at Millvale for months at a time. He is already cutting teeth at six months, and I wish to see every tooth erupt, as well as all the other milestones in his life, from crawling to walking and talking."

"We are a large family," Lucy said. "We enjoy one another's company immensely. I hope you will agree to bring your children to the Season, Rowena."

"I have never attended the Season," Dru said. "I wed Perry before I made my come-out and did not travel to town this past spring because I was as large as a whale. I gave birth to Beau in July, but I am eager to come to next Season and see what all the fuss is about. Perry and I will go to some of the events, but I think a majority of our time will be spent with family."

"I came out three years ago," Rowena shared. "I have had my fill of the Season. The *ton* is not kind to bluestockings such as myself."

"Well, I think you are delightful," Ariadne proclaimed. "You must go to a few events with Con, though. He is very proud of you and will want Polite Society to see his countess. Julian did not grow up in Polite Society. He worked on the London docks. We attend a few select events, but we mostly come to town to visit with my cousins and their families."

"I rather like the idea of focusing more on family than social affairs," she said. "I know Con is a bit sad that his sisters are living on the other side of the country from Marleyfield. Coming together each spring during the Season will give us an opportunity to catch up with one another and enjoy time together. As well as meet any new babes," she finished, thinking that would include her own children someday, hopefully sooner rather than later.

Ariadne spoke up. "I hope you do not think it too presumptuous of me, Rowena, but I have a modiste waiting upstairs. I did not know if you had already chosen a gown for your wedding, but Madame Laurent is here to measure you in case you might like something new to wear to the ceremony."

She had worried about what she would wear, not thinking she had anything suitable. Tears welled in her eyes.

"Thank you for your thoughtfulness, Ariadne. I would be

happy to meet with your modiste, but how could she finish a gown so quickly? I know we will wed in a few days."

"Now that the Season has ended, Madame's dress orders have dropped drastically. She has already been told that time is of the essence, and she and her assistants will make certain to finish your gown in time for the wedding."

Rowena and Ariadne excused themselves to meet with Madame Laurent. The modiste already had a few sketches of what the gown might look like. With Ariadne's guidance, Rowena chose one as well as the fabrics to use. Madame and her assistant quickly took her measurements and said work would commence immediately.

"We are staying at Lord Marley's townhouse, Miss Stanhope," the modiste told her. "We assumed you would be here frequently over the next few days. This way, there will be no traveling in traffic back and forth to my shop for fittings. It will save time. The gown you have selected is elegant, but simple, so it will not take long for us to create it."

"Thank you, Madame," Rowena said, returning with Ariadne to the drawing room.

She was entertaining them with stories from the recent house party and describing how five betrothals had come from it when the doors to the drawing room opened. A tall, confident woman entered, making her way to them. Rowena recognized her future mother-in-law from having seen Lady Marley at various *ton* events in the past. The countess was at the center of every activity of Polite Society. She was a most impressive woman, her skin still unlined at her age, her abundant gray hair piled high atop her head.

They all rose, and Lady Marley came to stand before her, the countess' eyes traveling up and down as she assessed Rowena. Thank goodness she wore gowns these days which fit her much better than those she had donned in the past.

"I know little of you, Miss Stanhope," the countess said. "Other than you are known for your intelligence. But my son would only wed for love, as his two sisters have, so I know you have captured his heart."

"I do love Lord Marley a great deal," she told the older woman.

"Then that is enough for me. Constantine is not easily satisfied. In all his years in Polite Society, he has never called upon a single woman. For him to have gone to a house party he held no invitation to merely to be in close proximity to you speaks a great deal of the affection he holds for you."

"You know of that?" she asked, bewildered how the countess would have learned of Con slipping into Lord and Lady Pebble's house party without an invitation.

"I received quite the letter from my son," her future mother-in-law revealed. "He usually keeps his thoughts to himself. For the first time, he poured out his heart to me. I know he wormed his way into the house party only because of your presence at it, Miss Stanhope. You must be quite an interesting lady for him to pursue you so fervently."

"I am fortunate to have gained his love, my lady."

Lady Marley sniffed. "I believe you to be quite formidable, Miss Stanhope. I would say my son is the fortunate one to have you as his future countess."

Soon after, the large party of gentlemen returned from their time at White's. Rowena quickly put given names with faces and remembered which husband belonged to which wife. She was thoroughly entertained by the stories they shared and knew she would no longer dread the approach of the Season each spring. Instead, she would celebrate it because she would be with family.

Her family . . .

She and Ollie wound up staying for dinner, as did Lucy and Dru and their husbands. The more she was around Con's sisters, the more she liked them. Lady Marley was not as friendly and open as her daughters, but Rowena knew she had the countess' approval.

Before she and Ollie left for the evening, Madame Laurent

asked if she might take a few minutes for an early fitting. Several hours had passed since she had first met with the modiste, and she was amazed at the progress already made on her wedding gown. She now felt fully confident that the gown would be finished in time for their wedding.

Returning downstairs, they said their goodbyes and went out to her fiancé's carriage, Con again escorting them to Ollie's townhouse.

Once inside, Con said, "Now that Mama has arrived in town, would you be amenable to the wedding taking place the day after tomorrow?"

"I think that would be lovely," she told him.

When they arrived at her former home, Ollie quickly bid them goodnight and exited the carriage, allowing them a few minutes alone for some stolen kisses.

"My sisters love you, just as I knew they would," he told her. "It seems you have taken to them, as well."

"They were so warm and welcoming to me. Ariadne and Eden, as well. You were right. Ariadne has offered the use of her townhouse for the wedding and the breakfast afterward."

"What did you think of Mama?" Con asked.

"She is much as I thought she would be. Lady Marley is not as open as the rest of your family, but I believe I have won her approval."

He brushed his lips softly against hers again. "I am so glad you finally arrived in town. It has been awful waiting for you. Tell me we will never part again, Rowena."

"You will be hard pressed to be rid of me, my lord," she said pertly.

Laughing, he kissed her again, hard, and then said, "I will see you inside. If I do not do so now, I will be lifting your skirts and making you scream my name."

"Don't tempt me," she said. "It is not every day a handsome lord offers to ravish me in a carriage. I believe I would rather like it."

His palm cradled her cheek. "I will do that very thing—once we are wed. It will give us something to look forward to."

Con saw her to the door, kissing her tenderly one final time. "I will see you tomorrow. And the day after, we will be joined as man and wife."

Epilogue

London—June 1813

It was the night of their annual ball. Not just any ball, but a ball given for family and friends.

And her husband would not let her out of bed.

"Con, darling, I must get dressed," Rowena protested, her wrists pinned to the pillow, her handsome husband hovering over her. "Our guests will be arriving soon."

"We should have made it a masquerade ball," he mused.

"What? Why?"

His wolfish smile caused desire to stir within her. "Because then we could have pretended to be downstairs and instead remained here and spent the night making love."

"Con!" she said, trying to look sternly at him and failing miserably. "You enjoy the ball we give each summer." Rowena gave him her own flirtatious smile. "And I promise you once it ends, I am yours."

A low growl sounded in his throat. "You are *always* mine, Wife."

He lowered his lips to hers, the hungry kiss drawing her in. His lips left hers, gliding down her body, his tongue a hot brand passing between her breasts. Along her belly. And finally stopping at her core. The familiar heat swept through her as he lapped at her.

A knock on the door sounded. "My lady," her maid anxiously said. "We must dress you for the ball."

Her fingers tightened in her husband's hair as his tongue

brought her closer to her climax.

"Just a few... more... minutes," she managed to shout before she whimpered.

"We will be waiting, my lord," Benchley boomed.

Con raised his head. "My valet sounds displeased."

Rowena gave him a haughty look. "I will be, too, unless you finish what you started, my lord."

Grinning, he said, "Right away, my lady."

Less than a minute later, she teetered on the precipice, falling over, the waves of pleasure causing her body to dance to the tune her husband had set.

Now limp, she asked, "How am I supposed to rise from this bed, much less dress myself for our guests?"

He brushed a swift kiss on her lips. "That is what your maid is for. Now, up, love. We truly do not want to keep our guests waiting."

Con leapt from the bed and reached for her. He swept her into his arms and started to head toward her bedchamber, where she dressed.

"My dressing gown," she called.

He dipped, grabbing it from the floor, and continued on his way. Once in her room, he set Rowena on her feet and held the dressing gown open so she could slip into it.

"I will return in fifteen minutes for you," he told her.

"That is not long enough," she pouted.

He arched one brow. "You never take longer than that, and you know it. Besides, I want to go and see the boys before the ball begins."

She opened her door, finding her maid standing outside, looking slightly put out.

"Come inside. His lordship will be back in a few minutes, and I better be ready when he appears."

"I do not like to rush getting you ready, my lady." Then the maid's face softened. "Then again, I am happy to be part of a household where the master and mistress are so much in love."

Rowena also liked being a part of such a household.

They would be wed five years this coming autumn, and every day she felt cherished. Con was an inventive, creative lover. He was also a wonderful father and excellent companion. They never tired of one another or ran out of things to talk over together.

The highlight of their marriage had been the births of their two boys. They had continued with the family tradition of naming their children after ancient emperors. Theodosius, known as Theo, would turn three at the end of August. He was a curious boy, sweet-natured, and very solicitous toward his younger brother. Leontius, whom they called Leo, was now eight months old and already crawling. He had six teeth and gnawed on everything he could get his chubby hands upon. Both boys had her golden-brown hair, and Theo had his father's amethyst eyes. Leo had been born with blue eyes, but Rowena had learned from the many births in their family that babes were often born with blue eyes, which altered in color as they matured. Already, she could see Leo's eyes beginning to change color and wondered if he would also share the amethyst eyes of his father and older brother.

After quickly washing and dabbing on some of her signature rosewater, she was dressed in her gown for tonight's ball. It was amber in color, and she knew Con would like it because he was always talking about the amber which ringed her brown eyes. He told her they would keep having children until he got at least three girls off her, and he hoped one of them would have her unique eyes. She did long for a daughter and hoped the next time they were blessed with a babe that it might be a girl.

She did her own hair, quickly twisting it into her usual chignon. The style was timeless and one she preferred because it involved so little fuss. While Rowena had allowed her lady's maid to experiment with different hairstyles, she always came back to her chignon.

Con appeared behind her as she checked her appearance in her mirror. Her maid knew to leave since her husband always wanted a few private moments with her before they entertained guests.

"I have something for you," he said, his voice husky, causing her to wish the ball was over and done and they could remain upstairs in their own world.

Glancing over her shoulder, she asked, "What is it?"

He handed her a small box, and she quickly opened it, finding a pair of amber earrings nestled inside.

"Oh, Con! They are beautiful."

His hands came to rest on her shoulders, his lips pressing a hot kiss upon her nape. "Not half as beautiful as my countess. Put them on, love."

Rowena fastened the earrings into place, admiring her image in the mirror. "What do you think?"

"I think they bring out the amber in your eyes," he said, nuzzling her neck. "And that makes me—"

"Do not say it, else we'll be back where we were half an hour ago, and our guests will be without their host and hostess."

He smiled lazily, their gazes meeting in the mirror. "Later tonight, when our guests have gone home, I want you to wear them. Only them."

She placed a hand over his. "Now, aren't you the cheeky one?"

Con pulled her to her feet, his arms going about her, his hands slipping to grasp her buttocks. "Oh, I can be cheeky. You just wait and see."

Giving him a coy smile, she said, "I look forward to your cheekiness, Husband."

They left her bedchamber and went upstairs to the nursery. A nursemaid sat rocking in a chair.

"Good evening, my lord. My lady. Both boys are down."

Rowena went to the bed where Theo slept. He looked much younger when asleep.

"He is already growing up so fast," she said wistfully.

"No matter how old he becomes, he will always be your little boy," Con assured her. "Even when he has a boy of his own."

She reached out and smoothed Theo's hair before kissing his cheek. Con did the same, and they moved to the crib, where Leo slept peacefully. Where Theo had been a restless babe, always moving, Leo's nature was placid. Once he was put down to sleep, he never seemed to stir. She cupped Leo's cheek and bent to kiss his brow.

"Goodnight, little one," Con said, escorting her from the nursery.

On their way downstairs, he said, "Although I hate putting you through it again, I am ready for us to have another child."

"I am always ready," she told him, slipping her arm through his and smiling up at him.

In the drawing room, they spoke briefly with Adams and Mrs. Adams, knowing their servants had everything well in hand. Dru had loaned them her cook for the evening, as well as a few scullery maids to help out their staff. Eden had recommended the string quartet which would play for the evening. As the French doors were opened by servants, Rowena could hear the strains of a waltz being played as the quartet warmed up outdoors.

Their guests began arriving. Instead of the typical receiving line, Con and Rowena met their guests in the drawing room. It was very informal as people entered, greeting others, including their host and hostess. Con had always liked the idea of dancing outdoors, and so this ball they held at the beginning of June each Season took place on the terrace, with the dancing there and spilling down to the grounds below, where the musicians sat. What made tonight special was that it was not a *ton* event. Only their family and close friends were invited, making for a relaxed atmosphere.

Besides the family she had gained through Con, they also had stayed in close touch with their friends from Lord and Lady Pebble's house party from years ago. That circle of friends had become as family to them.

Rowena now watched her brother and her best friend enter

the drawing room, and they made their way straight to Con and her. Ollie now had a son and daughter and had settled into married life and his role as a country gentleman with ease.

They embraced, and he asked, "How are my nephews?"

"We went to the nursery to see Theo and Leo before coming downstairs this evening," Con told them, pride on his face. "They were sleeping soundly and are such good boys."

Ollie turned to his wife, and she gave him a nod.

"We are to be parents again," he announced, causing more warm embraces to be exchanged.

Lord and Lady Cramer joined them. Lord Cramer was still a serious fellow, but his wife balanced him nicely with her friendliness and zest for living. The earl did open up with those he knew and trusted, and Rowena was glad the couple was a part of their group.

Lady Cramer asked, "Did I just hear that you are increasing?"

More congratulations were offered, and the two couples left to head outside, leaving Con and Rowena to continue to greet their guests. She visited with Lucy and Dru, who had truly become sisters to her in every way. Then Tia and Lia arrived with their husbands, Tia as effervescent as always.

Others began entering the drawing room, including Lord and Lady Rowland. The former Miss Lawson had wed the new earl six months after his father's passing, and they were an active part of the Mossleigh neighborhood. Occasionally, Rowena felt a bit wistful in having left Dorset, but she would not trade her life with Con in Somerset for anything.

Ariadne and Julian arrived in the company of Val and Eden. They were followed by Baron and Baroness Howell. In addition to Mary, Sarah had given birth to two boys. Lady Cramer had also birthed two sons, while Lord and Lady Rowland had two girls. The Dorset couples often teased about doing a little matchmaking between their children so that they might remain near Mossleigh.

Tray and his wife appeared, and soon Verina and Justina

arrived with their husbands, making the ball complete. Con asked if Rowena wished to go outside to begin the dancing, and she readily agreed. While she would never become a polished dancer, she enjoyed dancing with her handsome husband whenever the opportunity arose.

Con whistled loudly, gaining everyone's attention, and it made her think of Lady Pebble's bell tinkling so many years ago. Lord Pebble was not in good health, and they had remained at Pebblestone for this Season. Rowena hoped on their return to Marleyfield, they might go a bit out of their way in order to call upon the couple.

"Thank you again for coming to what has become our annual ball," Con said to their guests. "Balls usually have far too many people present and have never been to my liking. This one, however, is intimate, held so that our family and friends may mingle together and enjoy one another's company."

He laced his fingers through hers and brought their joined hands up to his lips for a tender kiss.

"The past few years of my life have been the best—because of this woman by my side. Rowena, I know no woman could have matched me as well as you have. You have given me two wonderful sons, and I look forward to each day we spend together, knowing we live it in love. My wife is the light of my life and has made me a far better man than I ever thought I could be."

Her husband gazed out across the terrace. "All of you feel the same about your spouses, as well. We are a most fortunate group of people within Polite Society." He glanced to the musicians. "Now, let the dancing commence with a waltz," Con commanded, and the musicians took up their instruments.

As the music began, her husband swept Rowena into his arms. She liked this new dance. The waltz was intimate, allowing a couple to be in close proximity with one another and gaze into each other's eyes, as well as converse, if they wished. It was almost like making love in public, which caused her to chuckle.

"What are you thinking of, love?" Con asked, his voice husky.

She smiled up at him. "Only about how happy I am with you. With our boys. And our life together."

"I will forever be in Tia's debt for asking me if I would do a favor for her—and ask her new friend, Miss Stanhope, to dance."

"And I shall be forever grateful that Lord Clay chose to remain in town and gamble his time and money away, allowing you to take his place at the Pebblestone house party."

They finished their waltz, but when the music ended, Con did not release her. Instead, her husband bent, giving her a lingering kiss. To have done so at a *ton* ball would have caused a bit of a scandal. Instead, in the privacy of their home, surrounded by their loved ones, no one thought a thing of it.

Con broke the kiss, and Rowena told him, "Each day, I grow to love you more and more. Thank you for loving me, Con. Thank you for changing my life and making me your wife."

He gazed down at her, and she saw the love for her shining in his eyes. "The best is yet to come, love. I promise you that."

The night passed quickly, with her dancing with many of their guests and being able to chat with everyone. Supper was early, held at ten that evening, and the dancing ended at midnight. All the parents longed to return to their homes, their children, and their beds.

After bidding the last guests goodnight, they went upstairs to the nursery for a final glimpse of Theo and Leo. Rowena glowed with pride, hoping the boys would get the best parts of Con and her.

Con led her to their bedchamber, and as he often did, he asked, "Would you play for me?"

She picked up the violin which stood in the corner of the room. Over the years, she had perfected her playing, and now the bow felt as natural in her grasp as her hands did when they tinkled the ivory keys of a pianoforte.

He sat in a chair, watching her play, his eyes smoldering with desire, heightening her own. When she finished the piece, he rose, taking the violin and bow from her and setting them aside.

"We have made two beautiful boys. Let us see if we can make another beautiful child tonight."

And they did.

About the Author

USA Today and Amazon Top 10 bestselling author Alexa Aston lives with her husband in a Dallas suburb, where she eats her fair share of dark chocolate and plots while she walks every morning. She enjoys travel and sports—and can't get enough of *Survivor* or *The Crown*.

Her Regency and Medieval historical romances bring to life loveable rogues and dashing knights. Her series include: *The Strongs of Shadowcrest, Suddenly a Duke, Second Sons of London, Dukes Done Wrong, Dukes of Distinction, Soldiers and Soulmates, The St. Clairs, The de Wolfes of Esterley Castle, The King's Cousins, Medieval Runaway Wives,* and *The Knights of Honor*.

www.ingramcontent.com/pod-product-compliance
Lightning Source LLC
LaVergne TN
LVHW011934070526
838202LV00054B/4630